HUNTED BY MAGIC

A NEW ADULT FANTASY NOVEL

JASMINE WALT

DYNAMO PRESS

Disappeared.

No, no, that can't be right, I thought to myself, clutching the sheets as ice crystalized inside my veins. People didn't disappear. Not really. They went missing, sure, but they didn't just vanish off the face of the planet. The idea that Iannis had disappeared, along with an entire dirigible of people, was impossible. He wasn't gone. He couldn't be.

"Sunaya." Lakin's hand was gentle as it pressed against my arm. His yellow-orange shifter eyes narrowed in concern. I could feel the weight of all my friends' eyes on me as well, who were gathered around my bed. "You're shredding the sheets."

I tore my gaze away from the messenger who'd delivered the news and looked down at my hands. Sure enough, my panther claws had extended, ripping through the comforter and sheets of my infirmary cot. Taking a deep breath, I slowly uncurled my fists from around the once-pristine white cloth, then tucked them beneath my armpits – I was ice-cold, something that was highly unusual for me. I didn't know if it was because I was still recovering from a near-lethal dose of silver poisoning, or because of the news I'd just heard.

"Disappeared?" Director Chen demanded, voicing the words I was too stunned to utter. "That doesn't make any sense. A dirigible is too large a contraption to simply go up in thin air, not without the assistance of extremely powerful magic. The Resistance doesn't have access to that kind of power."

The Resistance. Guilt flooded me. By Magorah, but this was all my fault. I'd failed to warn Iannis about the threat Rylan had delivered to me, the warning that I shouldn't accompany Iannis to the bi-annual Convention if I valued my life. I should have told him right away, but the Shifter Royale investigation had taken nearly all of my attention. Every time I'd had a chance to talk to him over the past few days, I'd been distracted with what seemed like, at the time, extremely urgent matters. I felt like the biggest idiot in Solantha for allowing this to happen.

"Clearly the Resistance *does* have that kind of power," I snapped, finally finding my voice again. "If not by magical means, they've found some other way to intercept that dirigible. If it didn't make it to the Convention with so many powerful mages aboard, something terrible must have happened. We have to find it." I pushed back the covers and struggled out of bed.

Director Chen held up a hand, and a gust of magic-laced wind smacked me flat back against the bed. "If by 'we' you mean myself and the Council, then yes, I agree we have to find it. But you are still recovering from an attack on your life, Miss Baine. If you come before the Council in your current state, no one will take you seriously. I suggest you stay here and regain some of your strength first."

"Like hell I will," I snarled, vaulting up off the bed, but Director Chen blasted me again, and I fell back against the pillows once more. Without another word, she swept out of the room, her bright silk robes billowing behind her. The messenger was quick to follow, and Fenris, after shooting me an apologetic look, jumped up and hurried after her as well.

"Much as I hate to say it, Director Chen is right," Annia remarked, concern in her dark eyes as she leaned forward and patted my shin from her place near the end of the bed. "The fact that you're still lying in bed instead of going after her tells me you've got a bit of resting up to do."

"Fuck that." But she was right, I admitted silently to myself as I struggled up into a sitting position. I was as weak as a newborn cub. "I'll be fine as soon as somebody can get some food into me. And when I am, I'm going after Iannis."

"Why?" Noria demanded. "He's a powerful mage and can take care of himself. You don't need to risk your life for him, Naya."

I lifted my chin to pin her with a glare. "He's also my teacher, and I owe my life to him. I can't leave him out there in danger without at least trying to help. Just because he's the Chief Mage doesn't mean he's invulnerable."

"Yes, and *you* aren't invulnerable either, as you've just proven once again." Noria stood, tossing her mane of fiery curls. "I think I'll go get that food for you. Maybe once your belly is full, you'll be able to think more clearly." Shoving her hands into the top pockets of her multi-pocketed jeans, she spun around and left the room.

"Noria!" Annia called sharply after her younger sister, twisting around in her chair to get up, but Comenius placed a hand on her shoulder.

"There's no point in talking to her about it right now," he said. "You know how she feels about mages in general. She'll just dig her heels in."

"Com's right." I sighed, dragging a hand through my mass of curly black hair. Despite the fact that she had a mage boyfriend, Noria was passionately anti-mage. She hated the unequal balance of power even more than I did, and was a huge fan of the Resistance, the freedom-fighter organization that wanted to overthrow the mages and level the playing field for shifters and humans. "Maybe when she comes back, she'll have cooled off a little."

"I'm sorry about her." Annia turned back, an apologetic look on her beautiful face. She was a more elegant version of Noria, her skin smoother, her hair straighter and darker, her curves more refined. "I thought that after this whole fiasco with the kidnapped shifters, she'd open her eyes to the fact that mages aren't the only ones capable of evil. But she's not ready to see that yet."

"She has true conviction," Elania, Comenius's lover and a talented witch, said in her throaty, accented voice. She'd been sitting silently next to Comenius the whole time, her hand on his thigh in a show of support. "Conviction can be a blessing because it gives us focus, but it can also blind us to certain truths."

"Conviction or not, I have to say I agree with Noria a little, and definitely with Director Chen," Lakin admitted. "Wouldn't it be better to wait until you're more healed before rushing out into who knows where to go after the Chief Mage?"

"I can't wait that long." I let out a shaky breath, my hands fisting in the shredded covers to keep them from trembling. "I've already lost Roanas. I'm not going to sit back and let the Resistance take Iannis too."

"Neither of those things were your fault," Comenius said, giving my shoulder a comforting squeeze. Roanas had been my mentor – he'd taken me in off the streets after my aunt Mafiela had kicked me out of the jaguar clan and raised me as his own, teaching me how to fight as well as fend for myself. I'd loved him as I would have loved my father, had he stepped up to take care of me instead of disappearing without a trace. When I'd found

Roanas in his living room two months ago, dying of silver poisoning, the loss had been nearly unbearable. My anger and bitterness against the Mages Guild coupled with my thirst for revenge were the only two things that kept me from descending into grief, and the wound was still fresh enough that I dared not give myself too much downtime to think about it. As my master, Iannis helped fill the hole in my life that Roanas had left behind, but my feelings for him ran along a different path.

No matter what, I couldn't lose Iannis too.

"Civil disturbance in Shiftertown square," a tinny voice announced. *"Please report immediately."*

"Shit." Lakin tugged the chain around his neck, pulling out the medallion that was normally hidden beneath his coat. The golden disc, stamped with a fang and edged with tiny runes, was the mark of his authority as the Shiftertown Inspector. "I have to go." He leaned in and briefly brushed his lips against my forehead. "Don't do anything stupid while I'm gone, okay?"

Shocked by the unexpected touch of his lips against my skin, I said nothing as he swept from the room. Silence descended upon the infirmary for a few moments, until I realized that everyone else was staring at me.

"What?" I snapped, turning to Comenius, whose eyebrows were arched higher than everybody else's.

"Nothing." Comenius's eyebrows lowered a fraction. "Just wondering if there's anything new in your life you'd care to share with us."

"No." Scowling, I crossed my arms over my chest. "There's nothing new going on in my life aside from the fact that my master is missing and I'm stuck in this stupid bed." Lakin had made his interest in me clear in the last week or so, but I'd already told him to back off. After the way he'd balked when I'd tried to disguise him with my magic, I'd realized that the two of us could never be a thing. My magic would always get in the way of any relationship I had with a shifter – I could no more deny it as a part of me than I could deny the panther that was a part of my soul.

"You're wrong."

"Huh?" Comenius scowled at me. "Wrong about what?"

"Wrong that it's not my fault." Tears stung at my eyes, and I blinked them back as I met Comenius's cornflower-blue eyes. "Not long after I defused the bomb on the Firegate Bridge, Rylan called me. He warned me not to accompany the Chief Mage on his trip to the Convention if I valued my life, and that if I warned him the Resistance would punish me accordingly. Of course I'd planned to tell Iannis anyway, but there was just so much going on that every time I tried, something more important came along and sidetracked me. I think I did try to tell him right before he left, but I was so out of it that I couldn't get the words out right."

"So this *is* the work of the Resistance, then." Annia's expression turned thunderous. "Just wait until Noria gets back here so I can tell her that. If she still hasn't changed her mind, I'll make *sure* Mom puts her under house arrest. There's no way she's joining up with them, not after this."

"I do not know your sister well, but from what I've seen, a curfew is hardly going to stop her," Elania observed dryly. "She is too strong of spirit, that one."

The scent of freshly-cooked meat caught my attention, and I lifted my head, hoping that was Noria coming back with the food. Footsteps sounded outside the hall, but only a servant entered the room, bearing a platter piled high with brisket, new potatoes, and green beans. My growling stomach sank as I realized that though Noria had indeed sent word that I needed food, she hadn't bothered to stick around.

"By Magorah." I raked my hands through my hair. "We're losing her."

"I'll go talk to her." Annia jumped to her feet. "Don't worry about it, Naya – she's my responsibility, not yours. You just eat and focus on getting well."

"Thanks." I gave Annia a wan smile, then accepted the platter from the server and dug in. "I'm getting out of bed as soon as I'm done with this food," I warned Comenius in between mouthfuls. "There's no way I'm letting Director Chen shove me out of this rescue mission."

Comenius opened his mouth, but Elania spoke smoothly over him. "Perhaps we can help you along in your recovery. Surely the Mages Guild has supplies that Comenius and I can use to mix you a strengthening tonic?"

I swallowed a mouthful of brisket to hide my surprise. I hadn't expected Elania to be so helpful. "They do, but I'm not certain they're going to be willing to hand them over."

"Oh, I can be very persuasive." Elania blinked as she got to her feet, and my eyes were drawn to the long, black dress that emphasized her curvaceous form. Comenius's were too, which was probably why he didn't protest when she curled her fingers around his upper arm and pulled him up with her. "Come, darling, and let's leave Sunaya to eat in peace. We may as well make ourselves useful instead of just sitting here."

"Alright." Comenius shot me a worried look as Elania pulled him from the room. "You'll be here when we get back, right?"

"Yes," I agreed, and settled back, albeit reluctantly, to wait. Com's herbal teas were always effective, and Elania was very popular for her potions. Much as I didn't want to sit in bed, I knew whatever they whipped up for me would be worth the wait.

2

T he tonic tasted pretty terrible, but it *was* worth the wait. My shifter metabolism digested it quickly, so within two minutes of choking it down a rush of energy hit me, driving the weakness from my limbs and filling my body with the same urgent fire that burned within my soul.

"Thanks guys," I told Comenius and Elania as I hurriedly shoved my legs into my leather pants. They'd been left on a chair near my bed along with the shirt I'd worn to the Royale, and though they still stank of fear and sweat and blood, they were a lot better than going before the Council wearing an infirmary gown. "I can take it from here."

"Nice try," Comenius said dryly, "but just because you're bright-eyed and bushy-tailed doesn't mean we're not going with you."

"Visiting hours are over," a guard announced brusquely, striding into the room. "All citizens who are not here on urgent Palace business need to vacate the premises immediately." He jerked his thumb toward the door.

"We're here to visit Sunaya Baine," Comenius said stiffly, not moving a single muscle. "She's the Chief Mage's apprentice, so I'd say that's Palace business."

"Perhaps, but not *urgent* Palace business." The guard's hand moved to the sword hanging at his hip. "Like I said, visiting hours are over."

"Just go," I muttered in Comenius's ear. He was normally quite level-headed, but like most Pernians, he had a deeply buried stubborn streak. "I'll meet up with you soon."

"You'd better," Comenius warned, squeezing my shoulder once more. "Stay safe, Naya."

"You too."

I waited until the guard had escorted them down the hall and the sound of their footsteps had faded before I headed downstairs toward the Mages Guild, where the Council room was located. My bare feet padded against wood and stone – whoever had left my clothes by my bedside hadn't seen fit to do so with my shoes or weapons. My weapons were spelled to return to me eventually, but the shoes were not, so I was a little annoyed that they were gone. Servants and mages went about their business, but there was a tightness in their expressions, and a few glared at me with more hatred than usual. Clearly the word that trouble was afoot was spreading, though it didn't seem that everybody knew the full story yet. The whole Palace would be in a panic if they knew their Chief Mage had vanished.

I hurried past the lobby of the Mages Guild, then took the hallway to my right, which I knew led to the Council room even though I hadn't been there before. If the Mages Guild logo emblazoned in gold across the heavy wooden door hadn't been enough, the cacophony of arguing voices beyond it would have told me I'd found the right place.

I pushed open the door and stepped into a long, rectangular room. Portraits of past Chief Mages covered all but the far wall, which was lined with windows overlooking the manicured gardens. Thick carpet cushioned my bare feet, a welcome change from the chilly stone. Two chandeliers dangled from the ceiling, one directly above me on my half of the room, and the other one above the large, round table on the other side, where the eight senior mages sat along with Director Chen. Fenris, ever the shadow, sat directly behind her seat in wolf form, and if not for the fact that her chair was faced sideways to me, I wouldn't have noticed him at all. Only one chair was empty, and my chest tightened as I realized it must be Iannis's seat.

All talking had ceased the moment I'd stepped in through the door, but the silence didn't last. "Miss Baine!" Director Chen exclaimed, jumping to her feet and frowning heavily. Fenris hastily scrambled backward to avoid being trampled, and I ignored him as he turned a reproachful glare my way. No doubt he thought I should still be abed. "What are you doing here?"

"The same as you." I planted my feet wide and stood my ground as I faced the Council. "I want to rescue the Chief Mage."

"You will have absolutely no part in this rescue mission!" One of the Council members, who I recognized as Omonas ar'Candar, jabbed a long, slightly crooked finger at me. Unlike some of the elders, he did nothing to hide his age – light glinted off his bald head, and the beard that brushed halfway down his navy robes was pure white. "You have been a bad influence on Lord Iannis, leading him to flaunt convention and ignore laws that have kept Canalo safe for many years. You had better pray to your god that the Chief Mage is still alive, because if not, you shall be tried and executed for your unsanctioned use of magic as you should have already been!"

The other mages were quick to chime in, shouting at Director Chen, ordering her to remove me. I saw a hint of regret in her dark eyes as she moved toward me, but her ivory face was stern, and I knew she wouldn't hesitate to kick me out.

"Wait." Fenris stepped in front of me, in human form, and I blinked – I'd been so focused on Omonas and his cronies that I hadn't noticed he'd changed. "Sunaya may not be a member of the Council, but she's a trained enforcer and has experience tracking down missing persons. She could be an asset in this emergency."

"What she is is a liability," Omonas snapped. "And might I remind you, Fenris, that you are not a member of this Council either? Frankly, I don't know what you're doing here. Shifters have no place in the Mages Guild."

Fenris stiffened. "I have always attended such meetings."

"Only because Lord Iannis permitted it," another mage sneered, turning in his chair to face Fenris. "But he is not here right now, so I don't see why you should be here either. There is nothing that the two of you can do that we are not capable of."

"Actually," I argued, remembering the charm I wore around my neck, "I do have a way to –"

"*Stop.*" Fenris's voice echoed sharply in my head, and my vocal chords froze. I tried to speak, and panic shot through me as nothing came out but air.

"What's wrong, Miss Baine?" Omonas taunted. "Cat got your tongue?"

I gritted my teeth, unconsciously taking a step forward – I *hated* that expression.

"We're just about to leave," Fenris said, clamping his hand around my arm in a vice-like grip. I shot a glare at him, but since I couldn't speak I had no choice but to go along. "Good day, Councilor."

"I'm sorry," Fenris said as he dragged me into one of the guest rooms in the east wing and shut the door behind us. "I couldn't let you tell them about the *serapha* charm. If they find out that Iannis gave you such an intimate gift, they would see you as an even bigger threat than they already do."

The tightness on my vocal chords eased, and I rounded on Fenris, fury crackling through my nerves. "Just what the hell was that?" I demanded. "How did you manage to stop me from speaking? Is it some kind of charm you're using?" I couldn't wrap my head around it. Fenris was a wolf shifter – he shouldn't have been able to freeze my vocal chords, not without some kind of magical device, but I hadn't seen him use anything.

"I've picked up a thing or two from Iannis, but that's not important just now," Fenris said coolly. He sat down in an ornately carved rose-colored chair in front of a vanity. "We must use the charm to see if Iannis is still alive." He remained calm outwardly, but I could tell that fear for Iannis bubbled beneath the surface of his cool exterior.

"Right." I pulled out the charm, a white tanzarite jewel with iridescent flecks hanging from a silver chain, from beneath the neckline of my shirt. As I focused on the pale stone, it began to glow blue. I let out a huge breath of relief.

"He's alive," Fenris said, his yellow eyes narrowed in concern as he stared at the charm, "but judging by the lackluster glow, he is not well."

My heart sank as I glanced down at the stone again. Fenris was right – when I'd first tested the charm the glow had been bright, nearly dazzling, but it was faint now, barely enough to draw attention.

"I guess that means we have to find him fast," I said, stuffing the charm back beneath my shirt. If Fenris was right, I shouldn't be advertising the damn thing. "Did you learn anything useful from the Council meeting, before they threw us out?"

"Nothing good." Fenris's expression shifted to worry. "They were mostly just shouting at each other, especially at Director

Chen. Because she's so new, they don't respect her authority. Showing you any overt support would endanger what leverage she has."

"Fine." I pressed my lips together for a moment, but decided to let it go. Director Chen's position had a lot to do with politics, something I didn't envy her at all. I couldn't really blame her for trying to keep her position secure when Iannis wasn't there to back her up. "Anything else?"

"They did agree to offer a reward of five hundred gold pieces for anyone who brings Iannis back alive."

"Five hundred?" My eyes nearly popped out of my skull. "With that amount, I'm surprised the entire Enforcers Guild isn't on the job."

"I'm sure they will be soon enough," Fenris said dryly. "And as you've proven more than once, not all of them can be trusted."

"All the more reason to find him first." I stood up. "Regardless of Chen's reasons for publicly tossing me to the dogs, I'm not letting her off the hook so easily. She's going to include me in this rescue mission, one way or another."

"Naya," Fenris protested as I turned for the door. "You really should keep a low profile right now. With Iannis gone, the other mages are looking for any reason to turn on you. For now, at least until we figure out a plan, you should keep your head down."

"You know I'm no good at keeping my head down," I told him as I opened the door. "But at least I'm good at keeping it on my shoulders."

I SLIPPED into Director Chen's office, plopping down into one of her visitors' chairs to wait for her return from the Council meeting. The hard wooden seat was decidedly uncomfortable; the cushion was barely there, and the relief of dragons carved into the back of the chair dug unpleasantly into my spine. I wondered if Director Chen had ordered these chairs because, like her, they were Garaian, or because she wanted to discourage visitors. They definitely went with the Garaian motif in the room, from the stylized porcelain vases decorating her shelves and sitting on her desk to the silk, dragon-printed curtains hanging from either side of the window behind her desk.

I was just considering abandoning my chair for hers when Director Chen stepped into the room. She froze, her dark eyes on mine as I twisted around to face her, but her surprise quickly melted away into the lake of calm I was accustomed to seeing from her.

"Miss Baine." Her voice was cool as she closed the door behind her. Silk robes rustled against skin as she moved around me to sit in her cushy chair, and the scent of jasmine tickled my nose. "As usual, you fail to stay out of places where you do not belong."

"Thankfully, I don't care whether or not you think I belong." I crossed my legs and regarded Director Chen steadily as she sat down. Curiously, she avoided my gaze and reached for a small, rectangular silk-covered box instead. She flipped open the little latch, revealing two brass-colored balls roughly the size of chicken eggs – Garaian meditation balls. She picked one up, her fine, delicate fingers wrapping around the brass as she finally turned to look at me.

"Stressed much?" I arched a brow.

Her expression didn't change, but her knuckles whitened as she squeezed a little tighter. "I find these help me focus in tumultuous times, which today certainly qualifies as. If you still hope to be included in the search party, I cannot help you, Miss Baine. You should leave while you can."

"Why?" I slapped my hand against the cherrywood edge of

the desk. The color of the smooth surface reminded me of Iannis's hair, hair that in my weaker, unguarded moments I'd envisioned running my hands through. "You *know* that I deserve to be part of this mission. The Chief Mage's decision to take me on as his apprentice is the only reason I'm still alive. I'm more motivated to find him than almost any other person in this city."

"That may be, but I cannot afford to take anyone along whose loyalty to Canalo is not above reproach. Though it may not be fair, the majority of the Council members do not trust you."

"Don't you think this might be a good opportunity for me to *earn* their trust?" I gripped the arms of my chair, hard. Normally I didn't give a rat's ass about earning the trust or respect of any of the mages, but clearly my refusal to pander was coming back to bite me now.

"Perhaps, but your shifter abilities are of little use on an airship, and I doubt the other participants would be comfortable sharing such a small space with you." She gripped the ball tighter, and I could tell she was hanging onto her patience by a thread.

"I could go in a separate ship." I was getting desperate, I knew, but dammit, I needed to be on this mission!

"If you have a spare ship lying around, feel free." Director Chen arched a brow. "The Guild's last available airship is needed by the Finance Secretary. He is the only delegate left from the original team, and Canalo *must* have at least one representative at the Convention."

"Ugh." I slumped back in my chair as I tried to think of something else, anything else. I almost considered mentioning that I had the charm to try and sway her, but Fenris and I had agreed to keep our mouths shut about it to all but my closest friends, and Director Chen most definitely was *not* in that camp. "Is there anything I *can* do to help?"

Director Chen regarded me for a long moment, a flicker of wary sympathy in her dark eyes. "I strongly suggest that you stay out of sight until we return with the Chief Mage. Without his protection, the senior mages have little reason to tolerate you. I would hate to return with Lord Iannis only to find that he's already lost his apprentice."

Since I didn't have anything to say to that, I rose, then inclined my head. "Alright. Thank you for your time, Director Chen."

I strode out, my mind already on the next plan, as I had absolutely no intention of following her suggestion.

3

I managed to catch Cirin Garidano, the Finance Secretary, in his office. He was hurriedly packing a satchel with documents and reports from his desk drawers and filing cabinets. His long, dark hair was a little ruffled, the skin around his eyes tight with stress, and the collar on his robe was slightly askew.

"In a hurry?" I asked, leaning against the doorjamb.

"Miss Baine." The Finance Secretary didn't even look up at me, which told me he already knew I was there. "To what do I owe the dubious pleasure?"

"I need your help."

"I'm in no position to offer any assistance to you." Grabbing a sheaf of papers from a file, he riffled through it, then pulled out a document and stuck it in the satchel. "I must leave immediately if I'm to make it to the Convention on time."

"Yeah, I know." I ventured further into his office, then shut the door behind me so that no one passing by would unwittingly hear our conversation. "I want to come with you."

This time the Finance Secretary did look up at me, his

eyebrows climbing across his high forehead. "To the Convention? What business do you have there?"

"None. I need you to drop me somewhere on your way to the Convention, though."

"I'm not a ferryman, Miss Baine, and I've no time for extra stops." The Finance Secretary put one last thing in his satchel, then snatched it up. "I don't blame you for wanting to flee the city right now, but –"

"I'm not fleeing the city," I snapped, annoyed now. Why did everyone think I was just going to tuck my tail between my legs and cower in a hole while Iannis's life was in danger? "I'm going to find the Chief Mage, but in order to do so I need transport."

"Find the Chief Mage?" The Finance Secretary narrowed his dark blue eyes. "Just how do you plan on doing that?"

"I'm following a hunch." My fingers twitched as I resisted the urge to touch the *serapha* charm tucked beneath my shirt. The Finance Secretary had been fairly helpful to me so far, assisting me in the recent investigation by giving me access to a ledger with important information, but that didn't mean he was my friend. "My hunches are usually pretty good."

"In that case, you should confide your hunch to the search party Director Chen and the Council are organizing, and let them follow up on it." The Finance Secretary picked up his satchel and made to move past me. "In the meantime, I have a dirigible to board. Good day."

"Wait!" I grabbed him by the sleeve of his dark purple robe. "Please, Secretary Garidano. You have to take me with you. You know how much is at stake if the Chief Mage isn't found."

The air heated up around the Finance Director sharply, and I hurriedly released him, backing away before he burned me to a crisp. He turned his head, and his dark blue eyes blazed with a fire very similar to what I saw in Iannis's violet eyes during the few times his fury was ignited.

"Miss Baine, I *cannot* help you with this," he said tightly, a muscle in his jaw twitching. "In case you haven't realized, the attack on Lord Iannis's dirigible, if that is what happened, was likely timed to ensure that no one from Canalo is able to vote at the Convention this year. If I do not make it there on time, the attackers will have achieved their aim. Lord Iannis would consider my timely arrival more important than your need to involve yourself in the search."

"Fine." I fisted my hands at my sides, but nodded tightly. I'd been so consumed with wanting to get Iannis back that I'd failed to consider the consequences resulting from the attack on him. Iannis was the Chief Mage first, my master second, and I knew he would want the Finance Director to arrive at the Convention on time. "I take your point."

"Good. In the meantime, be careful. In fact, you'd best leave the Palace as quickly and quietly as you can. I suspect the Council will be eager to incarcerate you as soon as they get the chance."

He swept out of the room then, his robes billowing about him as his warning sunk into my bones, filling me with nervous energy. Quickly, I cast an illusion spell transforming myself into one of the many maids the Palace employed, then waited until I heard no footsteps outside before stealing back into the hall. Getting thrown into jail wasn't going to help me rescue Iannis. I'd already done that song and dance, and there was no way in hell it was happening again.

"JUST WHERE DO you think you're going, young miss?"

I stopped short outside the side entrance of the Palace as a guard stepped in front of me, blocking my path to the street and relative freedom.

"I'm headed out to the market to fetch some supplies for the kitchen." I blinked innocently up at him as tightened my grip on the wicker basket I'd grabbed on my way out.

"I'm sorry, but nobody can leave." The guard looked apologetic, but he didn't budge. "There's trouble's brewing in the city, and it's not safe for the Palace staff to be out and about."

I shrugged. "Okay then. But the Council has called a huge meeting and is demanding food, and the kitchen is short on a few supplies. I'll just tell them that you wouldn't let me leave..." I leaned in to read the guard's name tag. "What did you say your name was again?"

"Oh, alright, alright," the guard snapped. He glanced nervously over his shoulder before stepping aside. "Go on, then. Let the damn councilors get their canapés." Derision briefly twisted his features before he schooled his expression again.

"Thank you." I smiled sweetly at him, then hefted my basket a little higher over my shoulder and headed for the street. That guard was the first human I'd run across in the Palace who had shown open disdain for the mages, and I couldn't help but wonder just how many of the humans employed there shared his feelings. It would be all too easy for the Resistance to infiltrate the Palace using these people, to make these bitter human workers the eyes and ears that allowed them to plot the airship attack against Iannis. The thought filled me with chills, and I cast a glance over my shoulder at the Palace, wondering just how many enemies were lurking in our midst.

One problem at a time, Naya. One problem at a time.

Since my beloved steambike had been lost in Durain, I had to walk all the way down to the Port. Underneath the illusion I was still barefoot, so I hitched rides on the backs of carriages whenever I could, but it still took me nearly an hour to make what would normally have been a ten-minute trip.

My sore feet breathed a sigh of relief as they finally hit the boardwalk. I made my way down to Witches' End, the place where magic users from other countries who'd managed to get permission to settle within the Federation ran their shops. There were apothecary shops, fortune tellers, psychics, and more here – because they were born and raised in other countries, they managed to escape the no-magic rule that plagued the rest of the non-mage families in the Northia Federation. They were all licensed and registered with the state and had to adhere to strict regulations, but it was still better than being forced to have your magic stripped away, or being executed – the two choices I'd hidden from my entire life, before the truth of my half-mage heritage had come to light.

My friend Comenius ran a small shop there, called Over the Hedge. As a hedgewitch he specialized in nature magic, and offered charms and potions that were basically natural remedies enhanced by magic, like the nasty tonic he and Elania had made for me back at the Palace. I could see through the windowpane that Comenius was manning the counter, so I pushed my way inside, the little bell on the door tinkling as I entered. Comenius looked up from the register, and relief crossed his face as I dropped the illusion, allowing my true form to surface again.

"Welche Erleichterung!" he exclaimed, hurrying around the counter – there was nobody else in the shop right now. "I'm so glad you're okay," he added, wrapping his arms around me.

I hugged him back, inhaling his woodsy, herbal scent, but didn't allow myself to get lost in his embrace for long – there was work to do. "Director Chen won't let me be part of the rescue mission, and neither will the Council. Apparently they don't trust me."

"I'd say it's gone a little beyond that," Comenius said darkly, flipping the OPEN sign on the door to CLOSED and locking it twice. "I had guards here less than half an hour ago searching for you. Apparently there is a warrant out for your arrest."

"Typical." I gnashed my teeth together as he drew me behind the counter and into the back room. Half the space was taken up by wooden shelves stocked with merchandise and supplies, and the other half was dominated by a large, flat table where Comenius mixed herbal remedies and made charms. Bypassing his work area, he pulled me up a wooden staircase that led to the apartment above the shop. "Iannis is missing, and the first thing they think of is using the opportunity to get rid of me."

"They see you as a threat, and not without reason," Comenius said as he opened the door to his apartment. "You've been encouraging the Chief Mage to dig into places the others might rather he not look at too closely. That kind of thing is bound to stir enemies out of the woodwork, for both him and yourself."

Nodding, I looked around as Comenius closed the door behind us. His place was twice the size of my apartment in Rowanville, with an open floor plan where the kitchen, living room, and dining area were separated by arches rather than doors. The only walled-off area was to the back, where Comenius's bedroom suite was – I had personal knowledge of that space, as we'd been lovers once upon a very long time ago. But though I still felt the occasional spark when we touched or locked eyes, there wasn't much more than friendship between us, especially now that Elania was in his life and Iannis was in mine.

Even if Iannis and I *were* off-limits to each other.

"Okay, so what do we do now?" I demanded, sitting down on the dark green futon Comenius used as a couch. "Do I just cower in your apartment, keeping my head down like everyone keeps insisting that I do?"

Comenius snorted as he put on a pot of tea and grabbed a tin of cookies from one of his cupboards. "Since I highly doubt you're capable of hiding out in my apartment even to save your own life, never mind the Chief Mage's, I'm not even going to suggest it. We will come up with a plan, which likely will revolve around the use of that charm you have."

"Yeah." I drew the chain out from beneath my jacket and stared down at the opal. As I focused my attention on it and thought of Iannis, it glowed blue again, and I felt a tug on my soul. The magic seemed to be pulling me in an easterly direction, which made sense since Dara, the Federation capital, was located on Northia's east coast. But that wasn't particularly helpful, because there was a vast amount of land between us and Dara. I really didn't have any more information than Chen's search party, now that I thought about it.

"From what I understand about *serapha* charms," Comenius said as he joined me on the sofa, "they won't pinpoint the location of the person tied to them, but so long as you follow that internal tug, it will lead you straight to the other half of the charm, and thus to the person wearing it."

"Maybe, but that means wandering across the country on foot for who knows how long. And even if it pulls me in the right direction, if I follow it blindly it'll probably lead me straight across a chasm with my luck." I scowled down at the stone, annoyed at how useless it was proving to be. But then again, Iannis had used it to find me, hadn't he? "There has to be a better way to go about this."

"I'm sure there is, but I'm afraid I'm not the one to do it." Comenius smiled. "Thankfully, we both know someone who is."

IT DIDN'T TAKE LONG for Elania to arrive. As soon as the shop's doorbell rang, Comenius was on his feet, hurrying down the stairs. It was both amusing and disconcerting, the way my normally level-headed friend seemed to be infatuated with Elania, the witch who ran the apothecary shop down at the other end of the pier. From what I understood, like many witches Elania could also do spellcasting, which was why Comenius was enlisting her help. It almost made me wonder whether Elania had somehow bewitched my friend, as it was precisely because of his cautious, level-headed nature that the two of us had called things off. But I didn't sense anything magically off about Comenius. The only magic he was caught up in was the magic of lust, and that was something we were all subject to, no magical potions or spells required.

I should know, because as a shifter, or at least half-shifter, lust was a much bigger inconvenience to me than it was for a human or mage. Twice a year, shifter females went into heat and became insatiable creatures, consumed by the urge to mate and little else. The clock reset every time it was over, regardless of whether or not we were impregnated, but during the period in between our hormones ramped up bit by bit until we exploded all over again.

My time was coming soon, in a matter of weeks. Normally I didn't concern myself overmuch with it, as I just found a reasonably willing male to take out my sexual energy on when the time came. But I'd never had my heart tangled up over anyone before, especially not someone like Iannis. When we'd first met, the attraction I'd felt had been instant, and I'd fought so hard to deny it that I'd blamed it on my hormones. But as time passed, I knew my impending heat was only partially to blame – the growing feelings in my heart had little to do with the growing heat in my loins, and in the past I'd always been able to distinguish between the two. The presence of someone in my life that I both wanted, needed, and couldn't have in more ways than one, was really fucking with me. Sometimes I wished that I'd never met the Chief Mage, because then at least I wouldn't be torn into two over the issue.

But I had met him, and even if I was conflicted, my life was in many ways better for having him in it. And besides, I owed him a debt that even rescuing him might not repay.

"Sunaya!" Elania greeted me in her throaty voice as she glided into the room. She'd changed and freshened up since I'd seen her in the infirmary – her thick, lustrous black hair was piled up atop her head in a complicated weave, her eyes were rimmed with fresh kohl, and the flowing red dress she wore matched her lipstick perfectly. Beneath one slender arm she held a long, rolled up piece of parchment, and in the other hand she carried a small wooden case. "I am glad to see you are looking better."

"Thank you." I stood up to embrace her – I figured as Comenius's new girlfriend, and a helpful one at that, it would be smart of me to warm up to her. "The tonic you and Comenius whipped up worked wonders."

"Of course it did," she said, winking as she embraced me. The dark, exotic scent of spices and woman surrounded me, and I filed it away in my memory banks. "There is nothing I make that doesn't do the job it is intended for."

"Well I sure hope that confidence of yours extends to finding the Chief Mage." I sat back down. I glanced at Comenius as he rejoined me, noticing the slight flush on his cheeks and the hint of lipstick on his mouth that he hadn't quite managed to wipe off. Jealousy burned briefly in my chest – not at Elania for her relationship with Comenius, but rather that the two of them were happy, and didn't have to fear judgment or flaunt convention to be together.

"We will find him," Elania assured me as she dragged a scoop-backed armchair a little closer to the coffee table that separated the space between us. She set the roll of paper onto the table along with her small wooden case. The case contained various pouches and bottles filled with liquid and powder and herbs, as well as several rocks – some pieces of crystal and other semi-precious stones. She spread the rolled-up piece of parchment out on the table, then placed four chunks of crystal at the edges of the parchment. I recognized it as a map of the Northia Federation. Not a very detailed one, as it didn't show all the different towns and cities, just the borders delineating the fifty states that made up the Federation.

"Are those stones supposed to mark cardinal directions?" I asked, pointing at the crystal.

"No. I'm just using them to hold down the parchment so it doesn't roll back up again." Elania's red lips twitched as she reached for a black velvet pouch inside the purse. "Sometimes we read meaning into things that are not there."

"Indeed," I said dryly. I actually felt a little foolish, but I wasn't about to show her that.

"It's alright, Naya." Comenius patted my knee briefly as he regarded Elania fondly. "Elania has many years of training, and you're still starting out."

"Thanks for the reminder," I muttered, unable to keep the edge out of my voice. I didn't mind that Elania was more competent than me – that would be like being annoyed at the sky for being blue. Rather, I was frustrated that I was so behind in my magical education to begin with. If my father, the mage who I'd inherited my powers from, had bothered to stick around long enough to teach me how to use my birthright, I would be able to rescue Iannis on my own.

Then again, if my father had raised and taught me like he was supposed to, I likely wouldn't have ever crossed paths with Iannis in the first place.

I watched as Elania tugged on the drawstring of the pouch, then poured a fine white powder into her hands. A cloud of dust poofed into the air above her hand, and my nose wrinkled as the scent wafted toward me. It smelled like magic, and something human, like...

"By Magorah," I exclaimed, "is that human bone?"

"Very good," Elania acknowledged as she scattered the powdered bone across the parchment, careful to cover the entire surface. "An ancestor's shinbone, to be specific. The bones of a dead witch hold magical properties, so we grind them up for use in certain spells and incantations, such as the one we are about to do."

"Interesting," I murmured, sitting back against the sofa – more to put some distance between myself and the disconcerting spell than to relax. I found what she was doing a little gruesome; not just the act, but the meaning behind it. We'd buried my mother after she'd died, returning her to the soil from whence she'd come so that she might serve as nourishment for other lifeforms. The idea of stripping her bones from her carcass and grinding them up to be used in spellcasting sent a shiver down my spine. I wondered if this was something mages did as well, and resolved to ask Iannis about it, if I managed to rescue him.

When I managed to rescue him, I corrected myself silently.

"Alright," Elania said softly. She dusted off the last remnants of bone from her palm, then held it out and looked up expectantly at me. "I will need your necklace now."

I hesitated, my fingers toying with the charm. "The Chief Mage said that I shouldn't take it off."

"It's alright, Naya," Comenius said gently, his hand on my shoulder. "Elania won't do anything to harm your *serapha* charm. She's just trying to help."

Nodding, I pushed my mass of curls over my right shoulder, then reached behind me to unfasten the necklace. My fingers trembled, so it took me three tries, but I finally got it off. As I handed it off to her, my chest ached a little, similar to the time when I'd first separated the tiny piece of my soul that I'd put into the matching charm Iannis had worn. That's how *serapha* charms worked – you gave the other person a small fragment of your spirit, so that you were bound to them and would always be able to find them via the charms so long as they continued to wear them. The necklace I wore held a piece of Iannis's soul, so it stood to reason that Elania could use it to locate him.

Elania dangled the necklace over the map and began chanting in a strange language. She moved her hand above the map, making sure to hover the stone over every state in a kind of zigzag pattern without actually touching the surface of the map.

"Ah," she murmured as the powder covering a section of the map began to turn a cobalt blue. She stopped there, and we watched as the color spread out to cover the southern half of Mexia, one of the southwestern states that jutted up directly against the Federation border, just two states east of Canalo. "Here he is."

I scowled as I stared down at the map. "That's easily fifty thousand square miles of territory to search."

"And much of it is uncultivated Coazi land," Elania added, looking troubled.

"Coazi?" I tried to match the name with a memory. "Aren't they a tribe?"

"Yes. I believe the Federation ceded most of the land in this area to them." Elania handed the *serapha* charm back to me, then carefully swept the bone dust away from the area so she could mark it off with a pen. "I suggest reading up on the Coazi before you head into their territory. I know no more about them than any of the other indigenous tribes that populate the Federation."

"Well, now would be a great time to have access to the Palace's library." I huffed out a breath as I refastened the chain around my neck. Relief spread through my chest as the stone came to rest against my breastbone, and the strange pain there eased. "I'm sure there'd be a tome in there somewhere that could tell me all about the Coazi, whoever they are."

"I'll see if there's anything I can dig up," Comenius said gently. "In the meantime, though, you should rest, Naya. The tonic we gave you will only last so long, and your body needs the time to heal itself naturally."

"No way." I shook my head, unable to even entertain the idea of falling asleep. "I've been passed out in that infirmary bed for who knows how long already. I need to focus on prepping this rescue mission."

Comenius scowled. "Yes, and you're already showing signs of fatigue again. You'll be useless to the mission if you're not properly healed and rested."

"Alright," I ceded reluctantly. The edges of fatigue were starting to drag at me, likely sped along by my use of the illusion spell. Using magic draws on my energy reserves, and if I were to venture out on my own to try and find research books I would have to disguise myself again, which in turn would sap even more energy. Not exactly conducive to preparing myself for a long journey. "I'll chill out here for a bit."

"I'll get you a blanket and pillow." Comenius patted my leg, then stood up and went into the bedroom. Elania went with him, and I could hear them talking quietly as I stretched myself out on the sofa. If I'd wanted to, I could have tuned in with my sensitive hearing and eavesdrop on them, but Com deserved privacy in his own home. And besides, my fatigue was growing with every second.

As I sat there waiting for him to come back up, I heard a soft thud as something landed on the sofa cushion next to me. Startled, I jerked toward the sound, then smiled at the sight of my chakram pouch and crescent knives sitting there. They'd returned sooner than I'd expected. Pleased, I reached over to grab my weapons so I could strap them to my thighs, but another wave of tiredness washed over me and my hand fell back to my side.

I'll take care of my weapons later, I thought as my eyes slid closed. Floorboards creaked, and Comenius murmured something as he tucked a blanket around me, but I didn't hear what he said as I slipped into a fog. Images of Iannis falling from the sky, terror in his brilliant eyes as he reached toward me, rippled through my mind over and over, and I screamed in frustration that I was unable to move, unable to reach him at all.

Sleep. Resinah's cool voice echoed in my head, banishing the vision. *All is not yet lost, child. Now sleep.*

4

"I don't think you should go, Naya. At least not by yourself."

Scowling, I slammed the thick, dusty tome that Elania had brought in this morning, and scowled up at Comenius. "I'm not abandoning Iannis just because of a couple of paragraphs in an old history text."

"That isn't just some dusty tome – it is part of a trusted and valuable encyclopedia," Comenius argued, sounding highly affronted. We were sitting at his dining table along with Elania, who'd arrived with a basket of freshly made scones and cookies. The food was especially welcome after going without for nearly twenty-four hours, though it would have been nice if there had been some meat too. "According to those *couple of paragraphs*, as you say, the Coazi are unpredictable in their treatment of outsiders, and they are ruled by shamans, some of whom are as powerful as mages."

I scoffed. "Give me a break. From what I understand, they're really uncivilized. Surely they can't be that powerful."

"Tribal shamans are not to be underestimated," Elania warned, setting down her teacup and regarding me with a frown. "Their magic relies heavily on nature and spirits, but it is old and powerful. If you run across a shaman who considers you an enemy, you may find yourself outmatched."

"Well then I guess I'd better be careful, but that doesn't mean I'm staying here." I huffed out a breath. "If Iannis is hurt and lying around in the wilderness, the last thing I need is for these Coazi to find him before I do."

Comenius opened his mouth, presumably to argue, then froze as the doorbell rang.

"Are we expecting someone?" I asked, my senses prickling. Because we were on the second floor, there was no way for me to scent whoever was at the door.

"I ran across Annia yesterday and asked her to bring some of your things by the apartment," Comenius said as he cautiously rose from his chair. "Perhaps it's her."

"I'll come with you –" I began as he made for the door, but Elania placed her hand on my shoulder.

"You have a bounty on your head right now, Sunaya," she reminded me. "Let Comenius answer his own door. He can handle himself."

"Alright." Forcing myself to relax, I grabbed a cookie and took a bite. Elania was right – there was no reason to risk myself needlessly, and this *was* Comenius's place, not mine. I didn't really have a leg to stand on if he didn't want me answering the door.

Faint conversation drifted to my ears, and though the front door of the shop was too far away for me to make out the words, the cadence of the visitor's tone was familiar. It took me a second to figure out who it was.

"Fenris!" I exclaimed, and in the next second I was through the door, bounding down the stairs.

"Sunaya!" Elania called after me, but I burst into the front of the shop, eager to see my friend. I'd felt bad about leaving the

Palace before meeting up with him again, especially since the Council seemed to have it in for him nearly as much as they did for me. Thankfully, he looked like he was in one piece, standing next to Comenius in the front of the shop, dressed in his customary dark tunic and leggings.

"Good morning –" Fenris began, then let out a small "oomph" as I wrapped my arms around him and crushed him tight to me.

"Good morning my ass," I chided as I squeezed him. "We both know this is a shitty morning. But I'm glad to see you. I was worried the Council mages had gotten to you or something."

"As was I about you." Fenris had frozen when I hugged him, but only momentarily, and his strong arms wrapped around me as he hugged me back. "I'm relieved you made it safely out of the Palace."

"Let's head upstairs," Comenius said, double-checking the lock on the front door. "We can catch up in my living room and finish breakfast."

I checked my watch as we headed up the stairs, and frowned. "Isn't it time for you to open the shop soon?"

"I already called my employees last night and gave them the day off," Comenius explained. "Word of the Chief Mage's disappearance is spreading throughout the city, and panic along with it, so I decided not to open my doors today. Elania and I have already reinforced the protection spells outside our shops, as have many of the other shop owners."

"Fair enough," I said as we walked back into the apartment. We rejoined Elania at the table, Fenris seating himself next to me, and though I was glad to see him safe, I was also perturbed at the prospect that unrest was spreading throughout the city while I was cooped up and powerless to do anything about it.

"Despite living in the Palace all this time, I too was slated for arrest," Fenris said with a tinge of bitterness. He accepted the cup of tea Elania handed him and selected a cookie from the platter. "I had to slip out of the Palace in disguise. All shifters are in danger just now, as well as anyone else suspected of sympathizing with the Resistance."

"Shifters?" I demanded, scowling. "Why shifters? Humans are just as big a part of the Resistance."

"Yes, but the shifter population is smaller and easier to target," Fenris pointed out. "Not to mention that there are still a number of mages who think that shifters should have remained slaves to the mages, as they were originally created to be."

I hissed at that – we were born out of magical experiments done with humans and animals, originally bred to be a kind of warrior race, and many of the mages still thought they owned us. If not for the Uprising, where our ancestors had revolted, as well as the assistance of mages who thought our subjugation unfair, we would still be slaves today.

"I should call Lakin, then," I said, hopping up out of my chair to get to the phone in Comenius's kitchen. "Make sure he's okay."

"You might not be able to reach him," Fenris warned as I picked up the phone. "He's probably got his hands full."

The phone rang for several seconds before it connected. "Inspector Lakin," a slightly breathless male voice answered, and relief swept over me.

"Boon," I said, using his first name despite my better judgment – I knew Lakin had feelings for me, so I usually did my best to keep him at arm's length. At this second, though, I was too happy to hear his voice to care about that. "How are things?"

"Crazy," he said, sounding distracted. I heard some rustling in the background, like he was looking for something. "There are mages here, both from the Enforcers Guild *and* the Mages Guild, stalking the streets of Shiftertown with warrants and looking for any excuse to snatch our people off the streets and throw them in jail. My deputies and I have mostly been trying to protect the residents and get people to safety before they are taken."

"By Magorah," I muttered, gripping the receiver tightly. "Is there anything I can do to help?"

"Not really," Lakin said dryly. "They're looking for you too, and between your bad rep and the bounty on your head, you'd be caught the second you set foot here."

I gritted my teeth again. Ever since my heritage as a half-mage had become public knowledge, the Shiftertown community regarded me with scorn and hatred. This largely had to do with the fact that most shifters disliked mages in general, so they viewed my half-mage status with a combination of disgust and jealousy, imagining that I enjoyed all kinds of unfair privileges as the Chief Mage's apprentice.

"Well I'm going to bring the Chief Mage home," I said after a moment. "So that should help with your situation."

"All by yourself?" Lakin demanded. "I can't imagine you're going with the official search party, since they've got a warrant for your arrest."

"Fenris is coming with me, and maybe Annia if I can convince her. But I'm going either way."

"How are you even going to find him? You don't have the kind of resources the Mages Guild does. You might be better off –"

"If you say 'keeping your head down' I'm going to reach into the phone and rip your throat out," I growled.

There was a moment of silence. "You can't actually do that, can you?" Lakin finally asked in a pained voice.

"I think we'd both rather not find out." I let out a small sigh. Of course I couldn't do that – I didn't even know if such a thing was possible. But for all that Lakin liked me, he was afraid of my magic, and in instances like this it showed. "My talents would be of better use doing something like, say, rescuing the Chief Mage."

"I would come with you, but Shiftertown is my first priority."

"I know, and I'm not expecting you to." Somebody needed to make sure the shifters stayed safe, and there was no one more qualified than Lakin for the job. "I just wanted to make sure you were okay."

"I'll be fine. It's you I'm worried about." Lakin paused. "You'll let me know when you leave? And when you come back?"

"No guarantees," I warned. "But I'll try to keep you updated."

"Good enough." There was a weary sigh on the other end of the line. "Stay safe, okay, Sunaya?"

"You too."

I hung up the phone, and then the doorbell rang again.

"This time it *has* to be Annia," Comenius said as he hurried to answer the door.

A moment later, he walked back in with Annia, whose expression was downright thunderous. She had my travel pack slung over her leather-clad shoulder, and she tossed it to me underhand as she kicked the door closed behind her.

"This is officially the worst day ever," she growled.

"For reasons other than the obvious?" I asked cautiously as I caught the pack. Damn, but it was heavy – she must have stuffed it to the gills. Annia might look slender and willowy, but she kept in good shape and was amazingly strong.

"Yes." Annia snatched up a cookie and glared at it. "Somebody fucking snuck into the holding cells under the Enforcer Headquarters and slit Danrian's throat."

"What!" I jumped to my feet, and my pack slid to the ground with a loud *thump*. "You've got to be kidding. Danrian's dead?" Warin Danrian was the local manager of Sandin National Bank. He'd been running an illegal fighting ring called the Shifter Royale in which he forced shifters who were indebted to Sandin to fight in the ring. He'd also nearly killed me by injecting a fatal dose of silver-laced drugs into my bloodstream.

"As a doornail." Annia bit into the cookie with a vicious intensity, her dark eyes burning. "It happened while I was at the Palace with you."

"Fuck." I shoved my hands into my curly hair, fingernails scraping against my scalp. "This is my fault. If I hadn't let him get the better of me –"

"It's not your fault." Annia's voice was firm. "I would have eventually left the Enforcers Guild for some other reason – the assassin was probably waiting until I did to strike. Maybe I'd have gotten more information out of him, maybe not. But either way, somebody wanted to silence Danrian, and that was going to happen no matter what we did."

"It's that damned Benefactor." I sat back down on the couch, taking slow breaths to calm my racing heart. Working myself up into a rage wasn't productive. "Danrian said he was working with the Benefactor on a larger scheme that was coming to fruition soon. His confederates wouldn't have wanted Danrian to spill the beans right when they were about to make their move."

"Did they mean the attack on Iannis's dirigible?" Fenris demanded, his yellow eyes narrowed. "Or something else, something more?"

"If there is something larger afoot, I have a feeling we're going to find out very soon," Comenius said, brows furrowed.

An uneasy silence descended on the room, and we all looked at each other, not knowing what to say. What if some other catastrophe hit Solantha while I was gone? Of course, Comenius and Elania were more than capable of handling themselves, but what about Noria? And so many of the other citizens who were just normal people trying to live their lives?

"By the way," Annia said, breaking the silence, "I tried to pack everything you need in there, but if you have to go back to your apartment for anything, I'd be very careful. I had to do some serious sneaking to get into your place."

"Let me guess," I sighed, sitting down on the sofa so I could open up the pack and riffle through it. Inside were several days of clothes and toiletries, a set of knives, and a pack of jerky, amongst other things. Annia knew me too well. "My apartment is being watched?"

"You got it." Annia plopped down in the chair I'd vacated and popped another cookie into her mouth. "Half of the Enforcers Guild is camped outside your place, and the other half is running around like a bunch of chickens with their heads cut off. The Courier is blaming the Mages Guild for the Chief Mage's disappearance, and the public is fighting back so hard against all these heavy-handed arrests that several enforcers have been badly wounded or killed. Many enforcers are refusing to cooperate with the Mages Guild's orders, and I can't blame them. Everyone's gone bat-shit crazy."

"Fuck," I muttered, dragging my nails across my scalp. "We have to get the Chief Mage back before the city devolves into a war zone."

"I'm all for that," Annia said around a mouthful of cookie. She swallowed before adding, "Especially now that I can't do anything more with the Shifter Royale case. Plus, I'll get to cash in on that reward they're offering. So what's the plan?"

"We don't have much of a plan," I admitted with a sigh. "Elania cast a spell to pinpoint the Chief Mage's location a little better, and we've determined he's somewhere in the southern half of Mexia. But that's about it."

"That's a good thousand miles away," Fenris said, his brow furrowing. "It would take several days to get there even on steambikes. The coal and water charms powering them would likely buckle under the constant stress, and that's not even factoring in the rough terrain we'd have to traverse as we pass through uncivilized territory."

"Yeah, and there's also the fact that my bike is still in Durain somewhere." I blew out a breath in frustration. I really wanted it back, but the priority was to find Iannis right now, and searching for my steambike wouldn't help. "I can travel pretty fast in panther form too, but not fast enough over such long distances."

"What we need is an airship," Fenris said. "And a pilot to man one."

"I can do the piloting," Annia offered, "so if you've got the funds to procure a ship we should be good to go."

I arched a brow. "Since when are you able to pilot an airship?"

Annia grinned. "I dated a freighter captain during my college days, and I spent a lot of time with him aboard his ship between breaks."

"Spending a few months aboard the ship doesn't necessarily qualify one as a pilot," Fenris pointed out, sounding skeptical. "Are you sure you can manage this?"

"Hey, give me some credit!" Annia sounded a bit miffed. "I didn't just spend time watching him pilot the ship – I made him teach me, and I was pretty close to getting my pilot's license when we broke up. I wouldn't offer to pilot the ship if I thought I was going to get us killed."

Unfortunately, it turned out that Annia's offer was useless, because despite calling around at all the likely places, we simply couldn't find any kind of airship. The few ones available to rent had already been snatched up by wealthy families looking to get out of Solantha before the shit hit the fan, and we didn't know anyone we could ask to borrow a ship from.

"Well this sucks," I said as I slammed the phone down on the receiver again. "How the fuck are we supposed to get to the Chief Mage if we can't get an airship?"

"I'm not sure," Fenris admitted, looking just as put out. "Right now we might have better chances of finding a dragon to take us than an actual airship."

"Since dragons don't exist, I find that really depressing."

"Actually," Annia said, holding up a finger in thought. "I might have an idea of where we might be able to get an airship. Or at least something like it."

"Oh yeah?" Hope blossomed in my chest. "Where?"

Annia winked. "Only our favorite little redhead, of course."

5

"I am *not* letting you guys borrow my balloon," Noria insisted, arms crossed over her chest as she scowled at us. Elnos stood behind her, dressed in a pair of patched robes streaked with grime – the two of them had been wrestling with some kind of large, mechanical device before we'd walked into the workshop space they rented at the Academy.

"Why the hell not?" I demanded, gesturing at said balloon. It took up the entire left half of the workshop space, and resembled a giant wicker basket with a strange blanket hanging off it that was bolted to some metallic contraption, presumably something from which to burn coal. "It doesn't look like you're using it, and we need it."

"Our magitech balloon is highly experimental, and not ready," Elnos protested, stepping forward to take control of the conversation. He spread his hands imploringly, as if trying to make us see reason. "We've never taken it farther than the bay, and we're still tweaking some of the mechanism. We have no idea if it would survive a trip all the way out to Mexia."

"Besides," Noria added, tossing her head, "I'm really not interested in helping the Mages Guild. With the Chief Mage gone, maybe the Resistance can finally get something done around here."

"Noria!" Annia snapped. "Without the Chief Mage to rein everyone in, all we're going to accomplish is turning Solantha into a messy battleground."

"So?" Noria lifted her chin. "You have to fight a few battles in order to win a war. Fighting for freedom means you have to be willing to suffer casualties."

"Fine," I said through gritted teeth, "but that doesn't mean the Chief Mage has to be one of those casualties."

Noria turned her scornful gaze on me. "You know, you've really changed, Naya. Just a few months ago, you wouldn't have lifted a single finger to help the Chief Mage or his band of entitled cronies."

"That was before the Chief Mage saved my life," I said evenly.

"Alright," Annia said before we could take the argument further. "Politics aside, you owe me a crapload of favors, Noria, and it's time for me to cash in now."

Noria paled. "You can't be serious. *This* is what you're calling in that favor for?"

"Damn straight. I want that bounty, and Naya wants the Chief Mage. We're killing two birds with one stone, and you're going to help us by giving me that balloon."

"And just how are you going to steer it?" Noria demanded. "We haven't perfected the steering mechanism yet; it still requires a mage to pilot." Her eyes shifted toward me. "Preferably one who knows what she's doing."

I hesitated, but to my surprise Fenris spoke up. "I'm sure we won't have a problem figuring it out. Elnos, you can show us the basics, can't you? Between Sunaya and myself we should be able to keep it going long enough to get us to our destination."

"Sure," Elnos agreed, ignoring Noria's death glare. A mage

himself, he was the strange exception in Noria's life, but only because he believed that magic should be equally accessible to all. Hence why they worked together experimenting with magitech – devices that were powered by both magic and technology. "I've no problem teaching you the basics. We don't want them to die, after all, now do we?" He arched his brows at Noria.

"Of course not." Noria huffed out a breath, crossing her arms again as she pinned Annia with a gimlet stare. "But after this, you and I are square. Clear?"

"Clear."

~

AFTER A BRIEF LESSON from Elnos on how to handle the balloon, we set out to gather supplies. Since Fenris couldn't get back into the Palace to retrieve anything, he and I had to go shopping for travel gear as well as camping supplies for all of us.

"This trip would be much simpler if we weren't bringing your friend Annia along," Fenris grumbled as he plucked a bedroll off the shelf of the only camping store that was even open today. I'd spelled us to look like a couple of human students so that we wouldn't draw attention. "She's just a human. If something happens to that balloon and we end up stranded somewhere, she's sure to be a hindrance."

"Maybe," I allowed as I inspected the spoons of one of the mess kits I'd put into our shopping basket. There was a tiny nick on the edge of the implement, and I turned back to the shelf I'd grabbed it from so I could replace it. "But Annia's a damn good enforcer, and I could use someone with fighting experience at my back."

"I'm perfectly capable of defending myself," Fenris said stiffly, tossing the bedroll back and choosing another.

I rolled my eyes, then grabbed his wrist and turned his palm up. "Not a single callus on these bad boys," I remarked pointedly. "I'm not going to pretend I know what your past is, but if you've done any fighting, it was long enough ago that there's no trace of it on your body."

"You're right." Fenris snatched his hand back, glaring at me with his yellow shifter eyes. "You don't know what my past is. As I've said, I'm perfectly capable of defending myself."

"That may be so, but I'm still taking Annia," I said coolly. "Remember that without her, we wouldn't have the balloon. So you'll have to put up with the 'inconvenience' of it, or find another mode of transportation."

Fenris held my gaze for a moment longer, then looked away and sighed. "I suppose I can't argue with that. It's just...this is a very sensitive mission, Sunaya. The more people involved, the greater the danger that things can go wrong. Her sister sides with the enemy."

"I get it, but we need Annia. Besides, I trust her implicitly. She's not going to fuck us over."

"For Iannis's sake, I hope you're right."

"Alright," I said when we were all gathered around the balloon outside the workshop. Elnos and Noria had dragged the contraption to the small lot behind the shop to prepare it for liftoff. It was already inflated, the magical coal activated and burning brightly. "Guess it's time for us to get on this thing."

Fenris winced a little as he took in the neon-bright purple and yellow fabric of the balloon itself. "We're not going to blend in very well."

"Yeah, well I wasn't exactly creating this for a stealth mission," Noria snapped. She stepped up onto the platform we were going to use to board the balloon, then tapped the sandbags hanging off the basket. "Remember, these guys stay on here. The whole point is to make sure the balloon doesn't rise too fast when you lift off. The only exception is if for some reason you guys lose altitude and you're plummeting to the ground too fast. Then you drop them to lighten your load and slow your descent."

"We get it, Noria," Annia said quietly. There was a sadness in her dark eyes as she looked at her sister, and I wondered if it was because of the rift that had sprung between them when Annia had demanded Noria give up the balloon, or because of Noria's pro-Resistance attitude.

"Alright, well if you're so sure, let's get you boarded." Noria's narrowed eyes surveyed us. "You guys sure about this? Once you're gone, it's pretty hard to come back."

"We're sure." I eyed Noria's stiffened spine and rock-hard shoulders, then stepped forward and embraced her. She jolted in surprise at my touch, and I felt guilty that she would react this way to a show of affection from me. "Thank you so much, Nor. You don't know how much this means to me."

Noria sighed a little, hugging me back, and when I pulled away I was surprised to see a film of tears in her eyes. "I just want you all to be safe, and going out there to rescue the Chief Mage, especially at a time like this, is reckless. He's got boatloads of magic, Naya – surely he can take care of himself."

I snorted. "You're here to talk to me about recklessness?" In that department Noria was even worse than I was. "Besides, if it were Elnos out there, wouldn't you be going regardless of the danger?"

"I *love* Elnos." Noria arched a brow. "Are you trying to tell me that you love the Chief Mage?"

"I wouldn't go that far," I said lightly, though my heartbeat began to pick up at the accusation. "But he's my mentor now, and I've already lost one of those this year. I don't want to lose another."

"Alright." Noria sighed, then stepped aside to give me access to the platform. "Go on, then."

"Wait!"

I turned at the sound of Comenius's voice, and a smile broke out across my face as I watched him hurry into the lot with Elania on his heels. His features sagged with relief as he took us all in. "Oh, I'm so glad I didn't miss you."

"Me too." I stepped forward and into Com's waiting embrace. "Will you check on Lakin for me whenever you get a moment? I know you're not really comfortable with being in Shiftertown, but I'm sure his hands are more than full, and there are probably many wounded that could use your assistance."

"I'll do what I can." Comenius hugged me tightly, and I laid my head on his shoulder, soaking up his comforting embrace. His herbal scent surrounded me, and as I glanced over his shoulder at Elania, I was surprised to see jealousy in her dark eyes as she regarded us silently. But as soon as I stepped out of the embrace, the look in her eyes was gone, and a warm smile spread across her features as she came to hug me as well.

"May the gods be with you, Sunaya," she told me.

"And you." Truthfully, I had no idea what she meant by that, as I'd always operated under the assumption that there was one god – Magorah. I'd only recently found out that mages worshipped a version of Him called the Creator, as well as His right-hand woman, the first mage Resinah. I was still trying to wrap my head around what was true, but I couldn't deny that I'd felt a strong, powerful presence in Resinah's temple, and more than once I'd even imagined hearing her voice.

I stepped onto the platform, then turned back to face Noria as a thought occurred to me. "Promise me something."

"What?"

"Will you wait to join the Resistance?" When Noria's face stiffened, I added, "At least until we get back? I'd hate to think this is the last time we'll see you." Once Noria joined up with the Resistance she would become an outlaw, and would have to flee to one of the Resistance's hidden camps.

"I'll try," she allowed, her voice tight. "But no promises."

I nodded, then boarded the balloon. It was the best I could hope for.

"Take care of my sister, will you?" Annia called to Elnos as she hopped into the basket with me.

"Of course." Elnos nodded solemnly. Although he wouldn't – or rather, couldn't – stop Noria from joining the Resistance, he wasn't a fan of the idea. He would try to hold her off as long as possible.

"Alright," Fenris said as he settled himself into the basket along with us. "Let's get going."

Noria and Elnos rushed to cut the ropes tying the balloon to the ground. As they did, I took hold of the rope dangling from above, which I was supposed to direct my magic through to steer the balloon. I gripped the edge of the basket with my other hand as the balloon began to rise into the air, slowly, ever so slowly, and I watched as we crested the tops of the various buildings that made up the compound of the Academy. Soon we were high enough to see all of Rowanville – I could make out my apartment building, clustered in between so many of the other buildings and shops in Rowanville, and further up, the Port, nestled alongside Solantha Bay's glittering coast. Turning my neck, I also caught sight of Solantha Palace, Iannis's home, its towers and turrets spearing the gorgeous blue sky. The sun was halfway up its ascent to noon, casting bright rays over the glittering Bay waters, and I felt a tug at my heart. Solantha might be unsafe for me right now, but it was still my home, and I hated to leave it.

"Sunaya." Fenris's voice was at my ear. "You need to steer now, or the wind is going to blow us off course."

"Right." The wind was already pushing the balloon in a northwesterly direction, and we needed to head southeast. I cast one last glance toward Solantha, my eyes briefly lingering on Hawk Hill across the bay where Resinah's temple was secluded, then turned away. Focusing, I mumbled the Words that Elnos had taught me, and the burnt-sugar scent of magic laced the air as the rope between my fingers began to glow. Some directional instinct activated inside of me, a product of the spell, and I tugged the rope in the direction I wanted the balloon to follow.

"Nice job," Annia said as the balloon began moving southeast. She braced her arms on the edge of the basket and looked out, her dark red hair streaming out behind her like a banner. The sun kissed her face, highlighting her skin with a peachy glow, and from the way Fenris was eyeing her I saw I wasn't the only one who'd noticed.

"What?" he asked defensively when he noticed I'd switched my gaze to his.

"Just wondering if you've got something to share with the class."

"You already know how I feel about having her here," he muttered, but he averted his gaze.

But as I continued to steer the balloon, I wondered if I really did know how he felt. Fenris had stressed the need for discretion on this mission, but I wasn't sure why. After all, there was a horde of people heading out to search for Iannis. Why did it make a difference that Annia was teaming up with us as opposed to going out on her own, or with a crew of enforcers? Was there some kind of secret that Fenris was worried she'd find out about?

He does seem to have his fair share of secrets, I thought as I looked out across the changing landscape. We'd cleared the city now, and rolling hills of green stretched out below us, side by side with plots of farmland and orchards. The trees beneath us were laden with fruit just ripe for the picking. Hopefully whatever part of Mexia we ended up in would also have fruit- laden bushes or trees, or at the very least plentiful game. But at least part of the Coazi area was supposed to be desert country, so perhaps that was overly optimistic.

So long as we find Iannis, I'll put up with anything, I thought, my eyes firmly on the horizon. I only hoped that we found him before it was too late.

6

"By the Ur-God," Annia swore, her teeth chattering, "is there anything we can do to make it less freezing in here?"

"Sorry, but the closest heat source we have is currently being used to power the balloon right now." I turned my head to look at Annia, who was huddled in a corner of the basket, her bedroll unwrapped and tucked around her. Her cheeks were pink from the cold, as I imagined mine were – they stung from constantly being slapped by the winds buffeting our balloon.

"I wish I'd packed more layers to wear," she groused, her dark brows drawn together in a scowl. "This drafty basket is letting in far more air than the airships I've traveled on. Honestly, you'd think it was winter up here!"

"It is rather cold," Fenris agreed. He was sitting on the opposite end of basket from Annia, his knees drawn up to his chest as well, but he'd forgone the bedroll – since he was a shifter, the cold didn't affect him as badly.

"Seriously, Naya," Annia said, "can't you use your magic to heat up the air or something?"

"Keeping the air warm in here would require constant use of

my magic, and I'm already using it to steer the balloon," I told her. "I'm not a never-ending power source, Annia – that would drain me eventually."

"Oh alright," she sighed, burrowing a little deeper into her bedroll. "But this still sucks."

"I told you we shouldn't have brought her." Fenris's voice echoed into my mind, a little smugly. *"She's clearly not cut out for this kind of travel."*

"You have no idea what Annia is and isn't cut out for." Annoyed, I turned to glare at him, but I found that he wasn't even looking at me. Rather, he was staring at Annia over his knees, his yellow eyes glimmering with ire.

My scowl melted away into a grin as an idea came to me. *"Go sit over there with her."*

Fenris's eyes snapped toward me. *"Excuse me?"*

"Oh you heard me right." My grin widened. *"Go get under the bedroll with Annia and share your body heat with her."*

"I'll do no such thing," Fenris bit out. *"You keep saying she can take care of herself. She doesn't need me."*

"Oh stop being such an ass." I would have been annoyed at his recalcitrance if I wasn't enjoying how uncomfortable he was becoming. I'd never seen Fenris so ruffled. *"You know why we need her, and there's no point in letting her suffer if we don't have to. Be a gentleman, for Magorah's sake! Unless you don't know how."*

"Of course I know how," Fenris snapped.

"Know how to do what?" Annia asked, and we both snapped our heads around to look at her. Her dark, thickly lashed eyes were peeking out from beneath the bedroll, and they latched onto Fenris hopefully. "Build a fire in here without setting the whole basket aflame?"

"No," Fenris sighed, his voice softening. He rolled onto his knees, and the basket rocked a little as he made his way toward

Annia. "But I suppose I can help warm you up with my body heat."

"Oooh." Annia waggled her eyebrows, and I nearly lost it. "Does that mean you're getting naked?"

"Hardly." Fenris kept his voice even, but his short, dark hair wasn't long enough to hide his ears, and I bit back a laugh as I watched them turn red. Annia lifted the bedroll and waved Fenris over – a gesture that cost her as the exposure caused her to start shivering again. Noticing, Fenris quickly got under the bedroll with her and tucked it around them both, pressing his stocky body close to Annia's.

"There," I said, grinning. "That wasn't so hard, was it?"

"You put him up to this?" Annia asked, her brows arched.

"Well, I didn't want my best friend turning into a popsicle. Feel free to snuggle in closer – he doesn't mind."

"What...?" Fenris started to protest as Annia did exactly that, and I let out a snicker. From the glint in her dark eyes, I knew she was playing along with me. Fenris was ridiculously easy to tease, and I found myself wondering why I hadn't done it before. Probably because we didn't really spend any idle time together. As I watched Fenris slowly begin to relax, I wondered if he spent idle time in the company of others at all. He was close friends with Iannis, sure, but I'd hardly ever heard the two of them talk of anything other than business, and he didn't appear to have close relationships with anyone else.

Then again, Fenris was a shifter, so should I really be surprised that he hadn't made friends with the others? The way the Council had turned on him so quickly the moment Iannis was out of sight was proof that without the Chief Mage's support, Fenris didn't hold much influence. It made me wonder if that was my fate, too – if I would always have to rely on Iannis to protect me from the wrath and prejudice of the Mages Guild.

Hell no, I thought, gripping the rope in my fist a little tighter.

I might need Iannis now, but no way was I going to be dependent on him for the rest of my life. I was going to become a mage in my own right, a force to be reckoned with, and the other mages would have to respect me.

"Is it just me, or are we swaying a little?"

Annia's voice startled me out of my thoughts, and I realized that my lapses in concentration were pulling the balloon in the wrong direction – a side effect of letting myself get caught up in my emotions.

"Sorry," I muttered, reining myself in. The balloon steadied again as I straightened out our course. "I wasn't paying attention."

"Do you need me to take over?" Fenris asked, sounding concerned. "It's important that you maintain your focus and control, Sunaya. We don't want to wreck the balloon."

"No, no, I'm fine." I waved Fenris away as he started to stand up. "I'll be good for another hour at least."

"Very well," he said, settling back in with Annia. I turned my attention back to the landscape, which was so very, very far below us. It had been six hours since we'd left, with at least another four to go until we crossed the border into Mexia. Right now we were hovering over the state of Aziana, the craggy, reddish-brown landscape peeking through the clouds below us. Mostly canyons and desert, with the occasional green patch of forest. I'd heard they had cacti there the size of trees, with arms sticking out to the sides and up, like a man holding up both hands in surrender. I wondered what the people there were like – I'd traveled all over Canalo on enforcer business, but never to other states, and it made me realize I knew very little about the rest of the Federation.

If we ever get out of this mess, and I ever get some time off, I'm going to travel, I decided. *From coast to coast, so I can see what this country is really like, and after that to other continents.*

I steered the balloon for another hour, then with Fenris's help landed it in a sheltered valley so we could make camp. The sun was setting, and none of us were keen on trying to steer the balloon through the night. Without light it would be tough to land safely, and the charm could well lead us to a forest or down a canyon. Also, my bladder was full to bursting – we'd had a bucket on board to relieve ourselves, of course, but I'd stubbornly held out until we landed.

"You two make camp," I told Fenris and Annia once we'd secured the balloon. "I'm going to see if I can scrounge up some dinner."

"Why?" Annia asked, frowning as she held up a sack. "We've got provisions."

"We shouldn't use them if we don't have to. Besides," I added, grinning a little, "I could use the exercise."

"Suit yourself." Annia turned away to unpack the small tent we'd bought. It turned out that she'd brought one of her own, so we had two shelters if the weather got rough. Thankfully it didn't seem like that was going to happen – the air here was dry and warm. Almost swelteringly so, especially considering that we'd been freezing our asses off just a little while ago. I hoped things cooled off a little bit, or I was going to have trouble getting to sleep.

Putting the worry out of my mind, I closed my eyes and reached for my inner beast. She sprang forth eagerly, and a white light enveloped me as uncomfortably hot tingles spread through my body. I stretched and changed shape, muscles, skin, and bones reforming, and when the white light faded, I was crouched on all fours, my tail swishing back and forth. Digging my claws into the reddish-brown dirt, I stretched and yawned, muscles rippling beneath my black fur. It felt good to be back in beast form again.

I spared one last look at Annia and Fenris, then bounded

forward, heading up into the tree-dotted hillside. Dirt and rocks shifted beneath my paws as I ran, and I opened up my senses to the wilderness. Birds twittered overhead, branches rustled as a squirrel hopped from one tree to another, and the scent of deer droppings mixed with the fresher scents of evergreens and shrubs urged me onward.

I tracked the deer droppings further north to a clearing, where a herd of deer grazed. I crouched in the tall grass for a little while, scoping out the options, and my eyes settled on an older female with a limp in her rear right leg. Settled on my choice, I sprang from my hiding place and bounded straight for her. The herd immediately took off, galloping to safety, and the female tried to follow, but her leg slowed her down as I'd expected. Within seconds I was on her, taking her down, my claws digging into her hide as she struggled vainly. Clamping my jaws around her long neck, I shook her neck to break the spine, the killing blow. A crack rent the air, and as the deer went limp, I pierced her jugular with my fangs. As her sweet blood coated my tongue, I was briefly overwhelmed by the urge to feast right then and there, but I held back. This kill wasn't just for myself, after all – it was for Annia and Fenris as well.

"Wow," Annia remarked as I dragged the deer back to camp. "You really know how to impress a girl, don't you?" She was sitting on a log in front of a campfire, stirring something in a pot.

"I told Annia to wait for you, but she insisted on using some of the rations," Fenris responded as I tossed my head, annoyed that Annia was cooking something else. He was sitting next to her on the log, though at a respectable distance. To the left, I noticed that the tents had been set up, and the balloon was properly secured.

Oh well. More for you and me, I guess. Come on then, let's eat.

Something very much like reluctance crossed Fenris's face, but then he nodded and stood. I dragged the deer carcass aside out of respect for Annia, and waited until Fenris had changed into wolf form before ripping into it. Shifters need a lot of food to begin with, and on top of that I'd been using my magic all day, so I was ravenous. Between the two of us, we managed to pick the bones clean in short order.

"Enjoy your meal?" Annia asked after we'd trotted back over to the campfire.

I bumped my head against her leg and made a purring sound in answer, then curled up by her feet and stared into the fire. With a full belly and nothing pressingly urgent to do, sleeping in front of the campfire sounded like a really nice idea right about now.

"I'm going to explore for a bit," Fenris told me. I cracked open an eye to see him standing under the trees, swishing his tail. *"You'll be staying here with Annia?"*

"Yeah. I've had my share of exercise, thanks."

Fenris inclined his head once, then bounded off into the forest. I didn't know where he got his energy from, but then again I'd done most of the steering today, so it stood to reason he wasn't as pooped as I was.

"So," Annia said just as I was about to drift off, "what's the deal with Fenris?"

Huffing, I lifted my head to glare at her. Couldn't a girl take a catnap? It wasn't like we could actually communicate while I was in beast form.

Annia only lifted an eyebrow. "Oh, give me a break and change back already. I'm not sitting out here by myself and talking to the air when I've got you for company."

I made a disgruntled noise in the back of my throat, but did as she asked and changed back into human form. Once I was on two legs again, I sat down on the log beside her and stared up at the sky. The sun had fully set, leaving only a tinge of purple at the edges of the dark sky. Out here in the wilderness, I could see more stars than sky, many of them more luminous than even the waxing moon hanging above our heads.

"Not sure what you want me to tell you about Fenris," I finally said. "I don't really know much about him."

"You have to know something," Annia said, looking at me curiously. "From what I understand, you two are the only shifters who spend any substantial length of time in the Palace. What's up with that?"

"Well, I know why *I* ended up in the Palace," I said, playing with the ends of my ponytail. I'd scooped my hair back and tied it with a leather band hours ago – the winds had kept blowing it in my face and making visibility difficult while I was steering the balloon. "The Chief Mage took an interest in my abilities, and he hasn't gotten tired of me yet. But I have no idea why he and Fenris are friends. It's not like Fenris is half-mage like me."

"If he's not a mage, then how is it that he was able to help you steer the balloon?" Annia asked, puzzled. "I thought you had to have magic in order to do that. Isn't that what Noria said?"

"I…" I opened my mouth, and then closed it again. I didn't have an answer for that. "He must have picked up some kind of trick from Iannis."

"How do you know he isn't a hybrid like you?"

"He's not." I shook my head emphatically – of this I was certain. "He smells like a full-blooded shifter to me." I slanted my eyes toward her. "Why are you so curious, anyway?"

"I like to know who I'm working with." Annia's lips curved into a small smile. "And besides, I'm curious as to why he's so stiff and fidgety around me. If it weren't for you, I'd think he'd never been around a woman before."

"I think he's just not used to new people." But my own lips twitched, and I had to stifle a laugh. "Just how 'stiff' was he under that blanket anyway?"

Annia snickered. "He wasn't *that* kind of stiff, you pervert." Her dark eyes twinkled with mirth as she shook her head at me. "In fact, I have to wonder if he's even into women."

"Wait a second." My mouth formed a little 'o' of horror as the implications of that dawned on me. "All the time he and Iannis spend together...do you think...?"

"Do you think what?" Fenris asked, emerging from the forest in human form.

"Nothing," Annia and I said in unison.

"Hmm." Fenris's yellow eyes narrowed, but he didn't press the matter further. "I suggest we get to sleep soon, so we can get an early start in the morning. The sooner we find Iannis, the better."

"Right." We cleaned up what mess we'd made from dinner, then established a watch schedule – Fenris was first, I was second, and Annia was taking third. Fenris settled down by the fire, and Annia and I bedded down in the tents, which were each only large enough to accommodate a single person. As I fastened the tent's entrance, I took a moment to study Fenris's profile. I'd always thought of him as Iannis's stalwart companion, a trusted advisor and friend. But what if they were more? What if Fenris's motivation for finding Iannis went beyond simple friendship?

But if that's the case, then why would Fenris have encouraged Iannis to exchange serapha *charms with me?*

"Do you need something, Sunaya?" Fenris asked, turning to look my way.

"No." I shook my head, my cheeks flushing a little at having been caught staring. "I just...it's nothing. Goodnight."

I finished zipping up the tent, then flopped back onto my bedroll. I was chasing my thoughts in circles around my head. If Fenris was in an intimate relationship with Iannis, he wouldn't have wanted us to exchange *serapha* charms. I hadn't known this at the time, but *serapha* charms were usually exchanged between engaged or married couples – they were a semi-permanent method of binding two souls together, so that each would always be able to find the other. Even though I hadn't known that at the time Iannis and I had made the charms, Fenris had. In fact, it had been his suggestion.

The only explanation that made sense was that Fenris and Iannis *weren't* lovers. I was worrying about nothing.

It doesn't matter, I told myself firmly. *You're all in this together regardless.* Wondering about Iannis's relationship with Fenris wasn't going to help me find him. Putting the matter aside, I forced myself to relax into sleep. There would be plenty of time to think about these things once Iannis was safely recovered. Or so I hoped.

7

The next day started off well enough. We rose early, broke camp, and managed to get the balloon into the air with only two false starts. Not too bad for a couple of amateurs. It was just as cold up in the air as it had been yesterday, but Fenris and I took turns sharing the bedroll with Annia and we made do.

As I steered the balloon again, looking out over the rugged Aziana landscape, I wondered how Iannis was faring. I assumed he was with the other delegates, but of course I could have been wrong about that. The rest of them could have all died, or they could have been separated somehow. Worse, the Resistance might have taken them alive to be tortured for information.

They'd have to have a very strong mage on their side to pull that off, I mused to myself. I still couldn't imagine someone as powerful as Iannis being taken captive by human means. A renegade mage on their side was the only logical explanation for how they'd taken a whole dirigible full of mages captive, if that was what had happened.

Wanting to reassure myself that Iannis was all right, I tugged my *serapha* charm from beneath the collar of my jacket and focused on it. At first, the little white stone did nothing, but then suddenly it burst into a brilliant glow.

"Guys!" I shrieked, so excited that I nearly dropped the steering rope. "Guys, look!" I turned to show them the blazing stone.

Fenris sat up straight. "That's great news!" he exclaimed, hope brightening his eyes.

"What's great news?" Annia wanted to know.

"The stone's glowing brightly again," I explained, grinning at her. "When we set out it was only giving off a dull light, which meant that Iannis was injured or sick. The fact that it's glowing so brightly must mean that he's healed. He must have found help or something."

"Well on the one hand, that's a relief, but on the other that might mean one of the search parties has already found him," Annia said with a huff. "I've heard many of them have brought healers. And if that's the case, I won't get any prize money."

Fenris glared at her. "I hope you didn't embark on this mission solely for financial gain."

"Well, Naya is my friend and I want to help her out, but so what if I did?" Annia argued. "I'm an enforcer. It's a money-motivated profession."

"Umm, guys," I interrupted, pointing to the sky. "We've got some bad news too."

"What – oh." Fenris went silent as he stared at the black clouds gathering in the sky. "We can't fly through that."

"We definitely can't," I agreed, worrying my bottom lip as anxiety began to brew in my gut. The fragile balloon wasn't meant to withstand a storm, but I didn't want to stop because it would mean losing at least half a day. Iannis might be feeling better, but that didn't mean he wasn't still in some kind of danger or in need of help.

"Annia, can you drag out the map?"

"Sure thing." Annia reached for her pack and withdrew the map of the Northia Federation that Elania had given us. She spread it out on the floor, and I muttered the Words to a location spell Fenris had taught me – something he'd claimed to have read from one of the Palace's library books. A greenish-blue dot lit up on the map, showing our exact location just inside the Mexian border.

"Hey! I didn't even realize we'd crossed the border," Annia exclaimed. "We must only be a few hours away from our target."

"Yeah." I glanced at the gathering storm clouds again. They were still some distance away. "I think we can get another hour of use out of this balloon."

"Sunaya." The warning tone in Fenris's voice was clear. "We're of no help to Iannis if we get struck down by lightning."

"I know, but that storm isn't on us yet." I put the map away and renewed my efforts in steering the balloon. "We can make it a little further before we have to land."

"Okay, so maybe I was wrong."

"Maybe!" Fenris shouted over the howling winds. "Your recklessness is going to get us killed!"

The storm clouds, it turned out, were not the only thing we had to worry about. As we drew closer to them, the winds started to pick up, and soon we were fighting a ridiculously strong, cold current that was pushing us in the opposite direction. The storm clouds were coming in a lot faster than I'd expected – if I didn't land the balloon soon, we were going to get caught in the middle of a lightning storm.

"Okay, okay, I get it!" Tightening my grip on the steering rope, I focused my attention on bringing us down. "We're going to land this thing safely, okay?"

A flash of lightning lit up the sky, and two seconds later a crashing boom of thunder raised the hair along my arms. Biting my lip, I concentrated on bringing the balloon down, trying to find a safe place to land. Unfortunately, we were passing over a mountain range, and the trees made it hard to figure out where exactly to aim for. I was going to have to get closer.

"Sunaya!" Fenris shouted. "Incoming!"

I looked to my left, then cursed at the sight of a huge flock of large, black birds with yellow bills headed straight for us. Rushing to the burners, I turned the knob to decrease the heat, and the balloon began to drop, putting us below the level that the flock was flying at.

"Phew –" I began to let out a sigh of relief, but froze as the little bastards changed altitude as well. "Oh, shit. Take cover!"

I crouched down inside the basket just as the flock hit us – and by that I meant literally. The sound of wings beating and beaks cawing created a cacophony that made my ears ring, and I resisted the urge to clap my hands over them to block out the noise. The balloon jostled and swayed as several of the large creatures bumped into it, and my heart dropped as I heard a loud ripping sound.

"Fuck!" I jumped to my feet, then hastily grabbed the edge of the basket for balance as we dropped several feet in altitude. Leaning out the side, I saw a flap of fabric whipping around in the wind, and gritted my teeth. One of those bastards had ripped a hole in our balloon! Frantically, I tore my knife out and sawed off the ropes holding the sandbags, hoping the loss of weight would help slow our descent.

Thunder rolled across the sky again, but I didn't even bother to look at the storm clouds now – we had bigger problems. Despite lightening the load, the balloon was dropping at an alarming rate, much faster than I wanted it to. I grabbed the steering rope as the mountainside we were headed for came closer and closer into view.

"Steer it that way!" Fenris had jumped to his feet to stand next to me, and was pointing to a patch of land on the mountainside that looked clearer than the rest. "If we can avoid the trees we might be able to patch the balloon up!"

"Okay!" I shouted over the roaring wind, and tugged the balloon in that direction.

"Isn't there any way to slow this thing down?" Annia asked. She was scrambling about on her hands and knees, securing our baggage as best she could in preparation for what was looking like an imminent crash-landing. "I'd rather not have my bones pulverized, thank you very much!"

"I'm doing the best I can!" I shouted back, keeping my eyes focused on our destination. We were close enough now that I could see the individual branches on the pine trees. My stomach twisted as the ground rushed into view and I realized we were headed straight for a very steep, very narrow ravine.

"Brace yourselves!" I cried as we cleared the treetops, and I ducked back down and grabbed onto the edge of the basket. I squeezed my eyes shut right before we crashed into the hard, unforgiving rock, and prayed to Magorah that we would survive this so that I could see Iannis again.

"WELL THAT WENT WELL," Annia said dryly as we stared up at the smashed remnants of the balloon. We'd hit the rocky wall of the ravine hard enough that the basket had been smashed beyond repair, and it had been wedged so tightly in the rock that we'd been trapped a good twenty feet off the ground. Even in panther form it had been challenging for me to climb out and make it to the ground, and once I did I'd had to help fashion a makeshift pulley system from a coil of rope and some bits from the balloon itself. Engineering wasn't exactly my strong suit, and I'd been sweating bullets as I'd lowered Annia and Fenris down, but we'd eventually managed to make it out safely.

"At least we have most of our supplies," I offered, hefting my pack a little higher on my shoulder.

"Yeah, but we've probably added several days to our journey."

"We survived," I pointed out. "We could have easily ended up as pulverized as the balloon."

"True." Annia shuddered a little as she glanced up at the contraption. "I'm not entirely sure why we weren't."

"It's a mystery," I said dryly, slanting a narrow-eyed look at Fenris. I'd scented magic just before we'd crashed into the rock face, and I had a suspicion he'd had something to do with it. But Fenris simply gave me a bland look before returning his yellow gaze to Annia.

"If you're worried about food, feel free to help yourself to most of the supplies," he said. "Sunaya and I will be able to hunt game, and we should encounter streams along the way to refill our canteens. In the meantime though, we should focus on finding Iannis. Sunaya, where does your *serapha* charm tell us to go?"

Closing my eyes, I focused in on the charm around my neck, paying careful attention to the tug at the center of my chest. "That way." I pointed, and then opened my eyes to find that I was jabbing my finger directly at the rock wall.

Fenris sighed. "We'd better figure a way out of this ravine, then."

We followed the ravine long enough to find the stream and refill our water bottles and then, with me in the lead, forged an impromptu trail towards Iannis.

The next couple of days were long and grueling – the mountainous terrain was challenging, with plenty of gorges and rocky ground to traverse, and little water to be found. Fenris and I spent more time than not in beast form, finding it easier to travel across the unforgiving landscape on all fours, but Annia didn't have that luxury, and we often had to slow down and wait for her.

Finally, on the third day, we emerged from the treacherous mountain range. Rocky terrain gave way to wide, rolling plains covered in tall yellow grass, with the occasional scruffy-looking tree jutting out of the landscape. The air was hot and dry, and we stopped at the top of a small hillock so I could take off my jacket and survey the landscape.

The *serapha* charm was still pointing us in the previous direction, so Director Chen's rescue team had not yet found Iannis either. But with every day we lost, Solantha was likely sliding deeper into chaos. Fear for the city and for Annia's sister kept us pushing to the limits of our endurance, and we struggled through the long days with little sleep.

"You sure we're going in the right direction?" Annia asked dubiously as she pushed her long, auburn hair out of her face. "I dunno about you, but the way I see it there seems to be a whole lot of nothing out here aside from those buffalo." She pointed out to a large group of brown clumps in the distance.

"Not quite," Fenris remarked as he stretched a finger in the opposite direction. "If you look out there, you'll see we've got company."

"Huh?" Annia squinted her dark eyes as she looked out in Fenris's direction. "I don't see anything."

"It's okay," I assured her with a pat on the shoulder. "They're little grey dots, and they're hard for even me to see." Especially with the backdrop of the purplish-grey mountains on the other side of the plains.

"Little grey dots," Annia repeated. A hot gust of wind blew

straight at us, rustling the grasses at our feet and sending Annia's hair flying. Not for the first time, I was grateful for the decision to tie my hair back. "So, what are those supposed to be? Little tents or something?"

Fenris shrugged. "They could be, though they would have to be rather large for us to see them at this distance. I'm not sure what sort of dwellings the Coazi use – these people may all look the same to us, but from what I understand, they actually differ from tribe to tribe in numerous ways."

"You seem to understand a lot," I commented, my eyes still scanning the landscape. Now that I looked more closely, I could see the dwellings in more than one location across the landscape. "It looks like they've got several settlements out here. Is that normal?"

"It's not unusual," Fenris confirmed. "Tribes have been known to split off into different clans, especially when their territory covers such great distances. Each one will likely have its own chieftain and shaman, and there is probably a central clan as well."

"Sounds like politics exist even amongst savages," Annia said, huffing out a breath.

Fenris turned a narrowed gaze in her direction. "Do not make the mistake of thinking these people are simple," he warned. "They may not speak our language or practice our customs, but their minds are as sharp as yours or mine. It wouldn't do to treat them like children or idiots and inadvertently insult them if we run across them."

"What do you think we should do if we do run across them?" I chewed my lower lip, worried about the possibility. "Do we fight first and ask questions later? That reference book Comenius dug up said their shamans can be very powerful, and I'd hate to be at the mercy of one."

Fenris sighed. "It's hard to know. Some of them might be

friendlier than others, and it would be a shame to make an enemy when we could find an ally instead. We'll have to reserve judgment until the moment actually arrives."

"Well, it's certainly not going to if we stay on this hill," I decided, squaring my shoulders. "Let's move on."

We trekked for another mile or so across the rolling hills, following the tug from the *serapha* charm's spell. It seemed to be a little stronger now that we were out of the mountains, and I was hoping that meant we would run across Iannis soon. Was he with one of the Coazi clans, wearing buckskin tunics and making clay pottery with his manicured hands? The idea made my lips twitch in amusement, and was far more appealing than the possibility that the Coazi were holding him hostage. Though admittedly I couldn't see either one of those things happening – Iannis was both too proud and too powerful.

And what about the other delegates and their flunkies who had been aboard the airship? Were they with the Coazi? Or had they all struck out together, perhaps even building a shelter of their own as they tried to figure out how to alert the Federal authorities to their plight? Were they all still alive? I had no idea how the airship had gone down – for all I knew it had gone up in flames and only Iannis had figured out how to survive, while everyone else had plunged into a fiery death.

A shudder went through my spine at the thought of dying by both air and fire. With the recent storm and crash we'd experienced, I was glad that I had both feet firmly on the ground. I just hoped they stayed that way until we found Iannis.

8

The *serapha* charm had us cutting across the plains diagonally. Up ahead I could see two large evergreen forests cutting into the plains and narrowing them into a small path that wound between the large swathes of trees. With luck that was where we'd find Iannis, hiding in the cool, dark safety of the pine boughs as he figured out his next move. That's what I would want to do if I were in his shoes. But then again, I was a panther shifter, and my beast was more comfortable in the mountains and trees than on these wide, open plains where there was very little cover.

The wind shifted direction. Fenris and I stiffened as an amalgamation of scents hit our nostrils. Clay, dried meat, bread, and...*humans.*

"Get down!" I hissed.

Annia immediately dropped onto her stomach between Fenris and myself, right at the base of a grassy knoll. I cursed inwardly at the tall grass, which would rustle whether we crawled or walked. My nose told me that the humans we'd scented weren't very far, and if they were trained warriors they would hear us coming. The air current had been shifting their scent away from us until it had changed direction – if not for that, we would have had more warning.

"We can't just lie here," Fenris murmured. "Unless you want to wait for who knows how long and risk them finding us, we need to get up that hillock and find out who we're dealing with."

I nodded, my lips pressed together. Turning to face Annia, I gave her a pointed look and jerked my head in the direction of the hillock. She nodded, and the three of us crawled up the side of the knoll as quietly as we could. We peered over the top of the crest to see a group of humans sitting cross-legged at the base of the knoll, enjoying a small meal of flatbread and dried meat. They had long, dark hair and brown skin with a reddish tint that I imagined was what chocolate would look like if it were mixed with magma. There were four men and three women, all dressed in beaded buckskin with moccasins on their feet. The women wore their hair in braids on either side of their heads with a part that fell in the middle, and the men either wore their hair loose, or in a topknot at the back of their heads, with bangs. Two of the men had red and white feathers woven into their fine black hair, and by their build and the weapons they had strapped to their persons I gathered they were the two warriors of the bunch, sent along to protect the party from strangers like us. Next to each of the non-warriors was a woven basket with a lid, meant to be carried like a backpack, and the smears of red on the weave drew my attention.

"What's the red stuff in the baskets?" I whispered to Fenris.

His yellow eyes narrowed as he considered. "I believe its clay."

Ah. Well that explained what I'd smelled earlier. So they weren't a scouting or hunting party – they'd come out to collect clay to make pottery or whatever else the Coazi did with the stuff. I started to relax a little, and let out a sigh of relief.

Instantly, two heads swung around in our direction – the two men I'd pegged as warriors earlier. They jumped to their feet, one drawing his bow, the other hefting his spear. I bit back a curse as we dropped back down behind the crest of the knoll, but it was too late – they'd already seen us.

"I don't suppose you speak Coazi?" Annia hissed at Fenris.

"Of course not." Fenris bristled. "Let us hope that one of them speaks our language."

Rather than waiting for them to find us cowering behind the hillock, we got to our feet slowly, our hands in the air to show that we meant no harm. The two warriors were already halfway up the hill, and they momentarily froze at the sight of us before leveling their weapons in our direction and shouting angrily.

"Please!" Fenris shouted, drawing their attention to him. "We mean no harm!"

"Why you come on our land?" the spear-toting warrior demanded. He wore his hair long and free, and was a taller, leaner version of the man next to him. Their features were similar enough that I wouldn't have been surprised if they were brothers, and I breathed a sigh of relief that they knew some Northian. "This not white man's land!"

"We are sorry for trespassing," Fenris said, lowering his head. He kept his hands in the air, his body language contrite and nonthreatening, and I forced myself to do the same even though the beast inside me growled at the idea of showing submission to a weaker life-form. Just because I was perfectly capable of killing these people didn't mean I wanted to. "We are looking for a friend of ours. He might be lost somewhere on your lands."

"Friend?" the other man asked. He was shorter and stockier than the other, and wore his hair in a topknot. His dark eyes were narrowed, and he kept his arrow firmly trained on me. "A white man?"

"Yes. A white man with red hair." Fenris gestured toward

Annia's flowing locks, though her auburn hair was much lighter than Iannis's. "Have you seen him?"

"He was flying in an airship," I added, drawing the taller man's attention toward me. "It may have crashed somewhere near here. Did you see anything big fall from the sky?"

The two men looked at each other out of the corner of their eyes. They immediately started talking to each other in low tones, which was unnecessary since we couldn't understand a single word they said. The fact that their broad shoulders had relaxed a little ignited a spark of hope in me.

"Do you think they've seen Iannis?" I asked Fenris.

"It's entirely possible."

"If we're lucky, he might even be at their camp!"

"Or unlucky, depending on what they're doing with him," Fenris warned.

Finally, the two Coazi males turned back to us. The stockier one met my gaze, and for the first time curiosity sparked in his dark eyes. "You are a man-beast, yes?"

"Huh?" My mouth dropped open, taken aback by the strange question.

"Woman-beast, then." The Coazi male gestured impatiently. "You can turn into an animal. I tell by your strange eyes."

"Yes." My lips quirked a little at his description of me – I'd been called a lot of things in my life, but "man-beast" was certainly a new one for me. "I turn into a panther."

The taller Coazi turned to his group and announced the news to them in their native tongue. The groups eyes widened, and then they broke out into wide smiles and started talking excitedly, jumping up and down on the balls of their feet.

"Er, what's happening?" I asked Fenris worriedly.

"Your guess is as good as mine."

The tall Coazi male turned back toward us. "We hear of the

strange man-beasts the mages who rule this land made, but never seen one. You show us?"

"You want to see me shift?" I asked incredulously. Part of me was stung by the idea – I wasn't some kind of pony to be paraded around for their amusement.

Fenris touched my elbow. *"I know it might seem demeaning, but I see no harm in doing this if it helps create goodwill with the Coazi."*

Swallowing a sigh, I took a step toward the Coazi. "Alright, I will do as you ask. You might want to take a step back."

They all stepped back hastily, and Fenris shot me a scowl as I fought against the urge to snicker. Of course there was no reason for them to step back, but I enjoyed the idea of screwing with them a little after being asked to put myself on display like this. Closing my eyes, I reached for my inner beast, and let the white light wash over me. I heard the Coazi gasp and murmur as my body stretched and changed, bone and muscle and skin reforming, fur sprouting, teeth and claws elongating. Delighted at the chance to break free, my beast purred loudly – we were the same person, and yet not, two sides of the same coin. It was hard to explain to someone who wasn't a shifter – a bit like having a split personality, except that my beast and I weren't really all that different when it came right down to it. My human instincts were simply more dominant in human form than they were when I shifted.

Opening my eyes, I surveyed my spellbound audience, and couldn't help but chuff in amusement at their wide-eyed stares. Wanting to milk it a little more, I stretched my long body, padding at the reddish dirt beneath my paws and allowing them to see my claws. Affecting lethargy, I gave them a wide yawn, exposing my long fangs, and they gasped.

"Fearsome," the stockier Coazi said, his dark eyes shining. "The legends we hear...they are true. But man-beasts are no longer slaves of the evil mages?"

"No, we are not," Fenris said, a little sharply. I slanted my gaze to him, wondering about the defensive tone in his voice. Maybe it was on behalf of Iannis, who wasn't there to defend the mages. "Shifters have not been bound by slavery for at least five hundred years."

"But mages and man-beasts not equal, no?" the Coazi male pressed.

Fenris opened his mouth, but he paused as the white light washed over me, and everyone else turned my way to watch as I changed back. A few moments later, I once again stood on the knoll in human form, my arms crossed beneath my breasts as I narrowed my gaze at the persistent Coazi.

"What's with all these questions?" I asked. "Are you really so interested in the welfare of shifters?"

"Shifters," the shorter male repeated, testing the word on his tongue.

"Not concerned with...welfare...but your interest in missing white man," the taller Coazi said. His dark eyes gleamed with something like mischief as he regarded me. "We know mages can fly in these machines, and the machine had mage...symbol painted on outside. Why is a man-beast trying to rescue evil mage?"

"Huh." I raised my eyebrows in surprise, starting to see the line of logic the Coazi male was following. Despite their strange looks and clothing and the heavy accent, they were quite intelligent. Much more than I had given them credit for, which made me feel guilty. Really, if I looked down on a group of people just because they were of another race and culture, was I any better than the mages who looked down on us shifters for similar reasons?

"So you want to know why a bunch of shifters and a human are out here looking for a mage?"

"Yes." The two men nodded, seeming pleased that I was finally understanding them.

"Well these two here happen to be friends of the man we're looking for." Annia stepped between Fenris and me, clapping a hand on each of our shoulders. "And I'm a friend of Naya here," she added, squeezing my shoulder to indicate who she was referring to. "But as far as I'm concerned, I'm here to collect a bounty. There's a reward out for whoever recovers the mage we're looking for."

"Ah. So missing mage is important." The Coazi's eyes gleamed at that.

My hackles rose at the crafty look in his eyes, and I took a step forward. "If you know anything at all about a missing white man, I suggest you tell us now." I was tired of whatever mind game they were playing with us, and I also didn't like the way they were looking at us. "If you are hiding him from us and plan to hurt him in any way, I will make you regret that decision for the rest of eternity." I bared my fangs at them.

The other Coazi stepped back, clothing rustling as they leveled spears and knives in my direction. But to my surprise, the tall Coazi just laughed. "You do not risk death for reward, no? White man you seek...he is one you love."

A blush rose to my cheeks at that, and my spine straightened. "I owe him a great debt, and I intend to see that repaid."

The man laughed at me again, and by the way his eyes sparkled I could tell he wasn't buying my explanation. But he finally lowered his spear, and his companion followed suit with the bow and arrow.

"I am Tsu-Wakan," the tall man said. He clapped his companion on the shoulder. "This my brother, Caranou. You come and spend night with us, speak with shaman. He tell you what you need."

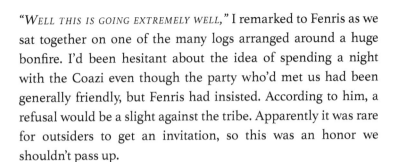

"*WELL THIS IS GOING EXTREMELY WELL,*" I remarked to Fenris as we sat together on one of the many logs arranged around a huge bonfire. I'd been hesitant about the idea of spending a night with the Coazi even though the party who'd met us had been generally friendly, but Fenris had insisted. According to him, a refusal would be a slight against the tribe. Apparently it was rare for outsiders to get an invitation, so this was an honor we shouldn't pass up.

"*Indeed,*" Fenris remarked dryly, his yellow eyes on Annia. She was dancing around the fire along with the younger Coazi, Caranou, who had welcomed us warmly enough after Tsu-Wakan had introduced us. By the time he'd led us back to their camp, which was several miles away, the sun was dipping beneath the horizon and our stomachs were rumbling with the need for dinner. Thankfully, the Coazi had been more than happy to accommodate us – they'd led us to one of the round grey dwellings I'd seen from a distance that were a cross between a hut and a tent, and had allowed us to rest our feet while they'd set up the bonfire and roasted meat and vegetables.

"*Yeah well you can't exactly blame Annia.*" Along with the food, they'd served us some kind of strong, fermented juice and passed a pipe around, which they'd insisted we smoke. Fenris and I remained unaffected because of our shifter metabolisms, but the alcohol and strange herbs had gotten to Annia. I snorted as I watched her stomp around in mini circles as she made her way around the bonfire, waving her hands in the air and shouting along with all the Coazi. Quite a few of them were bare-chested males wearing nothing but buckskin skirts, their bare feet stomping in the reddish brown dirt beneath us and sending up clouds of dust that made my nose itch. From the way their dark eyes lingered on Annia with admiration, I had a feeling she was getting laid tonight.

Lust surged through me at the idea, reminding me that my heat was barely two weeks away. I clenched my teeth as fire spread through my lower belly, hotter and more potent than the blaze in front of me. I already ached to quench it, although I knew it wouldn't matter. Having sex before the heat peaked didn't take the edge off – when the time came, it was always explosive and there was no escaping it.

Besides, there was only one person I wanted right now, and he was lost somewhere on these vast plains, close but nowhere near close enough.

"Your friend is very spirited." The log shifted a little as Aman-Wa, the tribe's shaman, sat down next to me. Grey streaked his dark hair, though aside from the deep laugh lines on his face he did not look so very old. His more colorful tunic separated his status from the other tribe members – the only person who was dressed more elaborately was the chieftain, who sat on the other side of the bonfire wearing a feathered headdress and beaded tunic, his arm slung across the slim shoulders of his wife as he talked and laughed with a tribe elder.

"Annia has always known how to have a good time." I grinned at the shaman, but Fenris shifted uncomfortably on my other side. I wondered if he was intimidated by the shaman, or if there was something else that bothered him about the man. My instincts told me Aman-Wa was easygoing and sincere, but then again I didn't know as much about these people as Fenris seemed to.

"She may have red hair and pale skin, but in spirit she could easily be one of us." The shaman's dark eyes sparkled as he watched Annia grab hands with one of the half-naked males and start dancing with him. "Our men have been eyeing her with more interest than perhaps is wise."

"Well, I hope none of them get too attached," I half-joked. "Annia is a bit of a heartbreaker, and we are leaving in the morning."

"To find your mage." Aman-Wa nodded soberly, turning his head to look at me. His eyes dropped down below my neck, right to where my *serapha* charm rested beneath my shirt. I'd removed my jacket due to the heat of the fire, and alarm raced through me as I wondered if he could see it through the cotton fabric.

Impossible. It's a black shirt and it's dark out. I had to fight against the urge to look down and check for myself.

"The stone you wear beneath your shirt, it holds a piece of the man you seek, does it not?"

I sucked in a breath, feeling like I'd been sucker-punched in the gut. "How the hell do you know that?"

The shaman smiled, and gently took my hands in his. "The spirits allow me to see what most cannot," he told me. "I know the one you seek is important to you, just as I know that you are not merely a man-beast. There is power inside you that is wild and untamed yet." He squeezed my hands gently.

I bit my lip as panic crackled through me. "Is this something you hold against me?"

"No," the shaman said. "While we do not like the mages who rule this country, you are more beast than mage, and your heart is pure. It is for this reason that I offer you advice."

"Advice?" I asked uneasily, and Fenris shifted behind me. I could practically hear his ears perking up.

"Should the stone fail to lead you to your friend, head in the direction of the mountains." He pointed to the mountain range opposite the one we'd crash landed in. "A group of white men are camped there, about a day's journey from where the flying machine crashed near the mountains. Our scouts have confirmed that they are holding prisoners."

Fenris stared at the shaman. "I always understood that Coazi fiercely defended their lands from invasion. How could there be a camp of white men there? Would you not chase them off?"

The shaman looked grave. "So we would, but they are in the area of another tribe. If Halyma wanted them gone, they would not dare stay there. Nobody defies Halyma." From his voice, I gathered that this Halyma, who must be the shaman or chieftain of the other tribe, was not a person Aman-Wa would lightly take to task.

Fenris and I exchanged a look of alarm. Had the Resistance bought off this other tribe somehow? If they were in league with the Coazi, that was more bad news.

I wanted to jump to my feet and take off in that direction so I could find out what was going on. Instead, I took a deep breath and squeezed the shaman's hands, which were still in mine. "Thank you for this information. We will use it wisely."

The shaman smiled. "I am sure you will. But let it sit in the back of your mind for now. You will have hard days ahead, so relax tonight." He patted my knee, then took his leave, disappearing around the bonfire to talk to someone else.

I immediately whirled around to face Fenris. "Did you hear everything he said?" I demanded.

"My ears are as good as yours," Fenris reminded me with an arched brow. "And yes, I heard what he said. There is a group of white men camped out in the plains."

"*And* they're holding prisoners!" I hissed, bracing my palms against the log as I leaned forward. "Iannis could be one of them! We have to go check it out."

"Right now? In the dark? While Annia is high as an airship?"

I growled, whipping my head around to find Annia. She was sitting on one of the logs with the man she'd been dancing with, halfway in his lap, with one hand on his broad shoulder and the other splayed across his chest. They were flirting heavily with each other, which was amazing because I doubted they were speaking the same language. But then, lust is a pretty universal emotion.

"She looks a little less goofy than she did before," I offered halfheartedly.

Fenris gave me a skeptical look. "She'll be useless for at least a few hours, and after those drugs wear off she'll be exhausted. Besides, we need sleep too. There is little point in charging into a Resistance camp tired and hungry. We need our wits about us, and you have not eaten enough."

I sighed, then looked down at my empty clay dish. I'd already eaten two helpings and meant to get more, but in the beginning we'd been chatted up a storm by everyone, including the chieftain, and afterwards I'd been so caught up watching the ceremonial dancing that I'd forgotten about food.

"If I scarfed down a bit more right now and changed into beast form, I could make it there to at least check it out while everyone is asleep."

"Sunaya." Fenris placed a hand on my shoulder and met my eyes. "Consult your *serapha* charm. What does it say?"

I closed my eyes and focused in on the amulet. It felt warm against my chest, and I wondered if onlookers would see it glowing brightly through my shirt. The familiar tug sprang to life inside me, and I followed it with my mind, seeking out the direction it was coming from.

I let out a breath that was half disappointed, half relieved. "The amulet is pointing northwest."

Fenris inclined his head. "Then that is where we will go. Finding Iannis is our priority. The camp the shaman was talking about may well be the Resistance, and it's plausible they may have captured some of the delegates. But if Iannis is not with them, we cannot waste time going there first."

"I hope this means he escaped when the Resistance came in and captured everyone." If that was even what happened. "How did they know to be here, though? This is only one of many territories that the airship was flying over. Did the Resistance somehow bring down the ship from the ground?"

"I know as much as you do," Fenris said regretfully. "Which unfortunately is very little. I doubt we'll get any answers until we find Iannis and he explains what happened."

"All the more reason to locate him, then."

"Yes. But for now, you should do as the shaman says and enjoy the celebration they've put together for us." Fenris smiled and patted my thigh one last time before he removed his hand. "I'm reasonably sure that venison is calling your name, and just because you can't get high doesn't mean you can't dance around the fire."

"In that case, I think you ought to take your own advice," I said, grinning a little as I grabbed Fenris by his hands. He yelped as I pulled him to his feet, and with more than a little glee I dragged him out to dance with me by the bonfire.

9

"Please remind me never to smoke a Coazi pipe again," Annia groaned, clutching her head with one hand as we trekked forward across the desert plains. "I don't know what the hell they put in that thing, but it's lethal."

I snorted as Fenris shook his head at her. "At least they have a remedy for it," I told her. "Pretty sure we wouldn't have been able to revive you if we hadn't forced that hangover concoction they gave us down your throat."

"Yeah well it's no wonder the stuff worked." Annia glared at the water skin clutched in her hand, which the Coazi had filled with more of the herbal potion to take on the journey. "This stuff tastes so horrible it would wake the dead." But she lifted it to her lips and took another swig nonetheless.

I simply shook my head and returned my attention to the landscape in front of us, glad that I was a shifter and that my system was unaffected by narcotics. If we'd all been as incapacitated as Annia was this morning, it would have slowed us down significantly.

Ahead, the rolling plains began to disappear into clusters of evergreen trees that encroached on either side of the vast landscape, leaving only a small stretch of plains in between the two forests. The sight ahead made me nervous, because people could be lurking within the darkness and safety of the trees, and we would be sitting ducks if we passed through the open space there.

Thankfully, the necklace tugged me toward the trees on the right side of the plains, so I led Fenris and Annia in that direction. After a quick consultation with Fenris, we both changed into beast form before venturing into the forest – we could move more quietly on paws than on booted feet, and could sneak up on anyone lurking beneath the evergreen limbs.

The shade of the forest was welcome after the hot sun that had continuously beaten down on us from the plains. The scents of woodland creatures met my nose, and I could hear them scampering around, both overhead as tree branches rustled and on the ground, darting between the meager shrubbery. The trees were spaced far enough apart that it was easy enough to walk a path through them, although there was still plenty of cover provided by the branches. If not for my keen sense of smell, we could easily walk past someone and never know about it.

I took the lead, with Fenris bringing up the rear and Annia in between. She had her short sword out and was scanning the trees with her dark eyes, forced to rely on her sight rather than the elevated sense of smell and hearing Fenris and I possessed. It was strange to be in a position where Annia actually envied me – usually I was jealous of her for leading the easy and relatively uncomplicated life of a human. But this time my shifter abilities gave me a clear advantage over her.

The tug in my chest grew stronger, and I huffed out a breath through my nostrils as a sensation not unlike heartburn began to spread through me. *"We're getting close,"* I told Fenris.

"Excellent." His excitement was palpable, and I picked up my

pace, eager to find Iannis. Could he sense my approach through his matching charm? I lifted my head as we trotted through the forest, peeling back my lips so I could probe the air with my scent glands. Surely if he was close, I'd be able to scent him by now? But maybe he was masking his scent with magic to keep predators away. The thought made me scowl. It figured that Iannis would somehow have to make this even harder – nothing about him was ever easy. Why was he even in this forest, anyway? Had he been taken in by the Coazi, who Fenris had said sometimes made their homes in the forest? The place didn't look inviting, but perhaps somewhere in all this greenery there was a clearing large enough to set up their huts.

As the tug grew stronger, I still didn't scent Iannis, but the sound of trickling water reached my ears. A few minutes later, we emerged onto the banks of a small stream running through the forest. Fenris and I stopped to lap from it while Annia refilled her canteen.

The charm's pulse was very strong here, the strongest I'd ever felt except in Iannis's presence. Once I was done drinking, I sat back on my haunches and changed back into human form so I could talk to Annia.

"What's up?" she asked, propping a hand on her hip. "How much farther do we have to go?"

I pulled out the *serapha* charm from beneath my jacket and scowled down at it. It was blazing white and hot to the touch. "According to this thing, I should be standing on top of the Chief Mage right now. But I don't see or scent him anywhere."

A worried look entered Annia's dark eyes. "Could he have lost the charm somehow?"

"I don't see how that's possible." I sucked in a breath through my teeth, looking down at the glowing charm. "They're not supposed to be able to be removed by anyone except the wearer."

"Sunaya," Fenris's voice was heavy with dread, and I turned to look at him as nerves prickled along my arms. *"Look up there."*

I followed to where his snout pointed, and my heart sank into my shoes. High up a tree across the stream, there was a tiny glowing stone winking from an empty nest.

"No. No, that's not possible." I took a step back as denial ripped through me. "That can't be right."

"Do you want me to retrieve it?" Fenris asked gently.

"No." I set my jaw. "I'll get it."

I leaped across the river, my booted feet landing firmly on the other side, then with a running jump grasped one of the lower-hanging, but sturdy branches. With a grunt, I hefted myself up, then continued climbing until I reached the branch the nest was sitting on. Tears filled my eyes as I recognized the thicker, more masculine silver links glittering between the small twigs and feathers of the nest – it was the same chain Iannis had put around my neck, and later his own, when we'd made these charms back in Solantha.

I took a deep breath and blinked the tears away, then reached out and carefully untangled the necklace from the nest. Instantly the throbbing pulse died away, only to be replaced by a hollow feeling of despair as I stared at the charm resting in the palm of my hand.

I'd thought that Iannis was going to be at the other end of this chain, but I was wrong. He'd taken it off, and now he was gone.

"Sunaya, you need to calm down."

"Calm down!" I whirled around, a snarl on my lips as I shot Fenris a death glare. He and Annia had been waiting for me to settle down so we could plan our next move, standing by as I paced furiously beneath the trees.

But I didn't want to calm down. My beast was close to the surface here, furious that I'd failed in my quest to find Iannis. The one advantage we'd held, the *serapha* charm, had proven to be utterly useless. Worse, from what I understood, the only way Iannis would have been separated from the charm was if he had taken it off voluntarily.

"Why would he take it off?" I raged, turning on my heel again so I could continue pacing. I wanted to punch something, and at the moment Iannis's face would have been the preferred target. What the fuck was he thinking, taking off the charm? "Did he decide that he didn't want to be found? That doesn't make any sense!"

"It is possible the charm was taken by force or trickery," Fenris said, his voice steady.

I turned again to face him. "How? Iannis said –"

"I *know* what Iannis said," Fenris snapped. "In case you've forgotten, it was my suggestion that he use the *serapha* charms in the first place. And while they generally cannot be removed by anyone other than the wearer, an unusually strong mage could find a way."

"What, you mean like by torture or mind control?" The very idea sent a shudder through me.

"Those are two possible options, yes." Fenris's voice calmed again. "I don't believe Iannis would willingly get rid of the charm, not when it's his only link to you, and the only way for you to seek him out."

I let out a breath as shame swept through me. Fenris was so calm and controlled, but the truth was he had every reason to be just as upset as I was. He'd known Iannis for much longer, and the two of them were very close. If he could keep his head under these circumstances, then so could I. I was letting my emotions get the better of me, and blaming Iannis for losing the charm wasn't going to help us find him.

"I guess now would be a good time to track down that Resistance camp the shaman was telling us about?" I asked as I fastened Iannis's chain around my neck. I'd considered stowing it in my pack, but wearing both charms together felt right. It helped settle the unease in my chest, and as the charm came to rest against my skin next to the other, a comforting feeling washed over me.

"That does seem to be our only option, yes." Fenris pulled out a compass from his pack and consulted it. "We'll likely be walking through this forest for a while yet. Perhaps you and I should change so we can make better use of our senses."

"How about one of you stays human for once?" Annia complained. "That way at least one of you can communicate with me if something goes wrong."

"Very well," Fenris conceded reluctantly. "I will remain in human form while Sunaya changes."

After I'd quickly shifted into panther form, we moved forward, using Fenris's compass as a guide to navigate the forest in the proper direction. I trotted through the forest silently on four legs, and though there was the occasional crunch of a twig or leaf beneath Annia's or Fenris's boots, for the most part we traveled soundlessly. There was evidence that humans had passed through this area, from footprints on the ground to the occasional bead or button from a piece of clothing. We even passed by the remains of a campfire in a clearing that was a few days old. I spent several minutes sniffing around the blackened wood and stones, hoping to catch a whiff of Iannis's scent, but his familiar mix of musk, sandalwood, and magic was nowhere to be found.

We made it several miles into the forest before I caught the fresh scent of humans, and I stopped dead. Fenris and Annia went still behind me as I lifted my head, trying to discern where the scent was coming from and any other information I could glean.

"*There's a group of humans up ahead,*" I told Fenris. "*At least three of them, all men.*"

"*It might be a scouting party,*" Fenris warned. "*We must proceed with caution.*" He relayed the message to Annia.

"*You two wait here,*" I said. "*I'll go ahead and check it out.*"

"*You shouldn't go alone,*" Fenris protested.

"*I'll be fine on my own against a couple of humans, and I want you here with Annia so I can report back to both of you on what I find. Besides, I doubt these humans will think I'm anything other than wild animal.*"

"*They may try to kill you,*" Fenris warned. "*Most humans see wildcats as a threat.*"

I gave him a slow wink. "*Then I'll just have to make sure they don't see me.*"

I slunk through the trees, silent as a wraith as I followed my nose toward the strangers. The sound of their voices grew louder as I approached, and a tingle went down my spine as I realized they were speaking Northian, not Coazi. Were these men from the camp the shaman had told us about? Or could they be some of the missing delegates?

I crouched behind a tree, peering through the leaves into a clearing. Three men dressed in dirty khakis sat with their backs up against the trees, legs extended as they munched on what looked to be an early lunch. They boasted red armbands tied around their upper right arms – the classic mark of Resistance members. My heart sank: so it really was the Resistance behind Iannis's disappearance.

"Say, d'you think we can finally get back to camp now?" the fellow closest to me asked around a mouthful of food. He had curly blond hair and a scruffy, tobacco-stained beard. "I figure we've combed these woods long enough. There's no one out here but us."

I held back a snort at that, glad that this particular scouting party didn't seem to have any shifters in it. If it had, they would have scented us already and we'd have been forced to fight.

"We gotta wait until Daresh's done sniffing around," another of the men said. "You know how fussy he is about this crap. Wants to make sure no stone is left unturned."

The blond rolled his eyes. "Can't we just leave his tiger-striped ass here? Surely he can catch up with us on those four legs of his."

I froze. So there *was* a shifter in their party after all. My senses went on high alert, trying to determine if there was a tiger shifter in the area, but I didn't scent or hear anyone other than the three humans before me.

"Fenris," I called as I began to creep away from the clearing. *"We need to get out of here. There's a tiger shifter on the prowl, and if he finds us —"*

The wind shifted, and I stiffened as I caught the scent of a tiger male. The rustle of a bush was the only warning I got before he sprang out of the undergrowth, claws extended and mouth open in a ferocious snarl. I leapt to the side, and he sailed past me, landing a good ten feet away. Heart pounding, I took off running at full speed before he had a chance to turn around, making sure to head away from Annia and Fenris. There was no way I was going to stand and fight a shifter who was three times my weight, when I was three times faster at top speed.

Unfortunately, the forest terrain meant I couldn't run at top speed, so I could hear Daresh crashing through the underbrush behind me. Sailing over a fallen tree log, I gave one last burst of speed, then took a flying leap into a tree. I scrambled up until I was out of the tiger's reach, digging my claws into the bark for purchase, then clung to a thick branch and changed back into human form.

The tiger shifter came into view just as the white light faded from my eyes, and I watched as he skidded to a stop in front of the tree. His orange eyes glowed malevolently as he snarled, but before he could jump up into the tree after me, I shot out my hand and shouted a Word. Ice blasted from my palm, and the tiger yelped, jumping back out of the way before the stream of magic hit him. It hit the ground instead, and a sheet of ice crackled across the surface like the top of a frozen lake. Except this was summer, so the ice started melting immediately.

Okay, so maybe using ice wasn't such a great idea. I would have preferred fire, but I didn't want to risk catching the entire forest ablaze.

Growling, the tiger shifter stretched a tentative paw toward the ice. He yelped as his pads came into contact with the frigid ground, then snatched the paw back and growled at me again. I lifted my hand threateningly in the air again, magic glowing around my palm, and he froze.

Stalemate.

Fuck this, I thought as the ice on the ground rapidly melted into a puddle of water. Iannis had been training me to rely on Words to cast spells, but my Loranian repertoire was limited, and that shifter's friends were going to be arriving soon. I could already hear them blundering through the woods, though still some way off. So instead I aimed my glowing hand at the shifter and willed him with all my might to freeze in place.

Magic shot out of my palm and blasted him straight in the chest. A blue-green glow rippled over the tiger as he froze in place, mouth still open in a soundless snarl. He stood stock-still, like a statue carved from orange, black, and white marble. If marble were fuzzy. And had really long fangs.

A ripple of fatigue washed over me, which was typical whenever I pulled magic directly from the well inside me instead of using Words. But I pushed it back, then used an illusion spell to make myself blend in with the tree. I watched the three humans charge into the clearing, weapons drawn as their eyes darted around anxiously.

"Fenris," I called out mentally, scenting him and Annia nearby. *"Hang back. I've got this."*

"Are you sure?"

"Yes. Stay back unless I call for you."

"What the fuck is going on?" the red-haired man snarled as he caught sight of the tiger shifter. "Daresh, why the hell are you just standing there?"

"Whoa," the blond said, crouching down in front of the tiger and waving a hand in front of his face. "He's like a statue or something."

"By the Ur-God." The third man, a stocky guy with long brown hair pulled back into a tail, grabbed blondie by the belt and dragged him away. "Someone's cast a spell on him! There must be a witch in this forest."

"It must be one of those shamans!" the redhead howled. "Daresh must've run across the Coazi, and now look what's happened!"

"Are they still somewhere around here?" Blondie swiveled his head around frantically.

"I dunno, but I'm not gonna wait to find out! I *knew* this was a bad idea, having them send us out without any kind of protection against these magic-wielding savages. You guys do whatever you want, I'm getting out of here before they come back and turn us all to stone!"

Red sprinted from the clearing as though his pants had caught fire, and his companions quickly followed, not even sparing a glance at their shifter comrade. I arched an eyebrow at the tiger shifter, who was still capable of glaring daggers at me – his eyes were practically shooting flames.

"*Guess your buddies aren't real big on loyalty, are they?*"

Surprise radiated from the tiger – he'd been so shocked by my spell he hadn't realized he could still use mindspeak. "*Their loyalty is to the Resistance, not to me specifically,*" he growled. "*I don't blame them for running from an abomination like you. What the fuck are you?*"

I dropped from the tree, landing in a crouch about ten feet away from the tiger, and gave him a taunting smile. "*Wouldn't you like to know?*"

"*A hybrid.*" Disgust rippled through his words. "*I've heard rumors a shifter with mage powers existed, but I thought it was a legend.*" He didn't sound impressed.

Ignoring him, I turned my head in the direction I'd scented Fenris and Annia from earlier. "*You guys can come out now. It's safe.*" Sitting down, I rested my back against the tree, then drew my knees to my chest and rested my forearms across them as I waited. A few minutes later, Fenris and Annia entered the small clearing. Their eyes widened at the sight of the frozen tiger shifter.

"Is that guy still alive?" Annia asked, awe in her voice as she crouched down in front of the tiger shifter and waved her hand in front of his face, much like his companion had done to him earlier. "He looks like a taxidermist went to town on him."

"*Tell her to get her hand out of my face,*" Daresh growled.

"*Or what?*" I sneered. "*You'll bite her hand off?*"

The tiger shifter said nothing, but the scorching fury burning inside him was so palpable I thought he'd set the tinder-dry forest on fire.

"Yes, he's still alive, and really put out about the fact that you're waving your hand in front of his face," I told Annia. "He told me to ask you to stop."

"Really?" Laughter tinged Annia's voice. "That is just too weird." Grinning, she patted the tiger on his head, then stood up and turned to face me. "How the hell did you do that to him?"

"I've got skills."

"Indeed," Fenris said dryly. "Have you used any of those skills to get information out of him, about the Resistance camp and Iannis's whereabouts?"

"Not yet. Figured I'd wait until you guys got here first. Do you want to do the honors?"

"Certainly." Fenris turned toward Daresh. "What business does a Resistance camp have in Coazi territory?"

"I'm not telling anything to the likes of you."

I stood up and approached the tiger shifter, lifting my right hand in the air as I did so. Blue-green fire snapped and crackled from my palm, the flames licking at my fingers. "I'm not sure if the rumors mentioned this or not, but fire is kind of my specialty. Now that you're not moving around anymore, there's no reason I can't slow-roast you."

"You wouldn't dare." The tiger sounded indignant and fearful all at once.

"Wanna bet?" Reaching out, I trailed my hand above his spine, letting the flames come within a breath of his fur.

"Alright, alright!" Panic screeched through the tiger's mental voice. *"I'll tell you. Just get that away from me!"*

"Talk first, and I might." I raised my hand slightly so that I wouldn't accidentally set him on fire, but remained close enough so that he could feel the heat of my flame.

"The Resistance has always had a camp out here," the tiger shifter said hurriedly. *"We negotiated with the Coazi a while back to let us hide out on their lands, as we do with a lot of the tribes across the country. They're not allies, but because they hate mages too, they let us stay here as long as we respect the land and follow their restrictions."*

"*So you're not out here for any* specific *reason?*" I pressed as Fenris relayed the information to Annia verbally. "*Like, say, to take down an airship of mages passing through?*"

"*We didn't take down the airship, but we were told to expect the delegates' arrival.*" Daresh's voice turned smug. "*We prepared some very special accommodations for them.*"

Fenris growled at that, but hope filled me – Daresh had just admitted the Resistance had the delegates. "*So you've taken all the delegates prisoner, then?*" I demanded.

"*All but the Chief Mage.*" Some of the smugness faded from Daresh's voice. "*The idiot we planted aboard the airship killed him.*"

No! I nearly screamed aloud as shock and grief rippled through me. But then I remembered the *serapha* charms around my chest, and forced myself to remain calm. The tiger shifter might have believed he was telling the truth, but his intel was wrong – Iannis was alive. The charm didn't lie.

"*How did he die?*" I asked, pretending I didn't know better.

"*We weren't given specifics. But trust me, if he'd been alive we would have brought him in. He was our main target.*"

I gritted my teeth – the tiger shifter had confirmed our suspicions, but we were still collecting more questions than answers.

"*Where is your camp?*" Fenris demanded.

The shifter hesitated, so I lowered my hand, allowing the flame to singe his orange fur. "*Oww, oww, oww! Okay! We've taken over an abandoned mining village at the base of the Sarania Mountain Range.*"

I frowned, calling up a mental image of the map we'd studied earlier. "*That's to the west, right?*" There were two mountain ranges flanking the plains here.

"*Yeah, if you head west through the forest, you'll come right to it.*"

I lifted my head to look at Fenris and Annia. "Guess we'd better head over there, huh?"

"It's the only lead we've got, so yeah." Annia sighed, running a hand through her hair as she looked off into the distance. "Not that we're going to find the Chief Mage there, since this asshole insists he's dead." She shot the shifter a glare, who returned it in full force.

"Even if he isn't there, the delegates are and we need to try and free them anyway," Fenris said. "They are mages, after all, and could be useful to us."

I groaned, not at all thrilled about the idea of working with a bunch of stuffy mages to rescue Iannis. But I couldn't deny the extra magepower would be useful. "Alright then, let's go."

"*Wait!*" The tiger shifter yelled. "*You're not just going to leave me like this, are you?*"

I turned back toward him and arched a brow. "*If you were in our position, what would you do?*"

"*I'd probably kill you,*" the tiger shifter admitted reluctantly.

"*Then you should thank Magorah that we're not you,*" I told him.

Hefting our packs higher onto our shoulders, we left the clearing and headed west, the tiger shifter cursing us all the way until we'd traveled out of mindspeak range.

"How long do you suppose it will take for the spell to wear off?" Annia asked after a while. "We'd better be gone from the camp by the time he storms in there, howling for revenge."

"Your guess is as good as mine." Perhaps we should have killed him after all. He would not show us any mercy when he recovered the use of his limbs.

"Two to three days," Fenris said, and we both turned to him, surprised by the certainty in his voice. "That should be time enough."

I arched a brow. "Are you sure about that?"

"Sure enough to bet our lives on it." Fenris strode past us, taking the lead with his compass firmly in his hand. "Now let's go and find these traitors before they kill the delegates they *do* have in their possession."

10

Three hours later, I stood on one of the topmost branches of a pine tree, one arm gripping the trunk as my other trained a telescope on the abandoned mining village at the base of the Sarania Mountain Range. Men were moving in between a handful of dilapidated brick buildings and sagging wooden cabins. The buildings had been painted over to approximate the dry, pale coloring of the desert landscape, making the compound difficult to spot from the sky. Many of the buildings sported boarded-up windows and missing slats in the siding. Only to be expected, considering that mining on tribal lands had been outlawed over a century ago, but I still wasn't looking forward to spending time here.

"Can't really see much going on from here," I admitted to Fenris, who was waiting on the ground with Annia. *"There are a few guys stationed at the entrance, and two on the rooftops with bows. A few guys are coming and going in the streets, but I have a feeling most everyone's indoors."*

"Very well. Why don't you come down then, before they spot you, so we can get on with our plan?"

I snorted. *"They're not going to spot me."* My perch was too far away for me to be easily spotted amongst the sea of trees, and I wasn't sticking my head out like an idiot for anyone to take a shot at me. But I shimmied back down onto the ground anyway.

"So what's our cover story?" Annia asked as I placed my hands on Fenris's shoulders and muttered an illusion spell to change his features. I lightened his hair, made him taller and thinner, and got rid of his beard. It was doubtful anyone out here would know him, but I was sure the higher-ups in the Resistance would be keeping tabs on Fenris because of his unusual relationship with Iannis. No way was I taking chances.

"We're going to tell them that we're recent recruits, and that Rylan Baine sent us out here." I stepped back from Fenris, then used the spell to give myself short, platinum blonde hair, yellow jaguar shifter eyes, and a shorter but curvier frame. "From what I can see, they don't have any electrical lines set up, so they won't be able to send telegrams. By the time they reach my cousin and ask him for confirmation, we'll be long gone."

"If they don't have electrical means of communication, it's highly likely they will have a bird shifter of some kind to relay messages," Fenris said, looking worried.

"Yeah, but even if they do, it'll take a while for him to deliver the message and then get an answer," Annia said. "At least a day or two. That's more than enough time to get the information we need."

It took us another thirty minutes to emerge from the tree line, and as soon as we did the guards stood up straight at the sight of us. The two guys on the roof trained their bows in our direction, and I was glad that we had a shooter on our side as well. Annia might not have had the eyesight of a shifter, but she was still damn good with her crossbow.

"Stop right there!" one of the guards stationed on the ground shouted, stepping forward. He was a human, with short black hair, and like his comrades was dressed in a long-sleeved khaki shirt and pants. The only bits of color were the red band tied around his upper arm, and a medal pinned above his heart that was shaped like a drop of blood. A hand went to the hilt of his sword, testing the blade's clearance, though he didn't draw. "Hands in the air!"

We halted immediately, doing as he said. I wasn't worried about the vulnerable position – my reflexes were faster, and I could slice his arm off with a chakram faster than he could draw his sword. Of course I had my magic too, but I didn't want to give that away since I was posing as a full-blooded shifter.

Seeing that we'd obeyed without hesitation, the guard relaxed fractionally, though his fingers didn't stray from his sword hilt. "What business do you have out here in Coazi territory?"

"We came to join the Resistance," I called back.

The guard cocked a brow. "Did you now? All by yourselves?" He looked skeptical. "New recruits must be vouched for by current members of the Resistance, and they never come to this particular place."

"I was given directions to this camp by my uncle, Rylan Baine," I told him. "As you can understand, he's a little too busy to bring us here himself."

The two guards exchanged a look – Rylan was an officer in the Resistance, and well known. "Rylan Baine's niece, eh? What's your name?"

"Mika Baine," I lied smoothly, using the name of my cousin Melantha's daughter, who I'd rescued from the Shifter Royale just days ago. It was better to use an actual family member's name than to make someone up – Rylan would have to ascertain Mika's whereabouts, which would be difficult since Solantha was in an uproar, and would buy us extra time. "These here are my friends, Felix Lamos and Anaris Maren." I gestured toward Annia and Fenris, who were standing to my right, without lowering my hands.

"Well it's nice to see some new faces," the other guard, a handsome blond with green eyes, spoke up for the first time. "Especially women, as not too many of those come our way." He sent Annia a wink, and she gave him a flirtatious smile. "I'm Private Willis, and this here is Sergeant Brun."

"Be that as it may," Brun growled, shooting his fellow soldier a look that said he didn't appreciate being introduced, "we can't just take your word at face value. We'll have to bring you three to the captain so he can decide what to do with you."

I shrugged as well as I could with my hands in the air. "Fine by me. When do we get to meet him?"

Brun sent Willis to fetch two more soldiers, then left them to guard the entrance to the town along with the archers while he took us to the Captain. Our hands were tightly bound in front of us with thick rope, and we were herded up a wide street flanked with two-story brick-and-wood buildings, every third of which was a crumbling ruin. The better-preserved houses had been patched up by the Resistance, newer pieces of cedar wood standing out against the older siding, and bits of plaster and glue were smeared around the edges of windows that had been replaced. The windows were small and covered with a film of dust, and none of the buildings had signs out front, so there was no way of telling which, if any of them, housed the prisoners we sought.

The soldiers led us into a two-story cabin that looked like it had seen better days, the siding worn rough by sandstorms and who knew what else, and the porch railing leaning sideways. The floorboards creaked under our feet as we were led onto the porch, and we stood under an awning that looked ready to collapse on top of our heads as Brun knocked on the door.

"Captain Milios?" he called. "It's Sergeant Brun."

"Come in," a deep, brusque voice answered.

Brun turned the wooden doorknob, and the door creaked loudly as he pushed it open. We followed after him into a small, rectangular room that had probably served as the house's kitchen and living area, judging by the wood-burning stove in the left corner. The empty, rickety-looking shelves on the walls would have once housed pots and pans as well as cooking supplies.

On the opposite side of the room was a large, rough-hewn desk covered with piles of paper and a typewriter that looked like it was on its last legs. Behind the desk sat a sturdy-looking man with salt-and-pepper hair and a weather-beaten face, who I could only assume was Captain Milios. His thin lips and hard, dark eyes told me he was not the cheerful sort, and I doubted he would show us any mercy if he found out who we really were.

"Sergeant." Milios narrowed his eyes. Like his soldiers, he was dressed in khakis, but he wore three blood-drop medals on his breast as opposed to the single one Sergeant Brun displayed. His medals were also gold rather than red, which I imagined went with his higher rank. He scowled at us before returning his attention to Brun. "Who are these people?"

"They claim to be new recruits, sent by Captain Rylan Baine," Brun explained. He jerked a thumb in my direction. "This one here says she's his niece."

Captain Milios's dark gaze snapped to mine. "Name?"

"Mika Baine."

"And the others?"

"I'm Felix –" Fenris began.

"Was I speaking to you?" the Captain snapped. He didn't

even bother to look at Fenris, his hard glare fixed on me like an arrow from a well-trained archer.

"No –,"

"Then shut up." He arched his brows at me. "What are their names?"

Fenris's lips pressed together so hard I thought he would swallow them, and I had to force myself not to laugh at the look of outrage burning in his eyes. He very clearly wasn't used to being a subordinate. "Felix Lamos and Anaris Maren."

"I've met Baine once," Milios said, his tone implying that he was not one of Rylan's fans. "He didn't mention a niece called Mika."

I snorted. "I bet you didn't mention any of your relatives to him either. Or do the members of the Resistance like to sit around and talk about their families?" I knew he was bluffing, trying to jab holes into my story, and I wasn't going to let him.

Captain Milios's cheeks reddened. "I don't like your tone, *shifter*. And I sure as hell don't trust you."

"You don't have to take my word for it," I said boldly. "Just ask Rylan. He'll vouch."

The Captain stared at us for a long moment, his dark eyes glittering. "I'll send him a message to verify your story," he said. "In the meantime, the three of you can do grunt work around here and earn your keep." He turned toward Brun. "Sergeant, assign these three quarters and put them to work. I want eyes on them at all times. They are not to leave the camp under any circumstances, and they are not allowed near the prisoners."

"Yes, sir."

"Dismissed."

"Grunt work?" Fenris seethed as we followed the sergeant outside. *"I can't remember the last time I've had to do something as menial as grunt work!"*

"Welcome to the life of an apprentice," I told him, and with great

effort managed to keep a straight face as Brun unwittingly led us into our new lives as undercover operatives.

AFTER HAVING our belongings thoroughly searched, Sergeant Brun showed us to our quarters. West of the main street were two rows of houses, mostly too dilapidated for use, but ten or so that were useable had been converted into makeshift quarters. The sergeant knocked on a door, and we stood outside the false-fronted cabin for at least a minute before it was yanked open by an orange-eyed shifter. His skin was the color of heavily-creamed coffee, and his thick, dark hair and rounded nose indicated Sandian descent.

"Sergeant." The tiger shifter saluted, and his dark brows furrowed as he took us in. "How can I help you?"

"We've got newcomers, and I'm assigning one of them to your barracks." Sergeant Brun motioned Fenris forward. "Recruit, this is Private Faresh Malara. Private, this is Felix Lamos, who is here on probation. Show him around and get him settled, then bring him to the mess hall for lunch."

"How much do you want to bet this is Daresh's brother?" I asked Fenris as unease shifted through my stomach.

"I would be willing to put significant coin down on that." Fenris didn't look my way, but I could sense his own discomfort. *"I can only hope that he never finds his brother, at least not until we are gone."*

"Yes, sir." Faresh saluted, then led Fenris into the house. I cursed silently as I watched them disappear, wishing that I'd slit Daresh's throat after all. The last thing I needed was Fenris being killed in his sleep for revenge.

We're just going to have to get out of here fast, I told myself as we followed Sergeant Brun through the rows of houses.

He stopped at a small, single-story shack at the end of one of the rows. There was no porch or false front, and the windows were boarded up, but the siding looked okay and I didn't see any obvious holes in the roof. I waited for the sergeant to knock on the door, but instead he opened it and walked right inside.

Annia and I exchanged a glance, then hurried inside after him. Peering into the dim interior, which was lit only by the rays of light seeping through the cracks of the boarded-up windows, I saw that it was a single-room dwelling, with two cots set up on opposite sides of the room, two chests, and two small, rough-hewn tables that held oil lamps waiting to be lit.

"Since you two are the only women here, you're getting your own space," the sergeant said, and he didn't sound too happy about it. "Women are born troublemakers, especially shifter females." He sent me a disapproving look. "I don't care who sleeps in which bed, but I expect you to keep it clean. There are two working outhouses in the area, one behind the barrack three houses down from you, and there's a well not too far from here where you can fetch water for sponge baths." He pointed to a rusty bucket.

"Yes sir," Annia and I both said. I fought against the urge to wrinkle my nose at the idea of going without a bath or shower for months on end – the sergeant would gleefully pounce on any opportunity to point out that a female like me was too pampered to be a soldier.

"You won't be getting uniforms until the Captain can verify your story, but later on today you can stop by the supply station and pick up basic toiletries. I'll make sure some are set aside for you."

"Thank you, sergeant," we both said.

"Alright, now set your things down here and come with me. It's time to put you two to work."

"Where exactly are you assigning us?" I asked. I hoped it was something that allowed me to move around the camp, so that we could discover the location of the prisoners.

"The kitchens, of course." The sergeant arched a brow, and for the first time his lips quirked into a smile. "It's about time someone brought a woman's touch to the slop they serve as food around here."

11

"This is unbelievable," I growled under my breath as I scrubbed furiously at a cast iron pan using coarse salt and steel wool. The sleeves of my shirt were rolled up to my elbows, and I was wearing a colorful rag wrapped around my head to keep my hair away from the food. "You'd think they'd at least give us a little bit of a learning curve before dumping us in here on our own."

"Yeah, right." Annia snorted from behind me as she wiped down the stove. "I swear the cook practically skipped out of the doors as soon as we arrived. Guy was fucking whistling a happy tune. Even if the sergeant had told him to stay, I bet he would have hightailed it as soon as we were left alone."

We talked quietly to make sure no one overheard us, though that was unlikely due to all the background noise. The mess hall was nearly full to bursting, with over a hundred men sitting ass to elbow at the picnic-style tables and stuffing food into their mouths from rough-hewn wooden trenchers. A third or so were shifters, and they mostly sat with each other. We'd had less than two hours to take the disgusting slop the former cook was putting together and turn it into a passable meal. I thanked

Magorah that Annia knew her way around a kitchen, because my own cooking skills were rudimentary at best. We'd turned out some decent sandwiches using canned meat, fried potatoes, and green beans, and you would have thought we'd served them a gourmet meal from the way the men's eyes lit up as they came up to the serving counter with their trenchers. Quite a few of them had complimented us on more than our culinary skills, their eyes lingering on the swell of our breasts beneath our shirts. It had taken me every ounce of willpower I had to smile flirtatiously at them, when what I really wanted to do was punch them in their leering faces. But if we wanted to find out where the prisoners were hidden, we had to start making some friends, and kicking these soldiers' asses wasn't going to help.

"I just wish we weren't stuck in here the entire day," I grumbled. "How are we supposed to talk to any of the men if they're out there and we're in here?" I spared a glance toward the mess hall, which I could see clearly through the large, rectangular opening in the wall. Fenris was sitting at one of the tables with several shifters, looking withdrawn and uncomfortable as he ate. The other shifters were ignoring him, and he made no effort to try and insert himself into the conversation. "Fenris certainly doesn't seem to be getting anywhere."

"Yeah, I noticed." Annia moved to cleaning the steel countertop in the center of the kitchen, and I had to move my cast iron off it to get out of her way. "I wouldn't worry about it too much, though. We're the only women around, and those men probably haven't seen a pretty face in months. I'll bet a few of them are going to wander back here. And besides, the guy who's on babysitting duty can't stop staring at my ass."

I flicked my gaze toward the soldier standing about twenty feet away in the mess hall next to the entrance nearest us. He was the classic tall, dark, and handsome human, with a day's growth of beard on his strong jaw, and his pale blue eyes seemed to follow Annia around the room. I met his eyes, and watched with amusement as his high cheekbones colored before he jerked his gaze away, scanning the rest of the mess hall. Right now there were three other soldiers policing the mess hall, mostly there to make sure the other soldiers played nice and didn't end up in a food fight or something worse, but he'd been here before lunch. I had a feeling he was stationed here at the captain's orders to make sure we didn't pull anything fishy.

"Well between the two of us, I'm pretty sure you've got the best shot at seducing info out of these guys," I admitted as I finished wiping out the cast iron pan. I hung it up on its hook by the stove, then grabbed a rag and started wiping down the cooking dishes that were hanging in the drying rack. "They don't seem to like me as much."

Annia shrugged. "If you were a human, they'd be just as into your ass as they are mine, especially since you've got more of it than I do." Annia grinned at me, and I stuck out my tongue – I was in good shape but I didn't have Annia's willowy figure. "You could probably get one of those shifter boys to tell you something, though."

"I think I'll leave the seducing up to you." There was only one male I wanted to get my hands on, a mage with violet eyes and dark hair the color of glossy cherrywood. Seduction wasn't really my strong suit – I just didn't have the patience for it, and besides, it was almost impossible to lie to a shifter about finding them attractive.

As the men finished eating, they brought their trenchers up one by one and thanked us for the meal. Annia stationed herself by the counter and took her time chatting each one up, giving them smiles and winks while I busied myself washing dishes. There wasn't really time for her to get any info out of the men, but we both knew they'd be thinking about her, and hopefully one of them would come back.

Fenris was one of the last to come up, and as he handed Annia a trencher, I heard him whisper "Good luck," to her under his breath. A smile curved my lips – he knew what she was doing just as well as I did. To me, he added, *"I've been put on maintenance crew, so I'll have more mobility around the camp than you. I'll tell you if I learn anything interesting, and let me know if there's anything I can do to help."*

"Will do," I told him, and then he left.

Soon, the hall was empty except for Tall, Dark, and Handsome, who was leaning against the wall, arms crossed as he watched us work – or rather Annia. I nearly rolled my eyes – his own were glued so firmly to her ass that I doubted he'd even noticed my expression.

"Showtime," Annia muttered as she grabbed a bucket and a rag. Now that lunch was over, it was time for us to clean up after the men. I took up a broom and started sweeping the kitchen, but kept one eye on Annia as she approached the table nearest to the mess hall and set her bucket of water down. She dunked her rag into the water, then leaned across the table and wiped it down, giving the soldier a great view of her cleavage. The guy's throat bobbed, and as his eyes brightened with lust I was sure there were things bobbing beneath his clothing too.

Annia chose that moment to straighten up and "accidentally" knock over the bucket of water. "Oh no!" she cried as liquid spilled all over the long-sleeved white shirt she wore. The wet fabric stuck to her like a second skin, becoming translucent. I had to choke back a laugh when the soldier's eyes nearly bugged out at the sight of Annia's nipples poking through the fabric. Men were so easy.

"A-are you alright?" the soldier asked, springing forward as his brain finally kicked into gear. "You're not hurt or anything, are you?"

"N-no." Annia shivered, pulling at her shirt. "I'm just cold and wet and oh, I hate this!" she wailed, actual tears gathering in her dark eyes. "I need to change my clothes now, but if I don't get this done in time, Captain Milios said he was going to have me thrown in the dungeon!"

"There, there, now." The soldier patted her arm, adopting the soothing and slightly patronizing tone men tended to use around hysterical women. "Captain Milios isn't going to throw you into the dungeon just for spilling water on yourself."

"That's what one of the soldiers told me," Annia sniffled. "And they've been here longer than I have."

"Yeah, well some of the guys here can be asses." The soldier shrugged off his khaki shirt and handed it to her, revealing an undershirt that clung to his muscular torso. I'd always assumed the Resistance was just a ragtag bunch, but the men I'd seen here were all in good fighting shape and uniformed. They weren't perfect, but they were far more disciplined than I'd anticipated. "Here, wear this."

"Thank you." Annia sniffled one more time, then gave the soldier a brilliant smile that had him blushing all over again. That blush crept all the way down his neck and disappeared beneath the neckline of his undershirt as Annia pulled off her sopping-wet top, leaving her standing there in nothing but pants and a white bra.

"So, is there really a dungeon around here?" Annia asked as she slowly slipped the soldier's shirt on, taking her time in adjusting the fabric around her shoulders, which were far too slim for the garment. "Or was that other soldier just making things up?"

"Not a dungeon, exactly," the soldier said, his eyes glued to the rounded flesh swelling over the cups of Annia's bra. "But we do use the old mineshaft to hold prisoners, and you could say that's kind of like a dungeon."

"Oh really?" Annia's dark eyes widened, her mouth forming

a small 'o' of shock. "So the soldier wasn't lying, I could be sent there?" She slipped the bottom button of the shirt through its hole as she spoke.

"I'm sure the captain wouldn't actually send you down there," the soldier assured her. "He wouldn't want you there with those vile mages."

"Mages?" Annia gasped.

The soldier stood up a little straighter, looking chagrined. "I think I've said too much."

"That's incredible!" Annia pressed a fluttering hand against her exposed bosom, and I had to admire how cleverly she directed the soldier's attention back to her body. "I had no idea this camp was so hardcore. I know the Resistance is fighting against the mages, but I didn't know we'd grown so strong that we could actually capture some of them."

The soldier's chest seemed to swell with pride at that. "Yeah, well, we had a pretty good plan –"

The door swung open, and Sergeant Brun stepped in. His eyes nearly bulged out of his head as he saw Annia standing there with the soldier's shirt only halfway buttoned. "Private Gilliam, what is the meaning of this!"

"Sir!" The private snapped to attention, his cheeks coloring once more, and I nearly snickered at the abject mortification in his pretty blue eyes. "I apologize, but the recruit here spilled water all over her shirt. I didn't think it was appropriate for her to be in a wet t-shirt, so I offered her my shirt to wear."

"And you think *this* is appropriate instead?" Sergeant Brun asked, swinging his baleful gaze toward Annia again. She'd hastily buttoned up her shirt and stood there with her hands behind her back and her head bowed, looking sheepish.

"I'm so sorry, sergeant," Annia said meekly. "It was an accident. I didn't mean to get Private Gilliam in trouble. He was just trying to help."

"I'm sure he was," Sergeant Brun said dryly. "But I can't have Private Gilliam on duty wearing only his undershirt. Go fetch another shirt from your quarters and change, and then hurry back here and give the private his shirt back."

"Yes sir." Annia saluted.

"And don't let this happen again. I don't need you distracting my soldiers with your charms." His eyes narrowed.

"It won't, sir," Annia assured him.

"Women," Brun muttered under his breath. It sounded like a curse. "Get going."

He stalked out of the mess hall, and Annia winked at me before following him outside. Guess we knew our next destination now – the mineshaft. But how were we supposed to get there when we had watchers following us around at all times?

12

"Man, that was exhausting," Annia groaned as she collapsed onto her cot. "I've never had to cook for so many people in my life."

"No kidding," I agreed, sitting down heavily on the edge of my own cot so I could pull off my boots. Annia hadn't even bothered taking her own shoes off – she lay sprawled out on her bed, eyes closed as the light from the lantern flickered across her face. "At least the job gives us full access to the pantry."

"Which you happily raided." Annia snorted. "I swear I don't understand how you eat so much, Naya. I'd look like a balloon if I packed in the amount of food you did this afternoon."

"Yeah, it's a real blessing having a food bill three times the size of yours." I rolled my eyes as I stretched out onto my cot. "The grass isn't always greener on the other side, you know."

"I do know." Annia opened her eyes as she rolled onto her side to face me. "I was just trying to lighten things up a bit. You've been pretty down in the dumps recently. Is it because of the dead end with the Chief Mage's necklace?" she asked, keeping her voice low in case someone outside was listening.

"That's a big part of it, yeah." Folding my arms beneath my

head, I stared up at the ceiling, tracing the old wooden beams through the darkness. "I thought for sure we were gonna find him at the other end of this necklace, so it's pretty discouraging that the plan didn't work out."

"True, but at least we know the Chief Mage is in this area, right? We never would have been able to narrow it down that far without your charm."

"Yeah, I guess so." Reaching beneath my shirt, I pulled out the two *serapha* charms and gazed at them. They blazed to life instantly beneath my scrutiny, like two tiny stars clutched in the palm of my hand, and a rush of longing hit me, so intense it was painful. "It's just...I want him to be *here*. With *me*."

There was a long, pregnant pause, and color rushed into my cheeks as I realized I'd said too much.

"Naya...do you have *feelings* for him?"

"We're master and apprentice," I insisted, stuffing the charms back down the front of my shirt. "It's not like I could help growing closer to him after all the time we've spent together."

Annia snorted again. "Yeah, but it doesn't seem like the kind of relationship you had with Roanas."

"No one can replace Roanas." A pang hit my chest at the mention of my dead mentor, the lion shifter and Shiftertown Inspector who'd taken me in after my aunt Mafiela had kicked me out of the jaguar clan. "He was the closest thing I ever had to a father."

"My point exactly."

I let out another huff. "What do you want me to say, Annia? That I wish I was a full mage, or that Iannis was a shifter, so that I could actually do something about my attraction to him?" My fists curled at my sides, and I itched to use them.

"You don't have to have either of those things to get what you want, if you want it bad enough."

I narrowed my gaze at Annia. "There's no way Iannis and I could ever be a couple. I'm the embodiment of why mages and shifters don't breed, and besides, masters and apprentices aren't supposed to have romantic relationships. Iannis would never break the rules just to be with me, especially as the Chief Mage."

"I dunno, Naya. He's already flaunted convention more than once on your behalf. When he made you his apprentice he was practically snubbing all the other mages to their faces, which they couldn't have been happy about. If he wants you badly enough, he'll figure out a way to make it happen."

"Yeah, well I'm not gonna bank on that. I don't really know how he feels about me." But warmth stole through me at the idea that maybe, just maybe, Iannis and I could be more. There were sparks between us, no question about that. On one or two occasions, those sparks had been hot enough that I'd been *sure* something was going to happen between us. But it never had, and I wasn't sure how much of that was because of my reservations or because of his. Just because Iannis found me attractive didn't mean he was going to act on it. Truthfully, if we were both smart, neither of us ever would.

"Sunaya?" Fenris's voice echoed in my head, drawing me away from my melancholy thoughts. *"Are you awake?"*

"Yeah." I sat up, instantly on alert. *"What's up?"*

"I've managed to figure out the shift schedule for the guards watching the prisoners. If we time this right, I think we can get you in to talk to the prisoners, so listen close and follow my directions..."

AN HOUR LATER, I was creeping down the dirt road leading from the town to the mineshaft where the Resistance housed their prisoners. I wore the illusion of Private Remis, the soldier Fenris said was due to replace the one on duty, or at least I hoped I was.

Fenris had described him in great detail, and I remembered handing him a trencher at both lunch and dinner, but there had been so many faces it was possible I could have made a mistake. To be safe, I was careful to stick to the shadows and remain as inconspicuous as possible.

The moon was over half full, providing plenty of illumination, and after about a ten-minute brisk walk the mine came into view. It was a large, vertical shaft carved into the base of the mountain, accessible only by a wire cage that could be hoisted up and down via a pulley system. Unfortunately, I wasn't going to be able to use the thing as the mule used to pull the primitive elevator was stabled for the night, but thanks to Fenris I had other options.

As Fenris had assured me, only a single guard was posted outside the mineshaft. He was leaning up against the wall, his stance relaxed and his eyes wandering, but he straightened abruptly at the sight of me.

"Remis! Is it time for shift change already?"

"Not yet," I admitted in a deep, gruff voice that matched my burly exterior. "I was having trouble sleeping, so I thought I'd come out early and keep you company."

"Yeah, I know what you mean," the soldier said as I approached, relaxing his stance. "Being stuck on night shift has been hell on my sleep schedule –"

I placed a hand on his shoulder, then murmured a Word that Fenris had taught me. Instantly, the man's eyes fluttered closed and he sank onto his bottom, head thunking against the rock wall as he slipped into a deep sleep. According to Fenris, he would be out until someone woke him up, presumably the very soldier I was impersonating when he arrived for shift change.

Pretty effective, I thought as I stared down at the soldier, who was snoring lightly. And this was just one of the spells Fenris had taught me tonight. I'd tried to get him to tell me how he knew them, but he'd brushed off my questions, telling me he didn't have time to explain. When we got out of this mess I was going to wring the truth out of him, but with less than half an hour left until shift change I didn't have time to ponder it.

Assured that the soldier wasn't going anywhere, I hurried to the edge of the shaft and peered down into the darkness. I could make out a very faint light from one of the tunnels that branched off from the main shaft, far below. I breathed a little sigh of relief – I had good night vision, but even I couldn't see in pitch darkness. Taking a deep breath, I muttered the Words to the second spell Fenris had taught me, and after a few moments my feet began to lift off the ground. A mixture of excitement and fear bubbled up inside me at the fact that I was *flying*, but I tamped down on it and focused on controlling my trajectory as I guided my floating body down the shaft. There was enough space around the cage that I was able to squeeze past it, and I floated down through the darkness, heading for the glow. It steadily grew brighter the further I sank, until finally a tunnel opening came into view, lit on both sides by torches bracketed into the rough-hewn walls. I wrinkled my nose as the scents of urine, feces, and unwashed bodies rolled over me, and knew without a doubt that this was where the delegates were being kept.

I floated into the tunnel, then released the levitation spell and touched down softly onto the hard-packed dirt. A wave of exhaustion hit me – the levitation spell used a constant stream of energy – and I pressed my hand against the dirt wall to steady myself. In the murky shadows beyond the torchlight, I could make out several bodies propped upright against the wall with their legs stretched out in front of them, heads hanging in apathy. I frowned as I realized I didn't see any chains or scent any magical wards holding them here, and wondered why they hadn't escaped yet. They were all mages with more experience than I – surely they could have magicked their way out of here by now? And why hadn't any of them noticed me?

Dirt shifted beneath my boots as I moved slowly toward them, and I raised a hand, conjuring a ball of fire for illumination. The sphere hovered inches from my palm, and as I held it high, it cast bluish-green light against the walls. The seven men stirred and moaned at the intrusion of light, and as I cast my gaze over their ornate but dirty robes I confirmed that they were, indeed, the delegates who'd accompanied Iannis on the dirigible. How different they looked now, from the proud officials who rarely gave me the time of day. I wrinkled my nose at the scent of vomit and other bodily excretions hanging in the air, and wished I'd brought something to tie around my face and block the smell.

One of them opened his eyes to stare at me, and I narrowed my own eyes at his blurry gaze and blown pupils that nearly eclipsed his grey-green eyes. "Wh-what do you want now?" he slurred, and my heart sank. No wonder the Resistance wasn't worried about the mages escaping. They'd been pumped full of drugs.

Crouching down in front of him, I tamped down the flame in my hand so I wouldn't continue to hurt his eyes. His dark brown hair was scraggly, his triangular jaw covered with a patchwork of stubble that told me growing a beard didn't come easily to him. "I'm looking for the Chief Mage," I said enunciating my words slowly and clearly. "Have you seen him?"

"'m not answering your questions." Those grey-green eyes flashed with contempt, and the mage inched himself a little more upright while doing his best to look down at me from his long nose even though my head was above his. "I don't... answer...to you."

I nearly snorted. Typical mage attitude, always acting superior even in the face of death and starvation. Truthfully, it was admirable, but a little annoying since we were both on the same side. Taking a gamble, I dropped the illusion and allowed my true form to show.

The delegate's eyes nearly popped out of his skull. "Y-you!"

"Shhh!" I clapped a hand over his mouth as the others stirred. "I remember you – you're Bosal ar'Nuris, the Secretary of Education and Culture." I tried to hide my shock at seeing him in such a state – I was used to seeing these mages striding briskly through the halls of the Palace, proud and aloof, not sitting here in their own excrement. "If you start yelling, you'll bring the whole Resistance camp down here!" The delegate struggled beneath my hand for a moment, but he was too weak and disoriented from the drugs, so eventually he subsided and I released him.

The delegate tried to speak again, but the drugs proved to be too much of an impediment for coherent speech. On instinct, I touched my hand to his shoulder and pushed some magic into him, visualizing the drugs leaving his body and energy filling him. My stomach pitched with nausea, and I tightened my grip on his shoulder as another wave of tiredness washed through me.

Beneath my hand, I felt the delegate's shoulders straighten. He sat up a little, some alertness returning to his eyes, and I let out a breath of relief. No, I hadn't healed him, but maybe I'd helped him enough that he could talk to me now.

"You're the...hybrid..." he slurred as he peered up at me through the darkness. "Lord Iannis's apprentice. Did he...send you here to free us?"

"No, though of course I'll do what I can. I came out here trying to find him. Why is he not with you?"

Bosal shrugged one shoulder. "Don't...remember. None of us do. We were on the airship one moment...down here the next. No idea where Lord Iannis is. Hoped he'd escaped back to

Solantha...but clearly hasn't, since you're here." Disappointment rang in his thick voice, mirroring my own.

"Do you have any idea what the Resistance is planning?" I pressed, hoping to get something, *anything* out of the mage. "What was their purpose in taking down the airship?"

"Wanted...to stop us from attending the Convention." The mage's voice seemed to be getting a little stronger, and I wondered if the dose they'd given him was starting to fade. "Don't know why, but they're planning something."

"Alright." I sighed, pinching the bridge of my nose with my free hand. A quick glance at my wristwatch told me my time was about up. "I'd better get back before someone misses me."

"Wait." The delegate's hand shot out, wrapping around my wrist with surprising strength. "You're not going...to leave us here, are you?"

"I would like to free you, Secretary," I said with regret, "but can you even stand? Do you have a spell to rouse the others, and get up the mineshaft?"

His growl of frustration sounded more like shifter than mage. "If we could, we'd be gone already. Don't know what that drug...they inject us with is, but it's too effective...and we don't get enough water. We need help."

"I'll come back with reinforcements as soon as I can," I promised. "But if I don't go now they'll just catch me too, and then nobody will find Lord Iannis."

"Al...right..." Bosal sighed, releasing my hand as he slumped against the wall. "Just hope you come back...before they decide to kill us."

Yeah, I thought as I took my leave. *I hope so too.*

13

I woke up the next morning with ravenous hunger clawing at my belly. By the time I'd made it back to the cabin last night, I'd been exhausted from all the magic I'd used, and had collapsed into bed after telling Annia and Fenris what I'd learned. Sleep had helped somewhat, but if I was going to recharge I needed food. Lots of food.

A tinge of pink washed over the dark sky as Annia and I made our way to the kitchens, a mere suggestion of dawn that made me grumpy as hell as I was *not* an early morning person. But we had to get the soldiers fed on time, and besides, I could use the opportunity to stuff my face so that I wouldn't be too irritable by the time everybody showed up.

"By the Ur-God," Annia muttered as she began opening tub-sized cans of corned beef hash. "We've been here less than twenty-four hours and it already feels like we've been assimilated into the camp." She spoke quietly so that the sleepy-eyed soldier on guard couldn't overhear.

"Tell me about it," I said around a mouthful of cookie as I kneaded dough. It honestly felt weird that we were feeding the very people who were responsible for Iannis's disappearance, but we didn't have nearly enough manpower to take them on, so we had to blend in. "If we don't get out of here soon, we might just find ourselves in uniform."

Annia snorted. "Do you really think that Rylan will slip up like that?"

"No," I admitted with a sigh. "He'll figure out what I'm up to, and since he's a lapdog for the Resistance he'll rat us out for sure. And don't forget the tiger shifter, Daresh. He'll denounce us in a heartbeat, when that spell wears off."

My heart ached at the thought of my cousin Rylan – he and I had been so close as cubs, and I hated that we were on opposite ends of this brewing war. He'd tried to get me to join the Resistance, and when that had failed, in an effort to keep me safe he'd warned me several times to keep my nose out of their plans. We still loved each other, but I knew that if the Resistance caught me here Rylan wouldn't lift a finger in my defense. To him, the cause was more important than family.

"The fact that Rylan would do that only makes me more certain that I don't want Noria anywhere near the Resistance," Annia whispered fiercely, the crackle of frying meat covering her vehement words. "When we get home, I'll knock some sense into that stubborn head of hers, even if it means sending her off to a foreign country."

"She'd either find her way back here or just join up with whatever passes for the Resistance over there." I shook my head as a wave of exhaustion that had nothing to do with my lack of sleep washed over me. "I'm starting to think that the only way to keep Noria safe is to help the mages crush the Resistance."

Annia's eyebrows shot up. "Never thought I'd hear you say those words."

My lips twisted in a wry smile. "Must be a sign of the end of times or something."

A somber mood settled over us. We quietly finished cooking

the rest of the meal and laying out the food on the serving counter for the men to help themselves. Soldiers started trickling in, and though they were a little bleary-eyed, their faces were washed and their uniforms were clean. The fact that these men took their duties seriously and had pride in their appearance told me that they were truly dedicated to their cause. I shuddered to think of the kind of force they would become if they had experienced military leaders commanding them.

As before, Annia took control of the serving line, greeting the soldiers with smiles and cheer that had them brightening up and grinning back at her. Even Captain Milios, who gave us both the stink-eye as he walked in, huffed out a reluctant greeting to her as she handed him his morning coffee. I watched him as he surveyed us with those keen eyes of his for a long moment before taking his food and sitting down at his table, which was angled perpendicular to the other tables and centered along the wall so that he could observe everyone at any given moment.

About ten minutes into breakfast, a soldier burst in through the doors and rushed straight to Milios's table. "Captain, captain!" he shouted. "There's an airship circling the plains, and it's passing near us!"

Instantly, soldiers rushed from their tables to peer through the windows set in the back and front walls. They ignored Milios's shouts, crowding around the few windows that weren't broken so they could see what was happening. Annia and I had our own window in the kitchen, so we hurried over to see what all the fuss was about.

I spotted the airship instantly – the taut canvas was tinted royal blue, and Canalo's emblem, stamped on the side in gold, shimmered in the early morning light. My fingers curled at my sides, and I sneered up at the rescue ship. Had the Council heeded my request to join their rescue team, we'd be a lot closer to finding Iannis. Instead, they were circling the plains fruitlessly, while we were stuck down here feeding these misguided soldiers. If the mages at least had a shifter aboard, Fenris and I could have communicated with them via mindspeak and gotten them to rescue their colleagues in that putrid mineshaft. Instead, I watched them sail by overhead with frustration searing my chest.

"ENOUGH!" the captain finally roared, silencing the fervent buzz that had spread throughout the room. "Stop acting like a bunch of hysterical housewives, the lot of you, and *sit down!*"

The men obeyed, returning to their seats with bowed shoulders, though plenty of them still glanced furtively in the direction of the windows.

Captain Milios huffed at the sight of his men. "You all are acting like a flock of hens who've had their feathers torn out," he scolded them. "That dirigible isn't going to spot us from so high up. We're too well camouflaged."

"With all due respect, captain, we're not worried about the town being discovered so much as the dirigible that Xiver took down," one of the soldiers, a skinny guy with mousy brown hair and a thin face, spoke up. He pointed toward a broad-shouldered man with inky-black hair and a square face sitting two tables away, who straightened instantly at the sound of his name. "If that airship finds the dirigible, they'll know the delegates went down near here."

"Don't you worry your pretty little head about that, Private," the captain scoffed. "That's why we've sent our resident mage out to take care of it. He should be done waving his magic fingers around by now. There won't be a single trace of that dirigible left behind."

"A mage!" Fenris shouted in my head as Annia and I exchanged a look. *"There's a mage helping them?"*

"Wipe that look off your face before someone sees it," I hissed back at him – his eyes were snapping fire, his cheeks turning a

brilliant shade of red. *"The last thing we need is for the captain to be even more suspicious of us!"*

"I don't think that search party'll find the dirigible, even if that mage doesn't do his job," Xiver drawled, a lazy grin on his face as his barrel chest puffed out. "I did a pretty damn good job hiding it away when I landed it in the mountains. And they're never gonna find the Chief Mage, not after what I did to him –"

"Thank you, Sergeant Xiver," the captain barked, cutting him off before Xiver could say anything more. "Now if you're done bragging about your piloting skills, let's finish breakfast so we can get started with our day."

"Yes sir." Xiver saluted the captain, but it was almost a lazy gesture, and the smirk didn't quite disappear from his face. The captain narrowed his eyes until Xiver finally turned back to his food, and the normal level of conversation resumed.

"I wonder who the mage is that's helping them?" Annia muttered as she brought some dirty dishes over to me. "Seems kind of strange that any mage would join up with the Resistance."

"Maybe they're getting offered some kind of deal," I suggested as I dunked my hands into the soapy water, fishing for the sponge I'd dropped. "Or they've got a bone to pick with the establishment."

"I guess, but I can't see the Resistance honoring any deal they make with a mage," Annia said dubiously. "Ultimately their goal is to remove the mages from power, so they couldn't have one amongst their ranks."

She went back to her station, and I mulled over her words for a few moments as I scrubbed dishes. Annia was right – the Resistance might be temporarily allying themselves with a mage, but there was no way that relationship was going to last.

"Sunaya." Fenris grabbed my attention again, his voice calm now, though ire still simmered beneath the surface. *"I've been*

listening to the captain and the sergeant talking. They're debating whether or not to execute the delegates."

I stiffened. *"What are they saying, exactly?"* I turned my head to look toward the front table. Captain Milios and Sergeant Brun had their heads close together, and they seemed to be arguing fiercely. I cursed myself for not being close enough to hear them – the noise in the mess hall combined with the fact that I was all the way in the kitchen rendered my super-hearing useless. Thankfully Fenris was only one table away, and though he kept his head down and appeared to be focused solely on his food, he clearly had an ear cocked toward the conversation.

"The sergeant is arguing that the delegates are draining camp resources, specifically the food, drugs, and manpower required to keep an eye on them. He and a number of the other men think the delegates should just be killed since they have no value and are enemies of the Resistance. But the captain is saying they need to wait on orders from the Benefactor first."

"The Benefactor!" The long stirring spoon I was holding slipped from my hands and clanged against the lip of the sink before disappearing beneath the soapy water. I fished it out and finished scrubbing it, then stuck it on the rapidly-filling drying rack. *"I didn't think that general members of the Resistance knew about the Benefactor."*

"Why wouldn't they?"

"Because Rylan didn't know, and he's the same rank as Captain Milios."

"Do you think it's possible that Rylan might not have been telling the truth?" Fenris asked cautiously.

"I don't see how. He was standing right in front of me when we had the conversation." Due to our heightened senses as well as sensitivity to body language, it was extremely difficult to lie to a shifter. Besides, I couldn't quite stomach the idea that Rylan and

I had grown so far apart that he was comfortable lying to my face.

"Perhaps the Benefactor, whoever he is, has become less careful about spreading their name around, now that their plans are coming to fruition," Fenris suggested, though he didn't sound completely convinced. *"In any case, we need to rescue the delegates sooner rather than later before the Resistance decides to execute them. Do you have any suggestions?"*

I nearly shook my head, but remembered just in time that I wasn't supposed to look like I was having a conversation. *"They're all heavily drugged, so they won't be able to offer any assistance, and we don't have the necessary manpower to go up against the whole camp. Not to mention that mage could be back soon, and we have no idea how powerful he is. For all we know, he could be as strong as Iannis."*

"Then our best option is to find Iannis fast, and bring him back here before it's too late," Fenris concluded. *"Unfortunately, the only lead we have is that obnoxious pilot."*

Finished with the dishes, I turned around to look at Xiver, who was joking around with the soldiers at his table, a shit-eating grin on his face. That grin widened as he caught me looking at him, and a lascivious glint entered his eyes that sent a shiver running down my spine.

"We'll take him tonight," I told Fenris as I turned my back on the pilot. *"Squeeze him for information and hope he gives us something useful."* He'd done something to Iannis, and when I got my hands on him I would make sure that grin was wiped from his face. Maybe even permanently.

14

Fenris might not have been much of a talker, but his keen eye and stellar observation skills were a huge help. During dinner service, he told me that he already knew which cabin Sergeant Xiver was staying in. The three of us hashed out a plan over dinner, one that I wasn't entirely happy with, but was fairly confident would work.

After our kitchen duties were done for the day, Annia and I headed back to our cabin. The shadow of the mountains loomed over the camp, but behind them the sky was streaked with brilliant shades of gold, purple, and orange as the sun bade us farewell. Annia received lots of catcalls and whistles as we walked past the men, but though she smiled and waved at them, she didn't stop to engage them in conversation. We had an agenda tonight, and the extra attention wouldn't help us with our mission.

"Alright you," Annia said, digging through her pack as I sat down on my cot. "Let's get you all prettied up for your starring role tonight."

"I can't believe you packed makeup," I groused as I watched her open a miniature makeup case and place it on her thigh.

"A lady has to be prepared for any situation," Annia said primly, arching her eyebrows and pursing her lips. I snickered, then yelped as she reached out and pinched my cheek. "Now, now, young lady. A lady never snickers."

"Yeah, yeah." I batted her hand away from my cheek. "Just get on with it already. I seriously doubt Xiver expects me to be a lady."

"Not in his bed, anyway," Annia agreed as she kneeled in front of me. She dipped a tiny brush into an equally tiny circle of bronze eyeshadow and instructed me to close my eyes. "Xiver looks like the kind of guy who'd fuck a woman and then slap her if she complained that she didn't get off."

"I bet he hasn't had the chance to do that in a long time," I mused as Annia brushed powder over my lids. "With the way he was looking at me today, I'm half surprised he didn't approach me himself."

"All the more reason that this'll work."

Annia finished making me up, and I changed out of the long-sleeved shirt I was wearing into a tank top I'd packed for hotter weather. The cotton garment showed off my toned arms, and more importantly my cleavage. Annia inspected me for a moment with pursed lips, then reached out and tugged my neckline a little lower.

"Perfect. He won't know what hit him."

We waited until darkness had fully settled over the village before I quietly slipped from our cabin. Following Fenris's directions, I headed for the cabin two rows behind us and one to the left. It had two stories, and I chewed my lip for a moment as I wondered which floor my target lived on. It would be easier if I could avoid his roommate.

I took a deep breath, then sauntered up to the door and knocked. A moment later, a tall, lanky soldier with dirty blond hair opened the door. His uniform discarded, he was dressed in a white t-shirt and underwear. Realization that I was a woman widened his eyes, and a blush sprouted from his hairline and spread all the way down to his collarbone before he shoved the door partially closed.

"C-can I help you, miss? I mean, recruit?" the soldier asked, his voice steadying now that he was partially shielded from sight. His pale blue eyes skittered over me, round as saucers. Judging by some of the looks we'd gotten, I was sure that if I hadn't been a shifter, more than a few of these men would have tried to sneak into our beds in the middle of the night.

"Sure." I leaned my shoulder against one of the rickety posts holding up the awning, careful not to put too much weight on the beam lest it collapse, and gave him my best coy smile. "I'm looking for Sergeant Xiver. Is he in?"

"Whatcha need him for?"

"I have a...message, that I need to deliver. Specifically for him."

"I see." The soldier looked disappointed. "Gimme a sec." He closed the door in my face, and I heard him hollering for Xiver.

"What is it?" the pilot snapped from the upper floor, and I groaned a little. It was going to be harder to take him if he was on the upper floor, though not impossible.

"One of the women is here to see you."

"Is that right?" The growl smoothly transitioned into an amused drawl, and I sucked my tongue between my teeth, annoyed. I could practically hear his ego swelling at the idea that he was the first man to be paid a visit by the new hussies in town. He was going to be in for an ugly surprise when he found out I wasn't here to suck his cock, but meanwhile....

The door swung open and Xiver's tall form filled the doorway. Unlike his roommate, he still had his uniform pants on, but he'd taken off the top and only a white cotton tank separated my gaze from his muscular torso. The patches of sweat on his tank top and the sheen on his tanned skin told me that he'd probably been doing push-ups or something – with the sun gone from the horizon, the temperature had cooled off considerably.

"What is it, woman?" He raked my form with his dark eyes. The glint in his pupils was identical to the one I'd seen in the cafeteria, and another small shiver worked its way down my spine. "Don't you know it's getting close to lights out?"

"Oh I know." I gave him a slow smile as I drew my gaze down his own body. "It gets cold here at night, though, and I was looking around the mess hall today for someone who could help keep me warm." I dropped my gaze meaningfully to his groin, then brought it back up to his face. "I was thinking maybe you were up to the job, but if not, I've got a few back-up options available."

Xiver snorted. "Those limp dicks wouldn't know what to do if you showed up on their doorstep." Another cold shiver crawled down my spine as he clamped a large hand around my wrist. "Come in and let me show you what a real man can do."

I let him pull me into the darkness of the cabin, prepared to follow him up the stairs, but as soon as he closed the door he pushed me up against the wall and crushed his body against mine. His chapped lips pressed roughly against my own, and I fought against the urge to gag as a combination of sour and smoky filled my senses.

A strangled noise in the background drew my attention to the fact that Xiver's roommate was still here. I seized on the excuse as I flattened my palms against the pilot's broad chest, pushing him away.

"I like a bit more privacy," I purred up at him as Xiver scowled, rubbing my hands up and down his chest to soften the insult.

Xiver glanced over his shoulder at his gaping roommate, who was sitting on his cot, eyes wide as he watched us. "What, you mean Wilton?" He laughed. "I planned on giving him a show. The way he blushes every time he sees you two in the mess hall, I figure he needs a crash course on how to handle a woman."

I arched a brow. "Before we do that, I need to make sure *you* can handle *me*." I pressed my tongue between my teeth as I grinned up at him. "I wouldn't want to embarrass you in front of your friend if I prove to be too much for you."

Xiver's upper lip curled. "I've never met a woman I couldn't handle, but if you insist." His hands were around my waist, and I turned my yelp of outrage into a girly squeal as he hauled me over his shoulder and carried me up the creaky stairs to his room. "Hang tight, Wilton!" he called down the stairs to his roommate. "As soon as I'm done with the shifter, you can have her next."

We entered the small upstairs room, which was barely big enough to hold the cot and dresser in it. Xiver didn't bother with a light – the window in his room was one of the few in this town that was still intact, and moonlight washed over the space. He tossed me unceremoniously onto the hard bed, and I considered kneeing him in the balls. But I didn't need his roommate running up here to see what all the crying was about.

"Strip," he ordered, his fingers moving to his belt.

I sat up and pretended to fumble with the buttons on my shirt. "I think I need some help," I said with a shy smile. "It's hard to see in the dark." I spread my legs apart, inviting him to step between them and giving him a hint of what he thought was coming.

His dark eyes gleamed with hunger, and he stepped between my legs without hesitation. As soon as he was close, I clamped my thighs around his hips, then drew him into my embrace and whispered the same Word I'd used on the soldier guarding the mineshaft. Xiver's body stiffened as the magic washed over him, and then every single muscle in his body relaxed as he slipped into a deep sleep.

"We've got him," I told Fenris as Xiver's forehead knocked against my shoulder and a loud snore erupted from him. *"Now come help me get him out of here before I change my mind and kill him after all."*

WITH OUR BAGS packed and a heavy, unconscious Xiver slung over our shoulders, Annia, Fenris, and I snuck out of the camp, heading back into the forest. Fenris and Annia carried him while I forged ahead, making liberal use of the sleeping spell Fenris had taught me on the few guards who were on night watch. I'd knocked out Xiver's roommate the same way – since we weren't planning on coming back until after we'd rescued Iannis, there was no longer any point in trying to hide my magic.

We trekked several miles into the forest before we decided we were far enough away that we could interrogate Xiver without interruption. My nose detected no scouting parties in the area, so we tied Xiver to a tree, and I delivered a good, hard slap across his face to wake him up. After the way he'd manhandled me, it felt good.

"Oww!" Xiver's eyes popped open, and he jerked, likely wanting to clap his hand across his stinging cheek. When he realized his arms weren't moving, he looked down at himself, and his eyes bulged as he realized he was strapped to a tree. "What the fuck is going on here?"

"Aww, does little Xiver not like being tied up?" I crooned. "I bet the delegates down in that mineshaft feel the same way."

His eyes narrowed. "So Captain Milios was right! You three *are* traitors."

"You're the traitor," Fenris growled, taking a step forward.

"You and the band of renegades you run around with, terrorizing good, innocent people in the name of justice."

"Those filthy mages we've got down in the mines aren't good or innocent," Xiver sneered. "They're part of the institution that oppresses us. What the fuck did they bribe you three with to get you on their side? You're all shifters and humans, the same as us. You should be helping *us*, not *them*."

"Thanks for the speech, but we're not interested," Annia interjected. "We brought you out here because you seem to be the only one who knows what happened to the Chief Mage, and I intend to drag his ass back to Solantha so I can cash in on the big pile of gold the government's put up as a reward. Now would be a good time to tell us what you know, before we disfigure something of yours." She pulled a knife from the sheath at her side and tested the point with her thumb.

"Like I'd help a gold-digging whore like you." Xiver spat at her feet, narrowly missing Annia's boots.

I cracked my palm across Xiver's face again, and his head snapped to the side. "You might want to use better manners on my friend. She's pretty good with that knife."

"I'm not scared of a little pain," Xiver snarled. The fear gleaming in his eyes told a different story, but I had to admire him a little for his refusal to give in. "You bitches probably don't even know how to use a blade outside the kitchen anyway."

The knife in Annia's hand landed with a thunk to the right of Xiver's head, slicing off a lock of his inky hair as it buried itself into the tree trunk. Xiver's face paled, and I snickered.

"I've got more of these," Annia warned, pulling another knife from her boot. As she straightened, the blade gleaming in her right hand, she pretended to yawn. "It's kinda late though, and I'm getting pretty tired, so my aim might not be the best—"

"Like chopping off my dick with that knife of yours is going to help you?" Xiver sneered. "You're not collecting that bounty no matter what you do, so go ahead and waste your time carving me up like a turkey."

Annia paused, and Fenris's face turned icy. "What do you mean by that, exactly?" I asked cautiously.

"I mean that your precious Chief Mage is dead!" Xiver laughed as he curled his lip at us. "I killed him myself, so you might as well tuck your tails between your legs and run on home!"

"How do you know he's dead?" I asked, resisting the urge to check the *serapha* charms resting against my chest. I'd last checked them only an hour ago, and Iannis had still been alive and well.

"Because I threw the bastard out the door, that's how!" Xiver boasted. "The plan was to put everyone to sleep with a special gas, but your precious Chief Mage wouldn't stay down, and he tried to kill me. So I lost my temper and threw him out the door, and then I landed the dirigible north of our camp, safe and sound. Things might not have gone exactly as planned, but I did my fucking job. Not many humans can say they faced down a Chief Mage and lived to tell the tale." His chest puffed up with pride.

"You lie!" Fenris cried, lunging forward. He wrapped his fingers around the straps of Xiver's tank top, pulling him close so that they were nose to nose. "There's no way you would be able to get rid of the Chief Mage so easily!"

"It was pretty damn easy if you ask me." Xiver smiled slyly. "The bastard was half paralyzed from all that gas, so he missed with whatever stupid spell he tried to cast on me. He was weak as a kitten when I grabbed his robe and shoved him out the door, so no way he survived the five-thousand-foot drop. He's burning in the afterlife right now for all his crimes against humanity."

Fenris let go of Xiver, his head bowed as he stepped back,

and for a moment I thought he was done. But then he lifted his head, eyes gleaming with fury as he pinned Xiver with the coldest, deadliest glare I'd ever seen.

"Your crimes are inexcusable," he whispered, raising his hands. My eyes widened as power crackled from his fingertips, the blue-green glow I associated with magic. "On behalf of the Federation, I sentence you to death."

Bolts of lightning erupted from Fenris's hands, hitting Xiver straight in the chest. Annia and I both clapped our hands over our ears, a second before a deafening crack ripped through the air. The soldier's mouth opened in a scream as the lightning tore through him, and I squeezed my eyes against the flash of purple and yellow that momentarily lit up the clearing. Spots danced beneath my closed eyelids, and I waited until the sizzle in the air subsided before opening my eyes.

What had been a healthy human male only a minute ago was now reduced to human-shaped chunk of blackened flesh. The stench of charred flesh coated my nostrils, but I was less stunned by Xiver's death than by the manner of how it had happened. Ripping my eyes away from Xiver's corpse, I stared at Fenris, whose chest heaved with exertion even as he continued to glare at the remnants of the human who'd inspired his wrath.

"Oh, that is *it!*" Annia stomped her foot, looking pissed as hell. She marched right up to Fenris and dug her fingers into the fabric of his shirt, pulling him around to face her. "I knew you've been hiding something since day one, and I can't take it anymore. You're going to spill the beans about what you really are, and you're going to do it *right now.*"

"Let go of me," Fenris snarled, ripping her hand away, but I stepped forward and placed my own hand on Fenris's shoulder, digging my fingers a little more firmly into his muscles than was perhaps necessary.

"Fuck that," I snapped, my anger rising quickly to match

Annia's. "You don't get to hide behind your excuses anymore, Fenris, not after that crazy fireworks show you put on for us. How the fuck did you do that?" I jabbed my finger in the direction of Xiver's corpse.

"He's got to be a hybrid," Annia declared, her eyes narrowed as she studied Fenris. "No wonder the Chief Mage took you in, Naya. Apparently you're not his first pet project."

"I am *not* Iannis's pet," Fenris growled. "Nor am I a *project*, as you so callously put it."

"But you're a hybrid, aren't you?" I pushed, noticing that he hadn't denied it. "I understand why you might want to hide that from everyone else, but why would you hide it from me?" I asked, hurt creeping into my voice. "I thought we were closer than this." I let the illusion spells drop from us, and Fenris's thick, dark hair and beard rematerialized along with his regular features. "Aren't there few of us as it is? Shouldn't we be sticking together instead of hiding our nature from each other?"

Fenris sighed, running a hand across his beard. "It isn't that simple, Sunaya. I'm not sure that the term 'hybrid' properly defines what I am."

"Well then tell us what does," Annia said, tapping her foot impatiently. "We've got time, and nobody but us is around to hear your secret."

Fenris pressed his lips together as he scanned the tree line, and I knew he was using his senses to try and determine if anyone was nearby. "This is extremely sensitive information," he said quietly. "If I share this with you, you must promise to tell no one. My life depends on it, and more importantly, Iannis's as well."

"Of course," I said, my anger dissipating as eager curiosity resurfaced. Excitement lit inside my chest at the idea that I might finally be able to unravel the mystery that was Fenris. "We won't tell a soul, right Annia?"

"I swear by the Ur-God," she said promptly. "Your secret is safe with me."

"Very well." Fenris stared up at the starry sky peeking through the tree branches, and I wondered if he was just gathering his thoughts or looking for guidance. "The truth is that I was not born as a shifter at all. I was born a mage, to a wealthy Federation family in Nebara."

"That's impossible." I gaped at him, dumbstruck. Nebara was two states north of Mexia, located almost directly in the center of the Federation. "Mages don't become shifters. Why the fuck would you do something like that?"

"In order to escape a death sentence."

Annia frowned. "But you said you were from a wealthy mage family. What could you have possibly done to earn a death sentence that they couldn't have saved you from?"

Fenris snorted. "Money and status doesn't protect you from everything, Annia. And besides, I wasn't just a mage from a wealthy family. I was the Chief Mage of Nebara."

"No fucking way." Annia's eyes nearly popped out of her skull. "You mean Polar ar'Tollis? The one who was sentenced to death by the Minister's Office for helping prisoners escape?"

"I believe that's what I just told you," Fenris said dryly.

"By Magorah." I sat down in the dirt, overwhelmed with what I'd just heard. Everybody knew about Polar. He'd helped a human family whose child had tested positively for magic escape across the northern border to avoid execution, and the Federation had decided to make an example of him by executing him in the child's place. "I can't believe it. No one was ever sure if you'd escaped, or if the Federation had decided to kill you quietly."

Fenris huffed. "The Federation wanted to make my death a public spectacle to discourage other mages from following in my footsteps. They would have succeeded had Iannis not intervened."

"I can't believe I'm hearing this." I leaned my head back against the tree trunk and pressed my palm against my forehead. "Are you telling me that *Iannis* turned you into a shifter?"

"Keep your voice down!" Fenris hissed, glaring at me. "If anyone overhears that and word gets back to the Federation, they'll have us *both* executed."

"You'll have to excuse us if we're a little shocked," Annia said, shaking her head. She sat down on a small rock in the middle of the clearing and stared at Fenris with something akin to awe. "It's not every day that we meet a shifter who used to be a Chief Mage."

"I didn't even know there were any mages around that still knew how to pull that off," I muttered. The practice of creating shifters had been banned nearly a thousand years ago, a long time ago even by mage standards.

"The act may have been banned, but the spells still exist, and are even practiced in secret in certain countries that choose to flaunt the Great Accord." Fenris sniffed at that. "Using an old and dangerous spell, Iannis and I managed to fake my death, and he transformed me in secret. I was in hiding for over a year before I came to live with him at Solantha Palace. You'll understand why I keep well away from naturally born shifters."

"Wow. That's incredible." My heart swelled with emotion at the thought that Iannis would do something so utterly selfless. I wished he were here so that I could throw my arms around him and hug him for it. The more I learned about him, the more I realized just how different he was from the stereotypical mage. "I guess you two must have been good friends."

"Yes...you learn who your true friends are when you're desperate. We met years ago in Manuc when I was traveling overseas, and kept up a correspondence. I backed him when the

Federation was voting on his appointment as Canalo's next Chief Mage. When he heard I was in trouble, he didn't hesitate." Fenris's shoulders slumped. "I suppose that's part of the reason why I lost my temper. Iannis saved me, and now that it's my turn to save him, I'm failing."

"We're not failing," I said firmly, taking his hand in mine and squeezing it. "We're hitting a few roadblocks, that's for sure, but we're not defeated and we're not going to be. As long as this thing is still glowing, we're going to keep searching." I pulled out the *serapha* charm that was tied to Iannis's soul, and light burst from it once more.

"You still haven't explained how it is that you can do magic," Annia said, frowning a little. "If the Chief Mage turned you into a shifter, shouldn't that mean you can't do magic anymore?"

"In theory you would be right," Fenris said, his lips quirking into a smile. "But shifters naturally have some magic at their disposal in order to shift, and Iannis tried to preserve as much of my power as possible during the transformation. I do not have the magical strength that I once did, and my skills are not what they used to be, but I still retain my knowledge and can do some spellwork." He closed his eyes as he wiped a hand over his face. "It is exhausting though, especially large bursts of magic such as frying someone with a lightning bolt."

"Here, let's eat." I pulled Fenris and Annia away from the stench of the charred body, then pulled out some dried meat for Fenris out of my backpack. We'd smuggled food from the pantry into our packs, stretching our supplies out a little longer. "We should replenish our strength as much as we can before we head out."

"To where, though?" Fenris demanded. "We've no clue where Iannis ended up."

"No, but Xiver did give us a good idea of where he parked that dirigible. Maybe we can find some clues there."

"Yeah, and didn't the captain say their mage went to destroy the dirigible?" Annia added. "If we can intercept him, maybe we can keep him from getting back to the camp so we can rescue the delegates without his interference."

"I would love to get my hands on that traitor," Fenris said, a hungry gleam in his eyes as he chewed his jerky. "Between the three of us there is a good chance we'd be able to subdue him."

"Alright." I patted Fenris on the back, then popped another piece of jerky into my mouth. And as we prepared to leave, I wondered just how much excitement I could look forward to now that Fenris was finally letting his bloodthirsty side show.

15

After our short rest, we headed back north into the mountain range in the direction we thought the dirigible might have ended up in. Unfortunately, Xiver hadn't been exaggerating when he'd said he'd hidden it well, and we searched for several hours without any sight of it. Between hiking up into the forest with Xiver, then back out again and up into the range, we were exhausted, so halfway through the night we collapsed in a cave and slept for a few hours. I had to admit I missed the cots we'd slept on at the Resistance camp, but I was so tired from all the magical and physical exertion that I couldn't bring myself to care overmuch.

The sound of unknown voices woke me, and I bolted upright to see that two Coazi males were standing at the entrance to our cave. Their forms were backlit by the morning sun rays streaming in, and I jumped to my feet, squinting against the light. Fenris and Annia, who'd been woken by my motion, quickly followed suit, and out of the corner of my eye I saw Annia nock an arrow and aim it at the intruders.

"Hold up," I said, raising my hands to indicate to the Coazi that I meant no harm. The spears in their hands were pointed downward, and I didn't think they intended to attack us, though they stiffened at Annia's aggressive stance. "They're not pointing any weapons at us, Annia, so I think we should do the same." I waited until she lowered her bow, then turned my attention back to the Coazi. "Good morning."

"Are you seeking Flying Man?" the one on the left asked as the two stepped a little further into the cave and out of the blinding light. Now that they were a little closer, I could see that though they wore the same buckskin tunics as the other tribe we'd encountered, the beads decorating their clothing were arranged in triangular patterns rather than the swirls the other tribe favored.

"Flying Man?" I echoed, confused but hopeful. Could he mean...?

The male nodded. "White man with purple eyes fell from the sky seven suns ago. Halyma saw a great spirit in him, and took him back to our village to be her *sharalli*."

"Uh-oh," Fenris said to me. *"I'm not sure exactly what a* sharalli *is, but I think it means consort or husband."*

"What!" I exclaimed aloud, and the two Coazi jumped, startled at my outburst.

"Is Flying Man your *sharalli*?" one of them inquired, looking at me curiously. "He say nothing about another woman."

"He was maybe afraid?" the other Coazi pondered. "Nobody says no to Halyma."

"Halyma is your shaman?" I asked.

"Yes." The two males nodded simultaneously. "She is chief shamaness of the Coazi. We do not like white man living among us, but Halyma has temper like raging buffalo, so we say nothing."

"Thank you for your assistance." Fenris stepped forward before I could ask anything more, taking control of the conversation. He waved a hand in the air and spoke a few Words, and immediately the males' eyes glazed over. "You will forget that you saw us, and return to your village." His voice resonated with power, and the burnt-sugar scent of magic stung the air.

The two Coazi blinked, then immediately turned on their heels and walked away. I opened my mouth to speak, but Fenris held up a hand.

"Stay silent until they are out of earshot."

"Why the hell did you do that?" I snapped, my fingernails digging into my palms. *"I wasn't done talking to them!"*

"They've told us all we need to know. Their shamaness is holding Iannis hostage, and we need to go to their village and get him back. Giving them more information about us isn't going to help, and if they warn the village we are coming that isn't going to help either."

I huffed out a breath, my ears telling me the Coazi were gone. "How do we know that Iannis is being held there against his will? I can't imagine any of the Coazi being strong enough to do that."

"Yes, and *I* can't imagine Iannis willingly choosing to remain with the Coazi when so much is at stake," Fenris pointed out. "From what these two men just told us, their shamaness is not only powerful, but she has a temper and her people are afraid of her. We need to get close enough to the village to do a proper reconnaissance so we can figure out the best way to extract Iannis."

"Well I know *that*," I said peevishly, turning my gaze toward the cave entrance. Honestly, I knew Fenris was right, and I'd been coming to the same conclusion myself. But as soon as the Coazi had said Iannis was their shamaness's new consort, the need to grill them and find out just what the hell that position entailed had consumed my mind. Did that mean the two of them were married? Was Iannis spending his days frolicking in the grass with her, and his nights rolling around in her bed? Iannis didn't even know this woman – how could she claim him so quickly? He was not hers to keep. My blood boiled, and I fisted my hands at my sides.

"Relax, Naya." Annia patted me on the shoulder, bringing me back to the present, and I turned to look at her. "We're not going to know for sure what's up with Iannis until we get there and see for ourselves. For all you know she's got him chained up in her tent, trying to force him into submission."

I laughed and winced all at once as an image of Iannis chained to the floor of a tent with a bunch of bearskin rugs underneath him and probably nothing covering him popped into my head. That wouldn't be so bad if I was there, but considering it was the shamaness...

"By Magorah, but we've got to hurry." Shaking my head, I cleared my mind of the image. It didn't matter what kind of state Iannis was in, we still had to get him back. Reaching for my beast, I shifted into panther form, then headed out with Fenris and Annia, hoping against hope that we'd get to Iannis in time to undo whatever spell the shamaness had put on him.

BACK IN BEAST FORM, Fenris and I were able to track the two Coazi males without difficulty despite the lead we'd given them. We followed at a distance, with Annia even further behind to make sure we drew no attention to ourselves. It took another couple of hours, but by early afternoon we arrived at the tribe's camp, set on a plateau at the edge of a large patch of forest high up on the mountainside.

Rather than following the two males into the camp, we hung back in the forest, shifting back into human form and climbing up tall pine trees so we could get a good view of the camp while remaining hidden from view. Perched securely on a branch, with my legs wrapped around the tree's trunk in case the branch wasn't as sturdy as I'd gauged, I fished out a spyglass and extended it, then fitted the lens to my eye.

Like the Coazi tribe we'd met on the plains, the mountain Coazi set up their dwellings in a circle. Unlike the plains Coazi, their huts were made out of wooden frames that were covered in what looked like woven mats and sheets of bark. In addition to several large looms where women sat and wove rugs, the center of the circle also housed a large, communal fire pit with logs set up around it for people to sit on. Several women were prepping the fire pit for cooking, and I noticed a woman watching from the side who was more elaborately dressed than the others. The feathers in her hair were a brilliant blue, and a colorful shawl with animal patterns woven expertly into the fabric was draped around her slim shoulders. The buckskin dress she wore flattered her shapely figure and regal bearing. Jealousy flashed low in my gut as I guessed that she must be Halyma.

"No sign of the Chief Mage yet," Annia commented as she studied the camp through a pair of bronze binoculars. "You think he's hiding out in one of those huts over there?"

A series of whoops and shouts echoed from the forest on the opposite side of the camp, and everyone in the clearing turned toward the sound as one. Both adults and children started jumping and shouting as well, and there was no mistaking their excitement as they all ran toward the edge of the forest.

A small group of Coazi men armed with spears and bows emerged from the forest, a pair of large hunting dogs dancing around their feet as they carried a huge elk back to the camp. I nearly fell out of the tree as I spotted Iannis at the head of the group, along with two other hunters. Brightly colored feathers very similar to the shamaness's were woven into his cherrywood locks, and he'd traded in his robes for buckskins. The tunic and leggings he wore showcased his tall, lean form in a way that his robes never did. I drank in the sight hungrily, my eyes roaming over his broad chest and shoulders, his lean waist, and long legs that I could tell were muscular even through the buckskin pants. His violet eyes glowed with health and vitality, and his white teeth gleamed as he flashed a brilliant smile.

Except that smile wasn't for me, I realized as I followed his gaze. That smile was for the shamaness, who had rushed forward to greet him along with the others. The whole tribe crowded around them, whooping and cheering at the sight of the elk, which had been bound to a long, sturdy tree log that all six of the men helped to carry. The shamaness gave Iannis a feline smile as she twined her arms around his neck, and I hissed as she pressed her slim curves against him. I saw lips move as words were exchanged, and Iannis lowered his head and kissed her.

"No fucking way!" Annia hissed as a red haze spread across my vision. My claws dug into the bark, and I realized a second later that I was snarling, my fangs bared. "Not only is he one of them, but he's standing there making out with that hussy shamaness while the rest of Solantha is losing their minds?"

I ground my teeth together, choosing not to respond because honestly, I didn't know what to say. I felt like someone had thrust a superheated blade straight through my heart. The searing agony made it hard to breathe, and hot tears gathered at the corners of my eyes. I'd come all the way out here to rescue Iannis, only to find that he'd thrown himself wholeheartedly at another woman. And from the way he was kissing her, it didn't seem like he had any plans on leaving.

"Your lack of faith is unbecoming, Sunaya," Fenris warned, his eyes narrowed as he read my emotions perfectly. Not that I imagined that was a great feat – I'm sure they were stamped across my face for the whole world to see. "You and I both know that Iannis would never willingly abandon his people to live amongst the Coazi. What we are seeing here is clearly a product of the shamaness's trickery."

"But –"

"This is the same man who took you in against the wishes of the Council and made you his apprentice. The same man who risked his life and reputation to save me from execution. Do you *really* think that he would willingly abandon his responsibilities now, when his people need him more than ever?"

"No." I let out a heavy sigh, and tried to push out all the negativity in my chest along with that breath. But it was hard, especially as I watched the two of them link hands and walk back into the camp with the rest of the Coazi. The group dispersed now that the welcome committee had done its job, the ones who'd been in the midst of chores returning to their tasks while others jumped in to help skin and prep the elk for dinner.

"I guess you're right, but it's hard to reconcile that logic with what my eyes are seeing," I told Fenris, ripping my gaze away from Iannis. I really didn't want to watch him hold hands with the shamaness anymore.

"I understand, but you have to put your emotions aside and focus on the mission," Fenris reminded me, his eyes softening with sympathy. "Besides, I imagine that when Iannis sees you again, he will have no trouble forgetting about the shamaness's charms." His lips curled into a smile.

"Yeah, right," I scoffed as a blush crept up my cheeks and butterflies erupted in my stomach. "Let's just focus on getting him out of there. The sooner we can get him away from that woman, the sooner we can beat some sense back into him."

"That's the spirit."

16

W e waited until the sun had set and the evening meal was in full swing before enacting our first plan. We'd gone through a couple of different options, including outright kidnapping Iannis, but even though he might have been under some kind of enchantment, there was no evidence that he didn't still have full use of his formidable powers. In fact, he was the only one of the hunters who didn't carry a weapon, so he was probably relying on magic even now.

"Alright," Fenris said as we watched Iannis leave the fire and head back into one of the tents. We'd already tried using mind-speak to reach him, but he hadn't responded, so our only choice was to get closer. "I'll head in now." He crouched down, white light enveloping him as he changed from man to wolf.

"Be careful," I told him as the light faded from his form, revealing a large wolf with coarse brown fur and yellow eyes. "The Coazi won't be happy if they see you anywhere near their children."

"Don't worry." Fenris shook himself, then stretched and yawned, revealing his sharp, white fangs. It was still hard to

believe that he'd once been a full-blooded mage, even with all the little clues I'd noticed before. *"I can be stealthy."*

Annia and I climbed up a tree and watched as Fenris quietly approached the camp. At first we thought things were going to be fine – nearly all of the Coazi were happily gathered near the fire, including the children, who were playing with the dogs.

The dogs.

"Oh fuck!" I cursed, suddenly realizing how stupid we were. *"Fenris, get out of there! The dogs—"*

But it was too late. One of the dogs had suddenly stopped playing, ears perked and nose in the air as he sniffed. Fenris, who was outside Iannis's tent, froze and the dog bayed as he caught the intruder's scent. The two huge beasts sprang forward, and Fenris made a run for it, but several Coazi rushed out of their tents, blocking his path as the slavering dogs closed in. My breath caught in my throat as I watched Iannis rush out of his tent, then stand by and do nothing as the two animals fell upon Fenris. There was no recognition in Iannis's eyes, only a bemused frown as he watched the three beasts roll around in the dirt, jaws snapping and snarling as they fought for the upper hand. The Coazi were closing in, already making a tight circle around the animals, so there was no way Fenris was escaping – the only way he was getting out of this was if he changed back into a human, and if he did that our cover would be blown.

Just as I was getting ready to jump out of the tree and charge into the camp, the shamaness stepped forward, her shawl fluttering around her slender arms as she made a cutting motion with her arm and shouted something. The dogs backed off instantly, returning to her side, and Fenris lay there panting for a moment, clearly weakened by the attack. Before he could get up, the shamaness reached into a pouch hanging from her belt and tossed some sort of powder at Fenris, then shouted something I could not understand. A purple glow enveloped Fenris, and my heart froze as he stopped moving.

"*Fenris!*" I cried out. "*What did she do to you? Are you hurt?*"

"*Not hurt...but extremely lethargic,*" Fenris answered as the Coazi tossed him into a wooden cage and tied it shut with leather ropes. "*You need to get to Iannis and break the spell on him – I could see the aura of a strong enchantment around him, and cannot not reach him with mindspeak even here. I have a feeling the shamaness has plans for me that I'm not going to enjoy, so please hurry.*" Beneath the urgency of his tone I could sense Fenris's disappointment, and I felt bad for him. Even though he knew Iannis had been under a spell, it must have cut Fenris deeply that his best friend had not recognized and aided him.

"*No kidding,*" I said as I watched the Coazi carry Fenris's cage into one of the huts that was near the fire. It was smaller than the others, and had some kind of ceremonial beading dripping from the entrance in lieu of a door, so I had a feeling the hut was used for rituals or important meetings. "*Are you sure we shouldn't just storm the camp and rescue you first? I really don't want them to sacrifice you to whatever gods or spirits they worship.*"

"*An attack now would be too dangerous, since Iannis is under the shamaness's control and will likely defend the tribe along with her. You need to get him alone and break through the spell clouding his mind. It's the only way.*"

"*And just how am I supposed to do that?*" I demanded, digging my claws into the pine bark as panic rose in my chest. "*He didn't recognize you at all, Fenris, and the two of you have known each other for years. What makes you think he's going to recognize me?*"

"*He probably won't,*" Fenris admitted heavily. "*But if you can get the* serapha *charm back around his neck, that might help you break the spell.*"

"Umm, so what's the plan, exactly?" Annia asked, sounding more than a little worried. "I'm going to assume you've been chatting with Fenris instead of staring dumbly off into space, and it would be nice to know what we're doing next."

"Fenris says I should try putting the *serapha* charm around Iannis's neck and see if that breaks the spell." I tugged the chain from beneath my shirt and stared down at the charm. "I guess if I do that, it'll remind him of our connection and hopefully get through to him. I just hope he doesn't see me as a threat and try to kill me."

"Just because the Chief Mage is dressing like a Coazi and under a spell doesn't mean he isn't the same person," Annia pointed out. "From what you've told me, the Chief Mage isn't a shoot first, ask questions later kind of guy. If you can get him alone for long enough, you might just be able to reason with him."

"I sure hope so, because it looks like I'm about to get my shot," I said as Iannis walked out of a hut with a small bundle beneath his arm. I watched as he headed in the direction of the woods he'd come from earlier, and my heart rate shot up as anticipation raced through me.

"I'll stay up here and make sure Fenris doesn't become dinner," Annia told me. "You go get the Chief Mage, and don't forget to take a piece out of that ass of his for putting you through the wringer."

"Damn right." I cracked a smile, then grew serious again. "If you see an opportunity to get Fenris out of there, jump on it."

"Will do."

I sprang out of the tree, then shifted into panther form and crept around the camp, careful to stay out of sight behind the tree line and downwind of the dogs. The last thing I needed was for the Coazi to find me and stick me in a cage next to Fenris. Thankfully they'd gone back to eating and dancing around the fire, and with my inky-black fur nobody would be able to spot me beneath the cover of the pines.

Once I'd made it around to the forest on the other side of the camp, I put my nose to the ground and started sniffing out Iannis's trail. It didn't take me long to find it, and I trotted uphill, winding my way through the trees and taking care not to rustle the needle-laden branches. I didn't want to alert Iannis to my presence – the last thing I needed was for him to blast me with his magic because he thought I was a wild animal that wanted him for dinner.

As Iannis's scent grew stronger, the sound of running water greeted my ears, followed by a splash. A gap in the trees brought the stream into view, and I nearly tripped over a pinecone as I caught sight of Iannis standing waist deep in the water without a stitch of clothing on. My mouth went dry as I watched the moonlight play over the muscles of his broad back, and I traced a line down his spine with my gaze until it disappeared beneath the silver ripples of the water. A flush spread across my skin, and suddenly I was too hot for my fur.

As Iannis dunked his head beneath the water, I shifted back into human form, figuring that was probably my safest bet. I stepped out of the tree line as he resurfaced, and swallowed hard as he tilted his head back and pushed his gleaming mane of hair back from his face. Silver moonlight played across the strong planes of his handsome face, highlighting the length of his nose, the edges of his high cheekbones, the strength of his triangular jaw. His sensual lips, normally so firm, parted on a contented sigh, and it struck me that I'd never seen him so relaxed. I wondered if he was like this in the privacy of his rooms, or if living out in the wilderness had softened him.

What if he really does want to be here?

As though he sensed my gaze, Iannis's whole body stiffened, and he turned sharply in my direction. Iridescent eyes clashed with mine, and an electric current zapped through me as he looked me up and down. Something like wary recognition flickered in his eyes, and I seized on that as hope filled me.

"Iannis." I took a cautious step forward, moving slowly as I might with a wild animal I was trying not to startle. "It's me, Sunaya. I've been looking for you."

"Looking for me?" His dark brows pulled together in a frown as confusion filled his gaze. "I am not lost."

"Yes, you are." I kept my voice low but firm as I stopped close to the edge of the stream. "You were flying to Dara in a dirigible bound for the Convention, but you never made it there. People have been looking everywhere for you. Solantha has been in a panic ever since we learned you were missing."

"Solantha," he said slowly, testing the word out on his tongue. "My city." A shadow passed through his eyes then, and he shook his head vehemently. "No, this is my home. I belong here with the Coazi."

"No, you don't!" My voice began to rise as agitation got the better of me. "These are not your people, Iannis. You have friends and colleagues who desperately need you. Not to mention that *I* desperately need you."

"You do?" Iannis looked positively bewildered. "What for?"

"Because I'm your apprentice!" I cried, throwing my hands up in the air. Not knowing what else to do, I tugged the chain I'd given to Iannis over my head and held it out to him. "We agreed to wear these, don't you remember? So that we could always find each other in case one of us was in trouble?"

The stone flared to life, and Iannis recoiled as if struck. "Get that away from me!" he cried, throwing his hands up as if to shield himself. A burst of magic emanated from his hands, and a hard gust of wind hit me, sending me flying backward. I sailed several feet through the air before landing hard on my butt with a yelp.

"By Magorah!" I shouted, struggling up into a sitting position. "What the hell was that for?"

"Halyma told me that the stone on that necklace was black magic, and it was preventing us from being together." Iannis scowled at the *serapha* charm, which was still clutched in my fist. "She said the pain in my chest would go away if I took it off, so I did. Why do you have it?"

"Because I was using it to track you down!" I snapped as I got back up to my feet. "Halyma is a liar, Iannis. She's using her shaman powers to trick you into believing that you're her lover, and that you belong here when you really don't. She didn't want you wearing the necklace because she didn't want me to find you."

Something flared in Iannis's eyes for a moment, and then that same shadow I'd seen earlier clouded his irises again. "Halyma is my *sharalla*. She wouldn't want to hurt me."

"She's selfish," I insisted. "Come here and let me prove it to you."

"No!" The shadow in his eyes darkened, and Iannis retreated to the other side of the stream. "You are the one who is trying to trick me."

I ground my teeth together, frustrated beyond belief with this game of cat and mouse. I wanted to jump into the water and wrestle the necklace over Iannis's head, but I knew he'd just hit me with his magic. Even if his brain seemed to be addled, he was still the Chief Mage, and there was no way I'd win that fight.

Then do not fight, a cool voice whispered in my head, one I'd heard before. *Sometimes it is better to use honey instead of flame.*

I sucked in another breath as another idea came to me, one that made me hot all over and incredibly nervous at the same time. It was risky, but probably the best shot I had at getting past Iannis's defenses. And right now, breaking the spell on him was more important than my pride.

"Are you giving up, then?" Iannis demanded as I took a step back from the edge of the stream and slipped the chain back around my neck. I could have sworn I saw something like disappointment in his eyes, but his jaw was set and his glare didn't waver.

"Well it's too bad you're not willing to listen to me," I said as I slid my pack from my back and dropped it on the ground near Iannis's buckskins. "But since I came all the way up here, I don't see why this whole trip has to be a whole waste. That stream looks pretty inviting, and I intend to have myself a bath."

"W-what?" Iannis's eyes widened as I tossed my jacket to the ground. By Magorah, but had I really just heard the unflappable Chief Mage *stammer*? "You can't use the stream while I'm here."

"Why not?" I asked innocently as I tugged my shirt off over my head. I stretched my arms overhead for a moment, giving Iannis a good view of my nearly bare torso, then allowed the shirt to flutter to the ground. "Is that some kind of Coazi law?"

"No, but Halyma would be furious..." Iannis momentarily lost his train of thought as I unhooked my bra from the front, letting my breasts spill from their confines. Hunger gleamed in his violet eyes, fanning the flames that were already spreading through my lower belly. He cleared his throat as I tossed the bra away. "She wouldn't want me to bathe with another woman, and might well hurt you in her displeasure."

At least he didn't want me to be harmed. Maybe this wasn't so hopeless after all.

"Who said anything about you bathing with me?" I undid my belt buckle, then slowly shimmied out of my pants and underwear all at once. My breasts swayed along with the movement, and I nearly grinned at the look of raw longing in Iannis's eyes. Damn, but why hadn't I done this sooner? "We're just sharing the same stream." I stepped out of my pants and toed them away as if my blood wasn't pumping with fear and excitement, as if my breath weren't coming short at the thought of entering the water with Iannis wearing nothing but my skin.

"I should leave," Iannis said, but he made no move as I stepped into the water. His violet eyes burned a trail of fire across my naked body as I slowly waded in, and though the cool water lapped at my skin, the fire inside me only built as I closed the distance between us. He was so close now, within arm's-length, and I held my breath as I approached. Part of me was afraid that this was just a dream, that in a few moments I would wake up and the glorious naked man before me would be gone.

But when my fingertips alighted on his chest, it didn't vanish into nothingness. The smooth, cream-colored flesh was real, as were the hard muscles that lay beneath the skin. A sharp, indrawn breath caused his chest to rise, and the crisp, dark hairs teased my skin as I flattened my hands against his chest. His heartbeat pumped hard against my palm, and I caught the flutter of his pulse at the base of his throat as I drew my gaze upward to his sternly handsome face.

"Why are you doing this?" he whispered.

"Because I need you," I murmured back, and my heart ached at the raw truth in those words. Sliding my hands into the hair at the base of his skull, I allowed myself to savor the feel of his silky cherrywood tresses gliding against my fingers, something I'd thought about more times than I could count but never imagined I'd actually experience. This moment was so surreal, and for a beat in time nothing else existed but the two of us. There were no consequences, no friends or family breathing down my shoulder, no past, no future, no anything. There was only the heartbeat beneath my palm, the water swirling around my hips, and a pair of iridescent eyes that blazed so hot I thought they might consume me whole.

Before either of us could change our minds, I unclasped the chain from around my neck, then slipped it around Iannis's neck while pulling his body into mine. Our lips clashed, and I nearly dropped the necklace into the water as a bolt of white hot heat lanced my body. Strong arms banded around me as the necklace clasped, and I could feel the heat of the two charms glowing between us as Iannis kissed me back, crushing his mouth against me as his fingers dug into my hips with bruising force. My knees went weak as his arousal pressed against my inner thigh, my fingers digging into his broad shoulders as I gasped, and then his tongue was in my mouth, tangling with mine. He tasted dark and sweet and spicy all at once, a flavor combination unlike anything I'd ever tasted, and I kissed him hungrily, wanting more, wanting everything he had to offer.

"I remember you now," he rasped, pulling back just far enough to let those glorious words feather over my lips. "I can't recall ever doing this, but I remember you. How could I have forgotten your fiery spirit for even a moment?" His hand drifted up to press against my cheek as his eyes burned into mine, and if I had been a lesser woman, or perhaps had a looser grip on Iannis's shoulders, I would have swooned.

"Yeah, well that shamaness did a number on you." I shifted a little, and my nipples scraped against his chest, sending little zings of pleasure through me. Iannis's eyes gleamed hungrily, and my lips parted as his head dipped down –

"Sunaya! Come quick!" Fenris cried, and I jumped, knocking my forehead against Iannis's. *"We're under attack!"*

"Shit!" I clapped my hand against my throbbing forehead. *"I'm coming, I'm coming!"*

"What's wrong?" Iannis demanded as I leapt from the stream and made a beeline for my clothing.

"Fenris just sent me an S.O.S.," I explained as I hurriedly dragged my clothing on. "I guess your shamaness friend is trying to kill him now."

"Damn," Iannis swore as he rushed out of the stream. I

forced my gaze away from his naked body – I couldn't afford the distraction – and focused on shoving my feet back into my boots. "That wolf who sneaked into the village was Fenris? Of course he was." He sounded chagrined as he grabbed for his own clothes. "Did you bring anyone else?"

"My friend Annia. I'm sure she's with Fenris right now."

Iannis and I sprinted down the hill, following the cacophony of shouts and cries. I was a little surprised that he was keeping up with me, but I didn't have time to dwell on that. We burst into the camp to see women herding their children into the safety of the huts, while pandemonium reigned closer to the fire pit. Annia and Fenris stood back to back near the fire, Annia with her bow drawn and Fenris in human form with his hands outstretched, power crackling at his fingertips. They were surrounded by warriors, and Halyma was facing down Fenris, a ferocious glare on her beautiful face as she held a feathered staff aloft and chanted some sort of spell that made the head of the staff glow bright with power.

"Halyma!" Iannis shouted, drawing the shamaness's attention away from Fenris. "Stop! These are my friends!"

"These people are outsiders!" Halyma's dark eyes flashed, and her nostrils flared as she caught sight of me. "Cursed man-beasts and white men, trespassing across our lands and trying to take what is ours!"

"They are not trying to take anything," Iannis said sternly, and I inwardly sighed with relief – he was sounding more like his old self. "They came here because they were concerned about me."

"They are trying to take you!" Halyma shrieked, her cheeks reddening with anger. "You are my *sharalli*, and I will not let them have you!" She leveled her staff in my direction, and a ball of deadly energy shot straight toward me.

Iannis shoved me to the side, and made a slicing motion

with his hand as he shouted a Word. A glowing force field materialized in front of him, deflecting the ball up into the sky where it dissipated.

"You...you defend her?" Halyma whispered, her dark eyes filling with tears. She looked so dejected that I would have felt sorry for her if she hadn't just tried to kill me.

"Of course." Iannis put his body between Halyma and me, partially blocking my view of the shamaness. "These people are my friends, Halyma. How could you try to hurt them, knowing that?"

"Because they are taking you from me." Halyma's voice hardened, though the tears did not disappear, and she pointed a shaking finger at me. "I knew that one would come eventually. That is why I told you to get rid of that necklace! And yet you defy me by wearing it again."

"I am not yours to command." Iannis's voice hardened as well, and the air around him crackled with power. "I am grateful that you found and healed me, Halyma, but you cannot keep me here against my will. My people are in danger, and I must go back to them. As a leader yourself, you must understand this."

Halyma was silent for a long moment, and for a second I thought she might actually let us go. But then she lifted her chin proudly and squared her jaw.

"I care nothing for mages or their troubles!" she spat, her dark eyes gleaming with anger. "I saw something in you that I thought would be different, but you are just like the rest, taking what you need from us and leaving us to suffer. If you want to leave me, I will send you to the afterlife!"

She pointed her staff in Iannis's direction and began a chant, but Iannis flung out a hand and shouted several Words. Some kind of strange, sizzling yellow and black energy shot out from his palm and slammed into the shamaness, knocking her flat on her back before she could complete her chant. Her body began to shake as energy crackled over her skin and clothing, and she bucked and writhed as though she were having a seizure.

"Come on!" I grabbed Fenris's hand. "Let's get out of here!" Raising a hand, I conjured a ball of fire and aimed it at the shamaness's tent. The structure burst into flame, and those of the Coazi who weren't trying to help the shamaness rushed to put out the fire, giving us the diversion we needed. The four of us made a run for it, sprinting from the camp as hard and fast as our legs could carry us, and I prayed to whatever god might be listening that we would make it out of this blasted mountain range alive.

17

It took over an hour to lose the Coazi – even though most of them stayed behind trying to save their shamaness and her burning hut, a good number of them still came after us. Iannis and Fenris took over the defense against the ones who chased us, deflecting arrows and spears with the use of magic. We did not retaliate as Iannis still seemed to have friendly feelings for them, and after all we were intruders on their land. We continued in our full-on sprint for a good two miles after the last confrontation before we finally slowed.

"Okay," Annia gasped, clutching at a stitch in her side. "We've got to stop or I'm going to explode. Surely we've lost them now, haven't we?"

"We have," Iannis confirmed as we slowed to a trot. I arched a brow, amazed that though his cheeks were flushed from the run, he was barely winded. "But the Coazi have small parties that roam these mountains, so it would not be wise to assume that we are safe. We really should keep moving."

"Well I'm sorry, but unlike you three I've got human limitations," Annia snapped, still clutching at her side. "I can't sprint for miles on end."

Iannis stopped abruptly, and I nearly ran into him. "Come here," he commanded.

Annia stopped as well. "Why?" she demanded, suspicion in her voice.

"So that I can help you," he said patiently. "There is little point in making you suffer through your 'human limitations,' as you call them, when I can provide a workaround."

"Alright." Annia stepped forward cautiously. "What do you want me to do?"

"Just stand there for a moment." Iannis squatted down, and Annia jumped a little as he wrapped his fingers around her ankles. He spoke a few Words, and glowing circles of magical energy formed around Annia's ankles. The energy spread up her legs and over the rest of her body, and her eyes widened as she was briefly enveloped in the strange glow. The magic hummed over her for a few moments, then disappeared in a shower of sparks.

"Wow." Annia ran her hands down her sides as Iannis rose. "What the hell did you do to me? I feel amazing."

"I gave you an energy boost," he said simply. "You should be able to run for several hours more without tiring. It will wear off eventually, but for now you should be able to keep up with us."

Sure enough, when we resumed our run, Annia kept up without complaint. We ran another eight miles, mostly downhill, until we came across a cave that looked suitable to bed down in for the night. Iannis and Fenris warded the entrance, and Annia and I built a small fire in the back of the cave where the glow could not be easily seen from a distance.

Once Iannis and Fenris had secured the entrance, they joined us around the fire. My eyes roamed over Iannis as he stared into the flames, the firelight flickering over his handsome features. When I'd first met him, I'd never thought I'd see him sitting cross-legged on a cavern floor in beaded buckskins, with his hair tousled and a healthy flush on his normally alabaster cheeks. It was a good look for him – no, better than good. He was downright sexy. No wonder that shamaness had desired him – any red-blooded woman would have. Even so, there was no way I could forgive her for putting that spell on him. What Halyma had done to Iannis was little better than slavery.

"Now that we've had a chance to catch our breath, why don't you fill us in on what happened?" Fenris asked as he handed Iannis a packet of beef jerky. "We've traveled quite a way to come to your rescue, at considerable risk. It would be nice to have the blanks filled in at last."

"Indeed, and I am grateful." Iannis's eyes swept over us all, lingering on me just a beat longer than everyone else. Heat swept through my stomach, and I fought the urge to bite my lip. "I am greatly in your debt, for going to such lengths to find me. If you had not, I might have lived for years or decades as Halyma's *sharalli*. Her mind magic is extremely potent."

"Just how the hell did she manage to bewitch you into staying with her in the first place?" I demanded, jealousy adding an edge to my voice. Even though I knew Iannis had been under a spell, it still chafed me that he'd allowed himself to be caught like that in the first place. I mean, he was one of the strongest mages in the Northia Federation. Shouldn't he have been able to resist one puny shamaness?

"These shamans are far more powerful than the public gives them credit for, and I suspect Halyma is special among them." Iannis arched a brow at me, no doubt reading my thoughts from the expression stamped across my face. "I woke up in the dirigible feeling disoriented and sluggish, and found my fellow passengers completely unconscious. Then the pilot came into the cabin, wearing a gas mask." His voice was suspiciously even, but I suspected that deep anger lay hidden underneath, like magma simmering beneath a seemingly dormant volcano. "I could not kill him since we needed him to land, so I tried to stun him instead. But the gas affected me more than I realized, for I missed, and he managed to throw me out the door of the airship." His voice turned arctic. "He will be punished."

"I took care of that for you," Fenris assured him.

"Oh?" Iannis arched a brow.

"Fenris lost his temper when we were questioning him," I remarked dryly. "He killed the pilot with a lightning bolt."

"Ah." Iannis looked surprised. "I suppose this means your secret is out now, Fenris."

"I was forced to explain my past to the girls after it was done," Fenris admitted with a sigh. "But never mind that, Iannis. What happened after you were thrown out the door? Even you cannot fly."

"I haven't come so close to death in several decades at the very least." A shadow passed over Iannis's face as he spoke. "I was hurtling through the cold air, my lungs aching from the gas, and it was too dark to see how far I was to the ground, so I invoked Resinah's strongest protection spell as well as another to make myself lighter so the impact would not be as great."

"Ah." Fenris nodded as though that made perfect sense to him.

"Wait a second," I objected. "Why couldn't you use a levitation spell to save yourself?" If Fenris was able to teach me how to do that, Iannis had to know how to use it too.

"The levitation spell is not powerful enough to halt a fall that rapid. It is meant for slow ascents and descents. At the rate I was falling, it would have barely slowed me at all."

"Oh." I frowned. It sounded like magic wasn't completely impervious to science. Clearly there was more to learn than I'd thought.

"In any case," Fenris said, moving the conversation along, "I imagine you did not come out of this unscathed."

"Certainly not," Iannis agreed. "I hit a tree, suffered numerous broken bones and lacerations, and was knocked unconscious by the impact. I only awoke when Halyma and her small group of Coazi found me, stuck in the top branches, and deduced I must have fallen from the sky. To give her credit, she is a very skilled healer. I could not have done it better myself. But by the time I was mobile again, she had used her powers to make me believe I was a member of the tribe, and in love with her." He shrugged, frowning deeply. "Had it not just happened, I never would have believed myself susceptible to such trickery." After a moment he added, "Now I know why she had to sacrifice some animal every day. It would have been difficult to keep up such a deep enchantment without constant reinforcement."

I huffed out a breath. "I guess I should take comfort in the fact that even you aren't infallible." I wanted to ask if he still had feelings for Halyma, but that would have sounded pathetic. "Still, it would have been nice if you could have kept the *serapha* charm around your neck. I about died when I found it in a bird's nest without you attached to it. I thought you'd decided to throw it away for some reason." My throat tightened, and I swallowed hard to get rid of the lump trying to form there.

"Halyma had a good idea of what it was, and she tricked me into giving it to her." Iannis's long fingers went to the charm, and butterflies fluttered in my belly as I watched him stroke the gem briefly. "I would have never taken it off willingly," he added, his voice softening.

"That's what I thought," Fenris said, sounding satisfied. "We could tell by the glow that you were still alive, so the charm was helpful to us regardless."

"How did you manage to locate me without it?" Iannis asked. "I hope you haven't just been aimlessly wandering around the plains."

"We decided to start with the Resistance camp at the base of the mountains," Annia said. "We'd heard from another group of Coazi that there was a camp holding prisoners, so we figured that was our best lead after hitting a dead end with your necklace."

"Prisoners?" Iannis's violet eyes snapped fire as he sat up straight. "Do you mean my delegates?"

"Yeah. They're being held in an abandoned mineshaft while the camp awaits orders on what to do with them. Naya can tell you the story, since she's the one who met with them." Annia jerked a thumb in my direction.

I sighed, then filled Iannis in on what we had discovered back at the camp – that the strike on the airship had been ordered by the Benefactor, targeting Iannis specifically, and that though they'd been waiting on orders from the Benefactor on what to do with the other delegates, they were leaning toward killing them. By the time I was done, Iannis's face had turned to stone, his eyes blazing with a cold fury that sent shivers down my spine.

"We must rescue them immediately," he said, pushing to his feet.

"Now?" Annia protested around a mouthful of beef jerky. "It's dark out. Everybody knows that you don't travel at night."

Iannis swung around to face her, and she flinched a little under the weight of his icy glare. "I cannot leave them to die, and besides, such missions are best performed under the cover of darkness. We will go now. Once the delegates are liberated and the Convention is over, I will stamp out the Resistance and their mysterious Benefactor once and for all."

18

With Iannis's mind made up, we packed up and headed for the Resistance camp. Fenris and I changed into beast form, and with the aid of Iannis's spell Annia was able to keep pace with us as we ran. The moon was nearly full now, and gave enough light for us to pick our way through the forest.

I wondered again just how it was that Iannis was able to keep up with us so easily. I hadn't seen him use the energizing spell on himself, and since expending any magic drained the body's energy, such a spell would only cancel itself out. I resolved to ask him about it later, when we weren't in the middle of a rescue mission, and also to fill him in on the problems back in Solantha.

Even at a steady run, it took us several hours to reach the abandoned mining town. By that time, dawn's fingers were painting the peaks of the mountains pink and gold. The camp was still covered in darkness, but I knew it wouldn't be long before the light washed over the tops of the rickety old cabins and the soldiers began stirring.

"I bet the cook is pissed that he's stuck back in the kitchen again," Annia muttered, and I snickered mentally.

"Stop." Iannis held up a hand, and we came to a halt. Standing between Iannis and Annia, I peered through the trees and tried to see what had caught Iannis's attention, but there was only the dark, barely visible outline of the crumbling buildings.

"What is it?" I asked Iannis.

"Someone has set up wards around the camp." His low voice simmered with anger. "It must be that renegade mage you and Fenris mentioned earlier."

"Shit." I squinted through the tree line again, trying to see whatever Iannis was looking at, but I couldn't. *"How the hell do you know there are wards out there?"*

"With enough practice you can train yourself to see the residue from active spells," Fenris explained. *"It takes years to master though, so in the meantime you'll have to trust us. I can see it too."*

"I don't see how the wards matter right now," Annia said. "We're heading for the mineshaft, not the camp. As long as there aren't any wards outside the mine it shouldn't be a problem, right?"

"True, but it's very likely the mage has warded the mineshaft as well," Iannis said tightly. "It's what I would do in his place. No matter though; I don't intend to walk away without confronting the traitor. Any mage foolish enough to side with the Resistance must answer to the Federation for his crimes."

"That sounds a little hypocritical, considering that you saved Fenris from execution for defying the Federation," I couldn't help pointing out. Even though I wasn't a fan of the Resistance, I did think that the current establishment needed to change. I liked the idea that maybe, just maybe, there was a mage out there who agreed and had the balls to join the fight for equality.

"*Now is* not *the time to debate politics,*" Iannis growled, and the hairs on my spine rose in challenge.

"*Maybe, but could you at least hold off on erasing the mage from existence until we find out a little more about him?*" I snapped back. Part of me couldn't believe I was saying this, but I'd come a long way from my black and white viewpoint about mages ever since I was forced to stay at Solantha Palace. "*If we could turn him back onto our side, he could help us bring the Benefactor down.*"

There was a long pause. "*I will consider your suggestion. In the meantime, lead the way to the mineshaft.*"

Who knew I could actually be the voice of reason? I thought as I changed back into human form. Once the glow had faded from my eyes, I swept my gaze across the horizon again...and in the growing daylight, spotted something I hadn't seen before.

"Guys," I muttered. "Any of you see that airship over there?"

Everyone turned their heads in the direction I was pointing. Settled about fifty yards from the camp was a small airship, with a wooden cabin attached under a faded canvas cylinder. It was half the size of those owned by the Mages Guild.

"I'm pretty sure that's how the camp receives their supplies. It could fit all four of us," Annia said, excitement in her voice. "Maybe we don't have to walk all the way back to Solantha after all!"

"You're forgetting about the delegates," Fenris said dryly. "Not to mention that Iannis needs to get to the Convention as soon as possible to thwart whatever the Benefactor is up to there. If we commandeer that dirigible, we'll be heading away from Solantha, not toward it."

"Okay, but we *are* agreeing that we're going to commandeer it, right?" Annia demanded. "The Chief Mage can send back a larger aircraft to pick up whoever is left behind, and any prisoners we take."

"Indeed." Iannis's eyes were focused on the dirigible. "Miss

Melcott, I suggest that you stay close to the dirigible to make sure that no one takes off in it, while Miss Baine, Fenris, and I rescue the delegates."

With that settled, we split up, Annia sneaking toward the dirigible while I led the way to the mines. The sun was creeping closer to the horizon now, bathing the dark, rocky mountain face with a muted glow, and we moved a little faster, not wanting to be caught in the sunlight where sentries might see us.

To our surprise, there were no wards set up around the entrance to the mineshaft, and nor was there a guard on duty. Were we too late? No – a grumpy-looking mule was harnessed to the pulley mechanism that operated the cage, and I could hear voices coming from below.

"Hang on," I said, lying flat on my belly at the edge of the shaft and tilting my ear toward the opening. "Let me see if I can hear what's going on before we go down there."

Fenris copied my pose while Iannis stood guard over us, and together we tuned in to listen to the furious argument occurring down in the mineshaft.

"You can't do this, Chartis!" Bosal, the delegate I'd spoken to earlier, shouted. I froze, straining to make sure I'd heard him right – his voice was thick and hoarse from the drugs in his system. "You're one of us! How could you side with these filthy mongrels and use your magic for their gain?"

"I *was* one of you," a cold voice answered, and a shiver crawled up my spine as I recognized Argon Chartis's superior tone. "But that was before Lord Iannis stripped me of my title and tossed me out into the cold, without so much as a recommendation. You did not lift a finger to help me then, Bosal."

"And so what, that justifies your becoming the tool of these barbaric humans instead?" the Secretary demanded. "I didn't realize you'd sunk so low, Argon. That *any* mage could sink so low."

"Silence!" There was a crack, and I imagined the delegate slumping against the wall beneath the force of one of Chartis's air-slaps. My cheek throbbed in sympathy – I'd been on the receiving end of a few of those from him myself. "The Resistance has offered me the means for getting my own back! Did all of you really expect me to just slink away after such injustice, like a chastised cur? A mage of my experience and standing?"

"Iannis!" I hissed, jumping to my feet. "It's Argon Chartis! *He's* the mage the Resistance recruited to help them, and he's about to execute the delegates now!"

Iannis swore, then sprinted for the mineshaft, speaking the Words of the levitation spell as he went. Rather than fumbling with the spell myself, which I still wasn't super confident with, I hopped onto Iannis's back as he dropped down into the mineshaft.

"Ciach," he swore as my arms and legs wrapped around his torso, but one of his hands wrapped around mine and squeezed, as if to reassure I was safe. "Are you trying to get us both killed?"

"I was going for efficiency," I muttered in his ear as we descended into the shaft, far faster and smoother than when I'd done it on my own. As the elevator cage came into view, I realized Iannis wasn't going to be able to squeeze by it with me on his back, so I dropped onto the top of the cage, then waited until Fenris floated past him before I swung myself over the side and dropped down into the tunnel.

Chartis swung around, his eyes wide with shock at the sight of us. Power crackled in his left hand, which was aimed at the delegate he'd been arguing with. All seven prisoners had been lined up against the wall, rune-engraved cuffs weighing down their wrists and preventing them from being able to use their magic. Four Resistance soldiers surrounded them in case one of them decided to attack, but it was hardly necessary – the mages could barely stand.

"You!" Chartis shouted, jabbing a crackling finger in Iannis's direction. Strangely, he almost looked triumphant at seeing the Chief Mage alive. "I *knew* you had somehow survived that fall."

"Well, I am a Chief Mage," Iannis said coldly, stepping forward. "It would be rather pitiful if I could be killed so easily. Step away from the delegates, Argon. I made the mistake of letting you go quietly, and I won't be doing that again. You are coming back with me to face trial for your treason."

"Come with you? Not in this life!" Chartis yelled, his eyes sparking with rage. He shouted a Word, and a bolt of lightning shot from his palm, heading straight for Iannis. Iannis raised a hand and shouted another spell as he caught the bolt in his hand. The deadly lightning dissipated, much to Chartis's fury. "You've already stripped me of my rank and thrown me out of the Guild – I won't allow you to humiliate me by putting me on a public trial as well!"

"Stop this!" Iannis commanded, his eyes flashing. "If you throw around magic like that in this tunnel, it will collapse and kill us all!"

"That doesn't sound so bad to me," Chartis sneered, raising his hand again. "It means I won't have to take the time to kill you all individually." He shot another bolt at Iannis, and as he did the soldiers rushed forward to attack me and Fenris.

"Help the delegates!" I shouted at Fenris as I charged forward to meet them. "I'll hold them off while you get them out of here!"

The next few minutes were utter pandemonium. Drawing my crescent knives, I blocked the first soldier's sword and knocked it away, then came in with a slash at his mid-section. A second soldier went for my ribs as I did so, and I was forced to twist away to avoid the bite of his blade. As a result, my slash didn't go as deep as I would have liked, and the first soldier jumped back, barely scathed. Out of the corner of my eye, I watched Fenris duck out of the way of another soldier's blade, then come in from underneath and slam his palms into the guy's chest while shouting a word. Ice spread like wildfire over the man's body, and the fourth soldier froze as he watched his comrade turn into a sculpture.

Inspired, I conjured a ball of fire in each hand, then tossed them both at the soldiers as they tried to rush me. The first one ducked it, but the second one didn't get out of the way in time, and he screamed as his clothing burst into flame, then dropped onto the ground and started rolling to stamp out the flames.

Out of the corner of my eye, I watched Argon and Iannis continue to fight. Iannis was on the defensive, working as hard as he could to try and absorb Argon's blasts so that they didn't hurt anyone or destabilize the tunnel. Unable to use full force against a well-shielded enemy, he was at a major disadvantage. If I didn't do something soon, Iannis was going to get hurt.

The hiss of a blade swinging through the air drew my attention to an attack from one of the remaining soldiers. I swung my crescent knife out to block the arc of his sword, but I didn't quite catch it at the right angle and his blade bit deeply into my fingers, straight into the bone. I cried out, my knife slipping from my mutilated fingers, and jumped back, out of the soldier's reach. He laughed at my pain, and the fear in my gut morphed into a towering flame of rage. Snarling, I lifted my other hand, then blasted him straight in the chest with a gout of flame. He flew backwards, landing hard on his ass, a scream erupting from his lips as the flames raced across his body, but I didn't wait around to see if he was going to do the stop, drop, and roll like his buddy. Instead, I drew a chakram from the pouch on my hip, then flung it at Chartis using my non-dominant hand. Too busy trying to blast Iannis and simultaneously shield against his attacks, Chartis didn't see the blade coming, and it sliced clean through his left leg. His scream echoed off the rocky walls, and blood spurted from the stump of his leg as he dropped onto his uninjured knee.

"You mangy beast!" he shouted, dark green eyes blazing with hatred as his gaze clashed with mine. He lifted a hand to blast me, but before he could, Iannis took advantage of Chartis's lowered shield and blasted him with a bolt of his own. Argon screamed as the electric shock ran through him, and he toppled to the ground. I watched him shake and tremble for several moments before he braced his hand against the wall and tried to rise.

"I wouldn't do that if I were you," Iannis said coldly. "In case you haven't noticed, you're surrounded and outnumbered."

It was true. Fenris had freed the delegates from their bonds, and they were on their feet now. Even though they looked like they could be knocked over by a stiff wind, they came to stand around the former Director of the Mages Guild, their lips tight and their eyes filled with the need for retribution. Fenris had his arm at the elbow of the oldest delegate, holding him steady, but I had no doubt that if Chartis tried anything, Fenris would kill him.

"This isn't how it was supposed to happen," Chartis cried in a trembling voice as his body collapsed against the dirt. Rivulets of blood seeped into the ground beneath him, and his face was growing paler by the second. "I should have been the next Chief Mage, not you! I was next in line for the position!"

"Had you been more interested in serving the people rather than serving yourself, perhaps you might have gotten the position," Iannis said. There wasn't an ounce of compassion in his stony voice. "Instead, you abused the position that you did have, and rather than trying to work your way back into the good graces of the Guild after I rightfully dismissed you, you've turned traitor." His eyes lifted to Fenris. "Bring me a set of those cuffs so I can bind him and cauterize his wound."

As Fenris went to gather a pair of the magic-suppressing cuffs lying on the ground, I noticed Chartis make a furtive move out of the corner of my eye. Turning, I saw that he was clutching a star-shaped charm, and though his lips were pressed together in agony, his eyes gleamed with a kind of triumph.

"No!" I shouted, jumping forward, but I was too late. Chartis spoke a Word, and the charm exploded with light, knocking us all back. I squeezed my eyelids shut against the blinding glare, bracing myself against the wall for whatever was to come. Power sizzled in the air as a tremor shook the ground, and rubble rained down onto my head.

"This is not the last you've seen of me!" Chartis's voice echoed through the tunnel as the light faded. When I opened my eyes, he was gone, the severed leg lying in a pool of bright red blood the only proof that he'd ever been here.

19

I turned to ask Iannis what the hell just happened, but before I could speak a portion of the ceiling at the back of the tunnel caved in. Clouds of dust and debris filled the air, making my eyes water and the flames in the torches sputter, and the ground beneath my feet began to tilt. Fuck. The whole damn tunnel was about to collapse on top of us!

"Come on!" I shouted, grabbing the sleeve of the nearest delegate and dragging him forward. He stumbled over the body of a fallen Resistance soldier, but I continued pulling him along. "We've got to get out of here!"

The delegates were too weak to levitate themselves out of the shaft, so Fenris and I ushered them into the elevator cage, choking on clouds of dust and rubble as we went. Fenris got into the cage with them, then shouted several Words. The elevator began to glow, then slowly rose up the shaft with a loud screech, taking the delegates to safety.

The next thing I knew, Iannis's arms were around me, and I bit back a scream of my own as he jumped out of the collapsing tunnel and straight into the abyss below. We fell for ten very long, very terrifying seconds, and then the levitation spell finally activated, dragging us to a halt. I sighed in relief as we began to float upward, leaning my head back against Iannis's chest.

"By Magorah," I said, then took in a deep breath to ease the tremors in my body. "You scared the living hell out of me."

Warmth swept through me as his arms tightened a little more snugly around me and he rested his triangular chin on the top of my head. "Are you alright, Sunaya?"

"Aside from my hand, I think I'm okay." There was also the fact that my stomach was doing somersaults right now, but there was no need to bring that up.

Iannis swore, and he gently grasped my hand and lifted it to the light filtering in from above. It was already starting to heal, but the slices were very deep, and now that adrenaline was wearing off the wound hurt like hell.

"I'll deal with this when we get topside," he promised.

"Thanks." I sighed, relieved that I wouldn't have to suffer with the pain for several hours.

"No, thank *you*." There was a hint of admiration in Iannis's tone. "If you hadn't severed Argon's leg just then, I'm not sure what would have happened."

"I'm sure you would have figured something out." But pride swelled my chest, and I grinned for a moment until I remembered that Argon had escaped. "How the hell did we lose him, though? I don't understand."

"He had a *gulaya*." Iannis's voice tightened. "It's an old-fashioned type of charm, very powerful and rare, that anchors the wearer to a particular place. It requires a lot of power to create, not to mention illegal ingredients, but if the charm is made properly the wearer can use it to teleport back to that single location at any time."

"Well fuck." I wanted to say more, but we floated out of the shaft, and I had to shield my gaze as my eyes worked to adjust to the morning sunlight spilling over the horizon. Iannis set me down, then gently encircled my wrist with his hand and spoke a few Words. A blue glow enveloped my hand, and I squeezed my eyes shut against the searing pain that ripped through my fingers as the magic knitted my flesh and bone back together.

After what seemed like an eternity, the pain faded. I opened my eyes to see that my hand was healed, and let out a breath I hadn't realized I'd been holding.

"There you are." Iannis let my hand fall to my side, and as I looked up at him, I was surprised to see his face was paler than usual. Maybe healing exhausted him more than I thought. "Are you alright now? I need to go speak to the other delegates."

"I'm fine," I said, biting back the questions that sprang to my lips. I stood to the side as Iannis went to talk to Fenris and the delegates, feeling a little bereft but knowing I couldn't monopolize his company. The way the delegates blinked in the light as they spoke to Iannis, a combination of awe and gratitude on their faces, was a little bemusing since I was used to seeing little to no emotion on their faces. But I guess being rescued from impending execution after several days of forced drug injections and incarceration would bring out emotion in anyone.

I wondered if Chartis would survive the blood loss, gulaya or not. The detached part of his leg lay buried under the rubble by now. But then, he was a powerful mage in his own right, and I imagined he'd be nearly as hard to kill as Iannis.

Bosal ar'Nuris, the Education Secretary, spotted me standing by the mineshaft entrance and struggled to his feet. Fenris caught him by the elbow and helped him the rest of the way, and when I realized he was making his way toward me I closed the distance so he wouldn't have to walk so far.

"Thank you for coming back for us," Bosal said, his voice steady despite the rings of exhaustion around his eyes. His long, pale hair was scraggly, his robes stained with dirt and who knew what else, but despite his ordeal he held himself with the dignity I'd come to expect of mages. "I am ashamed to say that I worried you might not, but glad that I misjudged you."

"You're welcome." I smiled and extended my hand. "I guess us shifters aren't so bad after all?"

"I don't know about all of them, but you and Fenris here are all right. I will try to keep an open mind about your species." He patted Fenris's hand, which was still firmly wrapped around his arm, then shook my offered hand. "If I can ever be of service to you, don't hesitate to ask."

The next couple of hours were spent rounding up the soldiers and securing the camp. With Chartis gone, it was easy enough for Iannis and the delegates to tamper with the wards, making it so that only mages could pass through the perimeter of the camp and effectively trapping the soldiers inside. The soldiers tried to stop us when they saw what we were doing, but between Annia, Fenris, and I, we managed to hold them off until the mages could finish their work. Once the soldiers were secured, we set up camp near the airship so that we could rest for a while and Iannis and Fenris could heal the delegates.

"By Magorah," I groaned to Annia, collapsing onto my bedroll, which I'd laid out in the middle of the grass. "I'm exhausted. How the hell does he do it?" I turned to look at Iannis, who was kneeling on the ground next to the ancient Legal Secretary. His hand was pressed against the other mage's forehead as he performed a healing spell. He'd been working on that particular delegate for at least twenty minutes, his eyes closed in concentration and his hands glowing with magic.

"I've heard that a mage's power grows along with their life-span," Annia, who was stretched out next to me, commented. "Maybe Iannis is really old. Have you never asked his age? Fenris might know. They age so slowly and use magic to make themselves look pretty, so I guess anything's possible."

"True." I bit my lip as I studied Iannis's smooth, unlined face and handsome features. It would be a shame if it turned out he was actually a wizened old man using magic to hide his features. But that seemed unlikely, considering how fit he was. An old mage might be able to hide his wrinkles, but that didn't mean he could make his body run like a young man's.

Once Iannis was done healing the others, he gathered us around for a meeting. "We need to take off for Dara immediately," he said. "As much as I'd like to stay and interrogate the soldiers here, the Convention is paramount, and we've already lost too much time."

"I agree, but the situation in Solantha also requires urgent intervention," Fenris said. "The Council did not take your disappearance well. All hell had broken loose by the time we left, only two days after your disappearance."

"We can't leave these Resistance members out here by themselves," one of the delegates' assistants protested. "If they have another mage in their employ, they could easily be freed. They must be taken back to Solantha and brought to justice." From the coldness in his voice, it was clear what kind of justice he had in mind.

"We are not going to leave them here by themselves," Iannis said. "I agree that it would be unwise to do so, and we cannot all fit on that small, rickety airship. Miss Melcott here is the only one who can pilot it, so she will be coming along, as well as Miss Baine. That means I can only take two more along."

"I'll be staying here," Fenris said. "I'm happy to work with whoever you choose to stay behind, interrogating the prisoners and keeping the camp secure until reinforcements arrive." It didn't surprise me that he was volunteering to stay behind – given his history, I figured he'd want to stay well away from the Convention. "We might also try to signal to Director Chen's airship for transport back home."

"Very well. I will take you, Bosal, and Asward as well." Iannis nodded to a dark-haired mage with olive skin, who bowed. "The others are too exhausted to travel yet, and the Convention is nearly over in any case."

"Just so you know, I can't actually fly the ship by myself," Annia spoke up. "Whoever comes along is going to have to be willing to take orders from me and help out. Even a small airship requires a crew."

"Very well, Captain Melcott." Iannis inclined his head to her, and I caught the ghost of a smile on his lips. "We will defer to you on all matters concerning the airship. Perhaps you can figure out a way to hail other ships we run across, so we might convince them to stop by the camp and help round up the prisoners. I will send a ship from Dara as well."

Iannis and Fenris went off to raid the camp's kitchens for supplies while I worked with Annia and the delegates to get the ship ready for takeoff. We scrambled around on the main deck, securing ropes and checking valves and doing whatever else Annia shouted at us to do. Since none of us were experienced with such engines, she had to do a lot of handholding, but eventually we were ready to go.

"Hey." I hopped over the side of the ship and landed in front of Fenris, who was talking with Iannis. "We're ready for takeoff."

"Very well," Iannis said. "I'm leaving you in charge, Fenris. Is there anything else you need?"

Fenris shook his head, smiling. "We've got everything in hand. You get on that ship, and wipe the smiles off the faces of whoever is resting on their laurels right now. I'm sure they'll be shocked to see you arrive not only in perfect health, but wearing aboriginal clothing." He grinned and clapped Iannis on the shoulder.

Iannis grinned back, a rare sight that caused my stomach to flip-flop again. "Strangely, I look forward to turning the attendees on their heads with my arrival. I may even miss these clothes," he added, running a hand down his buckskin tunic, and I snickered. I'd sort of gotten used to seeing Iannis dressed like a Coazi, but now that I thought about it, he was going to shock the shit out of the mages at the Convention, something I was really looking forward to.

"You take care, okay?" I told Fenris, wrapping my arms around him. He grunted a little as I squeezed tight, but his arms came around me and he hugged me back nonetheless. "I'm going to miss you."

"We'll see each other soon enough," Fenris assured me. "In the meantime, though, it will be a nice change of pace to be in charge here instead of being ordered around. Perhaps I'll have a little fun with Captain Milios."

I laughed as Iannis gave Fenris a stern look. "Not too much fun, please. The last thing I need is to receive news that the soldiers have escaped, after I've informed the Convention that we apprehended them."

"Don't worry," Fenris said dryly. "I'll be sure not to make you look bad."

I gave Fenris one last hug, then boarded the airship along with Iannis. A high-pitched whistle shrilled across the plains as Annia put the engine into gear, and as we lifted off, I looked toward the horizon and wondered exactly what was in store for us next.

20

"So we're finally here, huh?"

"Just about," Annia told me, drumming the fingers of her right hand against the helm. Her left hand firmly grasped one of the wooden handles jutting out from the wheel as she banked left, heading straight for the capital city. Dara glittered brightly in the reddish-gold sunset, gilding the roofs of the houses and buildings packed close together in the small coastal city. We could see the Capitol Dome from here, a great white marble dome with a golden statue of Jeremidah, one of the founding mages of the Federation, jutting out of the top. My heart began to drum a little faster – this was where the Convention was taking place. "Just need the Chief Mage to tell me where exactly to put the ship down."

"I'm sure he'll be up here soon," I said, my fingers lifting briefly to touch the *serapha* charm resting against my chest. As soon as Iannis hadn't been needed on deck anymore, he'd disappeared into the captain's cabin for some much-needed rest. We were all exhausted, but he'd used up loads of magic during our escape, so I couldn't blame him for wanting some shut-eye. Unlike Annia and myself, he actually had to attend the Convention and foil whatever new plot the Benefactor was hatching, so it was important that he and the other delegates were clear-headed upon arrival.

"Yeah, well you might want to tell him to rise and shine, because we're gonna be landing soon," Annia said. She brought her hand up to cover a yawn, then reached for her mug of coffee and took a long draught. "And he also better get me a five-star hotel, because after the day I've had I could sleep all week."

"Oh I'll make sure he does. You've been a lifesaver." I patted Annia on the back, then for good measure dug my thumbs into her shoulder muscles and started rubbing in circular motions. Since Annia was the only one who could fly this thing, she'd been attached to the helm all day, pushing us through the skies at top speed to get us to Dara before the day was out. Iannis and the other mages had helped by clearing the weather and ensuring the wind blew in a favorable direction, but without Annia there was no way we would have made this thing work.

"Ohhhh yeahhhhh," Annia groaned, arching her back as my right thumb found a knot. "You can keep that up for as long as you want."

I grinned. "Thanks, but I think I'll go get the Chief Mage now."

"Tease," Annia grumbled, shooting me a dirty look over her shoulder.

Laughing, I gave her shoulders one last squeeze, then vaulted over the railing and down to the main deck. There was no one to watch as I strolled across the wooden floorboards toward the tiny captain's cabin at the rear of the ship – the other delegates had taken refuge from the hot sun below decks. I would have to round them up soon, although maybe I'd leave that task up to Iannis. They were *his* delegates, after all.

As I lifted my knuckles to rap on the door, a ripple of nervous energy gave me pause. I stopped to examine the feeling, and realized that this would be the first time Iannis and I would have a one-on-one conversation since the little...incident back at the river. Heat rushed through me as I remembered the feeling of his hard, naked body pressed against mine. I licked my lips, convinced I could taste him on my tongue all over again.

We'd said things to each other at the river that I'm not sure would have ever slipped from our lips under other circumstances. I'd told him that I *needed* him, something I'd never told any man before, and part of me wished badly that I could take the words back. Saying them out loud had been admitting a weakness, and that was a dangerous thing to do around anyone, never mind someone as powerful as Iannis. He already held my life and fate in his hands – I didn't need to inflate his ego any further or allow him to think I was okay with being dependent on him.

But it was too late. I couldn't take back the words, nor could I take back the kiss we'd shared. And try as I might, I couldn't hide from the fact that I *did* need him. If not on an emotional level, then on a practical one, because he was the only mage around who was willing and able to teach me how to master my magic and control the volatile emotions preventing me from using it safely.

"Are you going to stand out there all day, or will you come in?"

I jumped, startled at the sound of Iannis's voice. A second later, heat flushed into my cheeks as I realized he'd known I was standing outside the door. Taking in a deep breath, I willed the blush to recede from my cheeks, then pushed the door open.

"How long did you know I was standing here?" I asked, then froze as I caught sight of Iannis standing on the other side of the bunk bed. He looked very much like his old self, dressed in a pair of blue and gold robes, his cherrywood hair tied back with a leather thong. No trace of the aboriginal remained in the lines of his face or the folds of his clothing, and his violet eyes were as cool and aloof as ever.

"Since I heard your boots stop outside my door." A slight frown creased his brow as he studied me. "You look...disappointed. Why is that?"

I thought about brushing off the question, but opted for honesty instead and grinned. "I was kind of hoping you'd show up to the Convention in your buckskins with the feathers in your hair," I admitted. "Where did you find those robes, anyway?" We'd found a few Resistance uniforms on the ship, but nothing resembling mage robes.

Iannis huffed. "I was joking when I said I was going to do that. After already missing half the Convention, I can't very well show up looking like a Coazi. The robes are an illusion that I will have to maintain until I can procure proper clothing."

"Oh really?" I arched a brow. "Does that mean you're still wearing the buckskins underneath?"

Iannis's lips twitched. "You seem awfully preoccupied with what I'm wearing, Sunaya," he remarked, walking around the narrow cot toward me.

"Yeah well, last time I was face-to-face with you alone, you weren't wearing much of anything," I murmured as he came closer. The smell of sandalwood and musk filled my senses, and I instinctively inhaled, wanting more of it.

"Indeed," he said softly, his eyes searching mine as he took my hand in his. "I wasn't exactly expecting company."

"Would you rather I had not come?" I asked nonchalantly, trying to act as though my pulse wasn't skyrocketing in response to his touch. His long fingers wrapped around mine, thumb stroking across the back of my hand, and my heart fluttered wildly. By Magorah, what was I getting myself into?

"Of course not. You saved me, broke through Halyma's spell and reminded me who I really am." His grip tightened on my hand. "You mentioned at the stream that you needed me. I think I am starting to realize that I need you too."

"Wait...what?" I gaped at him, stunned. "What could you possibly need me for, when you've got Fenris and the whole Mages Guild behind you?"

"Fenris is invaluable of course, and the Mages Guild has its role, but whenever there is trouble in my city, you always seem to find your way directly to the heart of it." Iannis smiled a little. "Those escapades of yours helped expose layers of corruption and decadence that I might not have otherwise noticed. Perhaps we should consider working together, instead of working around each other as we have been."

"Wait a minute." I couldn't believe what I was hearing. "Are you suggesting that we become partners?"

Iannis frowned. "'Partners' might be the wrong word, considering that we are master and apprentice. You would still be subject to my authority, and under my protection. But should you come across a case that has far-reaching ramifications, you may come to me and request my assistance at any time."

"Oh gee, thanks." I rolled my eyes as I sketched a mocking bow. "Your generosity abounds."

Iannis arched an eyebrow. "Did I say something to offend you?" He sounded genuinely curious, and if I bought into the brief flash of emotion I saw in his eyes, maybe a little hurt.

"No." I sighed, running a hand through my hair. "No, you said exactly what you're supposed to say." *Get real*, I told myself as I fought the sinking disappointment in my chest. The idea that Iannis would treat me as an equal, that he would profess to need me for emotional rather than practical reasons, was absurd. He was a mage, the Chief Mage, first and foremost, and mages and shifters just didn't mix.

But as Iannis studied my face for a long moment, something like regret flickered across his features, and I wondered if, like me, he really did want something more like a partnership. He opened his mouth to say something, then closed it again.

"What?" I snapped, annoyed that I was hanging on tenterhooks waiting for the words to spill out of his mouth.

He shook his head, then held out his hand. "Come here," he said. "I need to put an illusion on you."

"What for?" I asked as I approached cautiously.

Iannis took my hands again, and that familiar thrum of electricity started up in my nerves again, traveling up my arms and vibrating through my whole body.

"Dara is a very mage-centric city," he explained as magic began washing over my body. Sparks skipped up my arms and across my chest before sinking into my skin and filling me with more of that strange humming. "There are humans and a few shifters who live there, of course, but they are not allowed at the Convention. It would call too much attention to us if I brought a shifter with me, and you'll blend in far better as a mage."

The magic faded from around my body, and I looked down to see that I was dressed in a set of emerald green robes embroidered with delicate gold vines. A matching gold and green sash was tied around my waist, and the toes of soft gold slippers peeked out from the hem of my robe.

"There." Iannis took me by the shoulders and pulled me around to look into the small mirror hanging from the wall. "That wasn't so bad now, was it?"

I stared at my reflection in shock. My shifter eyes were gone, replaced by round human irises that allowed the whites of my eyes to shine through. They were still the same color, but it was a jarring contrast to what I was used to. My black hair was free of its tie now, cascading down my shoulders in glossy ringlets, and I wondered if that was illusion too or if Iannis had actually pulled the tie from my hair when I wasn't paying attention. The collar of the robe nearly grazed my chin, but from what I could see in the mirror the garment flattered my figure and was almost sexy despite the fact that it didn't show any skin.

Not that I wanted to show skin.

"So you think you've won by finally getting me into a robe, have you?" I asked Iannis as I turned to face him.

Iannis chuckled a little, shaking his head. "I wasn't aware this was a competition. But looking at you does make a man feel as though he's won something." His eyes roamed over me appreciatively. "You should wear these in real life. I'll buy some for you."

"Not a chance." But my chest swelled with pride at the compliment, and it was almost enough to make me consider wearing the robes again.

Almost.

"As soon as we reach our hotel room, you're getting these things off of me."

"Am I?" Iannis asked softly, interest flaring in his eyes. A blush heated my cheeks as I realized what I'd just said, and I cleared my throat.

"I didn't mean –"

"It would be impractical to rely on illusionary attire during the entire Convention," Iannis said. "As soon as we get settled, we must procure proper robes for all of us. That will make it easier to work together."

"Work together?" I pushed past the fog of lust clouding my brain to try and follow Iannis's logic. "You mean on finding out what the Resistance has planned here in Dara?"

"Exactly." Iannis nodded, his expression stony once more. "They did not want me to make it to the Convention for a reason. I fully intend on finding out why, and thwarting their plans. However, I must attend to delegate business and will be too busy to question whomever I like or snoop around. You, on the other hand, are free of official obligations, and your heightened senses may pick up on clues that I would otherwise miss."

"So you're saying you want me to be a spy?" A grin began to spread across my face.

"I suppose you could put it that way." Iannis arched a brow at my widening grin. "Unless of course you're not able to take the job seriously."

"Hell yeah I can take it seriously." I pumped my fist in the air at the idea that I was finally getting back to doing enforcer work again. "But that doesn't mean I can't get excited about it."

"Oi!" Annia's strident voice blared from the loudspeaker "Are you two lovebirds ever going to come out of there? This ship isn't going to land itself, you know!"

"Oops," I said, grinning up at an annoyed-looking Iannis. "I forgot to mention – the captain wants a word with you."

21

Walking up the front steps of the Federation Capitol Building at Iannis's side was entertaining, to say the least. The guards flanking the huge, gilded double doors stared in shock as they caught sight of him, and by the time they remembered to bow we were already past the threshold and stepping into the entrance hall. Glossy mosaic tiles patterned the floors and arching ceilings with runes, and in the center of the large space was a fountain sculpture of Jeremidah. This time he was flanked by Faonus and Micara, the other two mages that made up the Founding Trio. All three mages were carved as though they were the same height, suggesting that they were equals. I wondered how true that was, if at all. My Northia Federation history was a little rusty.

"Lord Iannis!" the receptionist manning the desk to the right of us exclaimed. She was a petite human dressed in a gold and white button-up blouse and high-waisted skirt. "Is it really you? They said that you were dead!" Her pale brown eyes, the same color as the hair piled atop her head, were wider than serving platters.

"As you can see, Pamina, I am alive and well." Iannis's voice was deadpan, but I caught the flicker of humor in his eyes and I knew he was enjoying the receptionist's reaction. "Would you mind telling me where the rest of the delegates are right now?"

"They're enjoying dinner in the banquet hall." Pamina's mouth formed a small 'o.' "You're going to cause an absolute sensation when you walk in. Do you need someone to escort you, Sir?"

"No need. We can manage on our own." Iannis inclined his head, then swept past her and headed down a long, wide hallway to our right. Huge portraits of various Chief Mages and Ministers lined the gold walls, and my slippers fell upon a richly patterned carpet that ran down the center of the hall, leaving the rune-covered tile to peek out along the sides. I followed after Iannis along with the two delegates, hurrying to keep up with his long-legged stride. We passed a number of humans along the way as they moved between various rooms connected off the hallway, all dressed in the same gold and white uniform as the receptionist and many of them carrying files and paperwork.

"I didn't think humans were allowed inside the Capitol," I remarked as Iannis led us up a set of carpeted stairs.

"They weren't, initially," Secretary Bosal explained to me. "But the Federation realized that it was a waste of resources to employ mages for menial tasks like filing when there were plenty of humans who needed the work. Now we allow humans to work at the Capitol, so long as they are willing to be magically bonded."

"Bonded?" I echoed. "You mean like magically sworn to secrecy?"

"Exactly," the delegate answered. "Any human who breaks the bond will instantly die by heart attack. It is a rather effective deterrent against stealing or selling state secrets."

"No kidding." I turned away before the Education Secretary could see the disgust twisting my expression. On the one hand I understood that the mages wanted to take precautions, but forcing humans to subject themselves to a death spell in exchange for work seemed a little over the top. What if someone captured one of them and tortured them for information? There would be no hope for survival in that situation. Was the information contained in those stupid little files really so valuable that they were worth the loss of human life?

"If humans are allowed in the building, then why don't I see any shifters here?" I asked Iannis.

"Shifters are trusted less by the mage community than humans, due to the hatred your species harbors for ours," Iannis remarked dryly. *"Given your origins as a species, it is only natural that we mages would rather not employ shifters in our main government building."*

The sound of violin music and chatter, which I'd caught strains of from the stairwell, grew louder, and I bit back a derisive snort as we turned a corner and came upon the banquet hall. The doors were thrown wide open, so music and light and tinkling laughter spilled freely into the hall, giving me an immediate impression of restrained elegance. More guards flanked the entrance, and expressions of shock crossed their faces before they stepped back to admit us.

The banquet hall was filled with round tables large enough to seat ten each. Most of the mages were seated at these tables, enjoying their food and wine and conversation, and my stomach grumbled at the enticing aromas of steak and salmon. A few people were standing around in small groups, some near the elaborate buffet toward the back of the room, and others near the entrance. The group nearest the doorway turned to look at us, and one of them dropped the glass of wine poised between her fingers.

"Lord Iannis!" the mage closest to us, a tall, slender man dressed in a set of silver robes that matched his short hair, exclaimed as the glass shattered into a million pieces. Dark red liquid spread quickly across the silver-veined marble, and the female mage who'd dropped it hastily scurried backward as a waiter swooped in to mop up the mess. "By the stars, but we thought you were dead!"

The entire room went silent at those words, and even the orchestra ceased playing for a few moments as everyone gaped at us in shock. Then the room exploded into pandemonium, and mages all around the room were jumping to their feet and rushing toward Iannis.

"Where have you been?"

"Do you realize you've missed over half of the Convention?"

"Was the Resistance responsible for your delay, or was there a mechanical malfunction?"

"Where are the rest of your delegates?"

"I'm very pleased to see you've brought him back here alive," a voice murmured in my ear. I looked over my shoulder to find that Cirin Garidano, the Solantha Finance Secretary, had somehow maneuvered his way behind me. He looked very stately in his gold and blue robes, the same ones as the illusion Iannis wore, and for a moment I was reminded of the time when Argon Chartis had taken up Iannis's seat in the audience chamber and worn his colors as well. But unlike Chartis, the Finance Secretary was acting with the blessing of the Mages Guild. It made sense for him to wear the colors of his state, as he'd been Canalo's only representative until our arrival.

"Yeah, no thanks to you," I jabbed, but only halfheartedly. "I had to hijack a hot air balloon in order to get to him."

"So that hunch of yours really did work out. I must confess I thought you were bluffing. How exactly did you find him?" the Finance Secretary wanted to know. His voice was pitched low, his lips so close to my ear I could feel his breath on my skin. "What a slap in the face for the Council, that you managed to locate Lord Iannis when they could not. You clearly must have had some sort of plan in place."

"It's a long story." I knew the Finance Secretary was trying to make sure he wasn't overheard, but despite his efforts and the loud noise in the room, I wasn't comfortable disclosing that information to him. Not to mention I still wasn't sure I could trust him. "I'll let the Chief Mage relay those details to you."

"And who is this young lady accompanying you?" the mage who'd 'greeted' us asked, drawing my attention back to the conversation.

"Narina Sernan," Iannis said, apparently inventing a name for me on the spot. I cursed him inwardly for not consulting with me first – he'd yet to pick an alias for me that I actually liked – but committed it to memory so I would know to answer to it. "She is my assistant, and she accompanied the search party which located me near the airship's crash site."

"I see." The mage inclined his head in my direction before turning back to Iannis. "While we are all grateful for her part in your rescue, I'll have to ask Miss Sernan to leave," he said sternly. "This particular banquet is for delegates only."

"Very well, Lord Bastien," Iannis said before I could protest. "In any case, we came straight here, and one of our party must secure our rooms at the Crystal Hotel."

"Are you serious?" I snapped, gritting my teeth in anger. *"You're going to send me off to run errands?"*

"The rules here are very strict," Iannis replied in mindspeak even as he went on talking to the other mages. *"Besides, I really do need you to secure our hotel rooms and purchase clothing and other necessities. Much as I wish you could stay here with me, it isn't possible, so please hold your temper and do as I ask. You'll have plenty of time to snoop around tomorrow."*

"Fine." His explanation was slightly mollifying, and I forced

myself to keep my expression calm even though what I really wanted to do was spit on Lord Bastien's shoe.

"That sounds like an excellent idea," Bastien said. He gestured to a guard, who instantly appeared at his side. "Help Miss Sernan procure transportation to the Crystal Hotel."

"Yes sir." The guard bowed, and I bit back a sigh. I didn't need an escort, but the warning look in Iannis's eyes was enough to make me think twice about kicking the guard to the curb. We were here on a mission, after all, and squabbling about petty matters wasn't going to help us get to the bottom of the attack on Iannis and the other delegates.

"Take this," Iannis said, pulling a leather pouch from the magical vortex that seemed to exist inside his sleeve. I took it from him and resisted the urge to test the weight of the pouch in my hand – I figured such behavior was unbecoming amongst the wealthy, and besides, I could already tell it had significant heft. "That should be more than enough to cover expenses."

"Thank you." With nothing left to say, I bowed to the delegates around us, then followed the guard out of the banquet hall, leaving Iannis to fend for himself against the pack of vultures descending on him en masse.

PLAYING the part Iannis had assigned, I allowed the guard to escort me outside and hail a cab, but stopped short of having him actually accompany me to the hotel. An escort was all well and good, but I didn't need a babysitter.

As I listened to the clip-clop of the horses' hooves, I peered through the cab's curtains and studied the city. Unlike Solantha, the majority of the people walking these broad streets were mages, dressed in robes that varied in color, style, and material. As we passed through a trendy shopping district, I watched a woman glide out of a carriage and take the arm of a man I assumed to be her husband. She was dressed in an ermine-trimmed fuchsia robe and sparkling gemstones, and her dark red hair was twisted up into two elaborate knots at the top of her head. Her husband was dressed in similar fashion, though his robes were black and more masculine in style. The two of them headed into a fancy restaurant, and I wondered if that was just their normal idea of a date night, or if they had important business there. Conversely, just across the street a pair of mages dressed in plain, monochromatic robes walked out of a bookshop, both carrying thick leather tomes in their arms as they chattered earnestly about whatever scholarly topic they were pursuing.

There were humans walking these streets too, nearly as many as there were mages, and though there were a few upper-class citizens around, most humans looked to be lower middle-class workers at best. Interestingly, I didn't see any shifters around, and I wondered if perhaps there was more of a stigma against them here in the capital city than Dara was letting on. Perhaps we'd made less progress than I'd thought regarding shifter rights. I thought we'd had it bad in Solantha, but at least in my hometown shifters were allowed to share the same streets and walk through the same neighborhoods as everyone else. It was little wonder that Iannis had wanted to disguise me.

The carriage turned off the main street and into the roundabout of the hotel, and I craned my neck so I could catch a glimpse of the building. It was four stories high, constructed of pale stone that you could hardly even see for the rows and rows of windows that circled the round structure. They sparkled in the light of the nearly full moon, catching the rays and reflecting them back in icy splendor, and I had to admit the hotel's name was well chosen.

The driver handed me down from the carriage, and I

pressed a coin into his palm before making my way through the revolving doors. More crystal greeted me here, from the chandeliers dripping from the ceilings to the flower-filled vases sitting atop glass tables. I took a deep breath and inhaled blossoms, perfume, expensive chocolates, and magic. The last scent didn't surprise me at all, considering there were mages everywhere, lounging in the sitting area or walking between the restaurant to the elevators that led to the rooms upstairs. Judging by their understated but high-quality robes, they were probably companions or assistants to the delegates who had flown into the Convention, forced to languish here at this fancy hotel while the delegates were enjoying their exclusive dinner.

I received curious stares from the mages in the sitting area, but I ignored them and approached the concierge instead. A human female with chestnut hair, wearing a starched white shirt and light blue vest, looked up at me through her wire-rimmed glasses, then straightened and smiled as she caught sight of my mage robes.

"Good evening, ma'am, and welcome to the Crystal Hotel," she said. "How can I help you this evening?"

"I believe you have rooms reserved for the delegation from Canalo," I told her. "Can I have the keys now, to inspect them?"

A frown creased the woman's smooth forehead. "The delegates from Canalo?" She pulled a large, leather-bound book from a drawer and placed it atop the desk, which like many other things in this hotel seemed to be entirely carved from crystal. "We already checked in the delegates from Canalo – one delegate to be precise. A Mr. Cirin Garidano."

"Yes, he was the only one who could make it out initially," I said, impatience tinging my voice. "The rest of the delegation was delayed, but we are here now. Unless you'd rather I tell the Chief Mage of Canalo that the Crystal Hotel took his money and then gave the rooms to someone else?" I arched an eyebrow at the concierge.

The woman's skin turned ice-white, and she quickly excused herself before hurrying into a back room, presumably to consult with someone. A few moments later, a manager came out, and there was some hurried discussion as they tried to figure out what to do.

"Ma'am, I apologize for the inconvenience, but it does appear that your rooms were mistakenly assigned to other guests." The manager bowed his head, sounding very apologetic. "I can recommend another hotel for your delegates to stay in, if you'd like, and we shall of course refund your deposit and provide compensation for the inconvenience."

"Compensation?" I hissed, curling my fingers around the edge of the reception desk and leaning in close. "Are you suggesting that I tell Lord Iannis, the Chief Mage of Canalo, that the Crystal Hotel was so desperate for coin that they couldn't hold his reservation for a few days? And that your idea of 'compensation' is to give him *money* when he has more than enough gold?"

The manager's cheek's reddened. "We are not desperate," he said stiffly. "This is a prestigious hotel, and our hotel rooms are very much in demand. You can't expect us to hold a room for an entire week."

"Very well," I said lightly, easing back from the counter. "I'll simply mention to the other delegates that the Crystal Hotel would rather turn out a Chief Mage in favor of putting up some vacationers instead. I'm sure you will be very popular at the next Convention." I turned away.

"Wait!" the manager cried as I took a step toward the exit.

I paused, looking over my shoulder at him. "Yes?"

"Please, come back ma'am." The manager gave me a pained smile. "I'm sure that we can work something out."

It took them nearly twenty minutes, but with some fancy maneuvering they managed to vacate the original suite for Iannis. However, as I had no reservation, they couldn't get a separate room for me, so I was given the choice between sharing a suite with the Finance Secretary and the other delegates, or taking the extra room in Iannis's suite.

I wasn't exactly comfortable with either, but I had a lot of questions for Iannis so I figured sharing a suite with him would be my best bet. So I smiled and thanked the concierge, then took the keys to our suite and made my way up to the third floor by way of one of the elevators.

The suite was pretty much what I expected – white couches, carpeting, and curtains; crystal vases and glass tables; and huge windows that overlooked the city as well as the Eastern Sea beyond. Too tired to enjoy the view, I wandered into the smaller bedroom and flopped onto the bed, then groaned as my body sank into the soft mattress.

Turning my head, I noticed a phone on my nightstand, so I picked it up and asked the operator to connect me to the Golden Tree Inn. The phone rang for a few moments before someone from the front desk answered, and I asked them to connect me to Annia's room.

"H'llo?" a sleepy voice slurred.

"Hey there. Just wanted to check in and see if you got that feather mattress you've been dreaming about."

"Oh hell yeah." Annia groaned, and I had the idea she was stretching her back. "This bed is ridiculously comfortable, and the room is incredible. Amazing what you can buy with a huge pouch of gold. It's almost enough to make me forget about cashing in on the bounty. Almost."

"Hey, well if you want to share some of that bounty money with yours truly, my pockets are wide open." I chuckled a little. Iannis had given Annia said huge pouch of gold, along with the

Golden Tree Inn as a recommendation for lodgings since she couldn't very well stay with us. The airship we had commandeered would be confiscated by the Federation since it belonged to the Resistance, but Iannis planned to hook her up with another pilot with a larger ship, and the two of them would lead reinforcements back to the Resistance camp to round up the rebel soldiers.

"So what's the Convention like?" Annia asked, sounding marginally more alert now. "I hope you're not getting too much snob on you from all that elbow-rubbing."

I snorted. "I don't think I'm in any danger of that," I told her. "The mage who greeted us kicked me out of the Capitol Building because they were hosting a delegates-only dinner. I was sent off to procure hotel rooms and clothing for everyone instead."

"Clothing?" Annia perked right up at that. "Does that mean you're going shopping?"

I paused. "I guess I am," I said reluctantly. "Although considering how late it is, not until tomorrow morning."

"Well, the pilot I'm supposed to meet up with isn't getting in until the afternoon, so I'll meet you in the shopping district at what, ten a.m.? We'll make a girls' date out of it."

I snorted with laughter. "I'm not sure how Iannis is going to feel about the two of us parading around Dara spending his gold."

"Well then, we'll just have to make it worthwhile, won't we?"

22

A fter getting off the phone with Annia, I crashed so hard that I never heard Iannis come into the suite. But the scent of coffee roused me bright and early from my slumber, and as my nose twitched, scenting the air, I also caught the briefest whiff of Iannis's scent.

Sitting up, I rubbed at my bleary eyes and checked the crystal clock on my nightstand. Seven fifteen. Far too early for a nocturnal panther girl to be awake. But Iannis was going to have to leave for the Convention sooner rather than later, so I hopped out of bed, snagged the fluffy white robe hanging on the outside of my bathroom door, then belted it around my waist before wandering out into the living area.

Iannis stood behind the glossy island countertop in the kitchen, already dressed in a set of blue and gold robes with the Canalo Mages Guild Emblem stitched above his heart. He glanced over at me from above the rim of his mug as he sipped his coffee, violet eyes studying me as I made a beeline for the coffee pot.

"I noticed that you didn't procure clothing or toiletries last night," he said mildly as I poured myself a steaming cup of my own.

"Yeah well, by the time I was done wrestling with the concierge and manager downstairs, I was pretty pooped." I added a hefty amount of cream and sugar to my coffee, then lifted the mug in both hands and blew across the top to cool the piping-hot liquid. "I figured you guys could make do with the hotel-provided stuff in the meantime, and it looks like you're still working that illusion."

"I'm actually not," Iannis said dryly. "These are Cirin's robes. He and I are of a similar size, so he leant me a set. The other delegates will have to make do, but it is rather unbecoming of us to show up wearing illusionary clothing. Other mages can tell."

I blinked. "They can?"

"Just like Fenris and I were able to see the wards around the Resistance camp, a well-trained mage can detect illusion. That is, they can tell that there is some kind of magic being used, and it wouldn't take much to deduce what kind. At least a few of my colleagues are bound to notice." Iannis arched an eyebrow. "It would be embarrassing for a Chief Mage to be unable to afford proper clothing."

"Yeah, I get it." I took a sip of my coffee, then closed my eyes and enjoyed the taste of rich, creamy caffeine sinking into my tongue. "I'm going shopping this morning, so I'll get all your stuff. Would help if I knew your measurements, though."

"I already wrote them down, as well as those of the other delegates." Iannis pulled a small, black leather notebook from his sleeve, tore out a cream-colored page, and handed it to me. "I suggest you procure robes for yourself too, and formalwear for all of us. There will be a ball tonight that is open to special guests as well as the delegates and their associates. I would like you to attend and make use of those heightened senses of yours."

"Sounds good." Nervous energy bounced through me as I tucked the piece of paper into the front pocket of my robe. I'd never been to a formal ball before, and I wasn't sure what would be expected of me. Was I going to have to socialize with the other mages? Were people going to ask me to dance?

"All of the above," Iannis confirmed.

I blinked. "Huh? Were...were you reading my *mind*?"

"It wasn't necessary. You were talking out loud."

"Oh." A blush rose to my cheeks, and I pressed a hand to my lips, then picked up my mug again. I took another drink – though the coffee didn't actually work on me, just like other drugs, I still liked the taste, and the morning ritual helped wake me up. As my head finally began to clear, another question popped into my head, one I'd been meaning to ask but hadn't had the opportunity yet.

"When we were escaping from the Coazi, how is it that you were able to run so fast and for so long?" I asked. "Unless I'm mistaken, you can't just spell yourself that way, and you didn't have any charms that would boost your speed or energy."

Iannis went still beneath my gaze, and if I didn't know better I would have thought he was nervous. "It's not something I like to discuss," he said carefully.

"Yeah, I've heard that before." My gaze narrowed. "Back on the Firegate Bridge, when you did that weird thing where you slipped inside my body with me." Chills still vibrated through me whenever I relived that moment – it had been truly unreal. "You're only going to be able to get away with that for so long before I start investigating."

Iannis scowled. "You've no right to go digging into my past," he snapped. "My business is just that, mine."

I folded my arms across my chest and scowled right back. "This may come as a surprise to you, but you're not a one-man show anymore, buddy. Especially not since you decided to bind us together by giving me a charm that, apparently, is usually exchanged by couples who are married or who intend to get married." I tugged the *serapha* charm from beneath the fluffy collar of my robe and held it up. "Were you ever gonna tell me about *that* one?"

Iannis frowned. "It wasn't intended as a wedding gift at the time I gave it to you. Who told you that?"

"Comenius and Elania, his witch girlfriend." I tried to ignore the little jab to my heart at his rejection. "They're not even mages, so that means this sort of thing is public knowledge."

Iannis sighed, running his long fingers through his cherry-wood locks. They gleamed in the morning sunlight streaming through the picture window to his left, the rays highlighting the notes of red and making his violet eyes glow.

"You said that you wanted me to trust you more, right?" I persisted. "Well that means you've got to do some trusting yourself. Whatever secret you're sitting on, I promise it will never leave this room. And it would really help, the next time you rope me into some kind of magical spell, if you told me all the fine print."

Iannis cracked a smile. "Very well. I will endeavor to do so, although I doubt such a situation will come up very often. As to my abilities...they come from a part of my heritage that is only known to a select few."

My ears perked right up at that. "And that would be...?"

"My mother. She is half-Tua."

"*What?*" I nearly dropped my coffee cup. Dark liquid sloshed over the side, and I yelped as the hot liquid splattered across my hand and stained the sleeve of my shirt. Setting the cup down on the table, I hastily grabbed the sponge sitting near the kitchen sink and used it to mop up the spill as best I could. I grimaced as I dabbed at the dark stain across my pristine robe – that wasn't going to be easy to get out.

"Here, let me help you." Iannis was at my side, gently taking the sponge from my hand. My breath caught as I felt the heat radiating from his body, and I bit my lower lip as his fingers gently grasped the wrist of the hand I'd burned.

"Are you alright?" he asked. I hissed as he stroked his thumb over my skin.

"I'll live." The skin had been bright red, but the color was already fading thanks to my superhuman healing abilities. "Not the first time I've burned myself."

"And probably not the last, either." Iannis's lips twitched as he stretched out the cloth of the robe and briskly rubbed the sponge over it. "You know, this isn't really necessary. The hotel staff will launder the robe and provide you with another. All you have to do is toss this into the hamper."

"You're trying to change the subject," I managed, fighting against the heat spreading through my body. I didn't point out that if I tossed my robe in the hamper, I would be left without a stitch of clothing on – the right side of my robe had slipped from my shoulder, and Iannis's gaze was fixed on the patch of bare skin I'd inadvertently revealed. "You were telling me about how your mother is half-Tua." Something I was still having trouble wrapping my head around. The Tua were an ancient, near-mythical race that dwelled in a world that was anchored to our own world, Recca. When they did cross over to our world, they were commonly sighted in Manuc, which I understood to be Iannis's homeland. The lore surrounding them suggested that they predated human life.

"Yes." With a little sigh, Iannis dropped my arm and tossed the sponge over his shoulder. It landed in the sink with a wet plop, and I arched my eyebrow at the effortlessly perfect aim. "My grandmother on my mother's side is Tua, and so my mother is half. As you may know, the Tua are near-immortal, and have powerful abilities beyond the scope of human comprehension. If not for the fact that they generally enjoy their own world more than ours, I shudder to think what would become of us."

I arched an eyebrow. "It sounds like you're afraid of them."

"It would be foolish not to be." Iannis's eyes were hard, glittering chips of amethyst now. "They are largely amoral as a race, and any interaction they have with our world is but a trifling amusement, such as when my grandmother decided to take a human lover. She abducted my grandfather shortly after he was married and bewitched him. Not unlike what Halyma did to me, but Tua magic is infinitely more powerful. She eventually returned him to his wife when she tired of him, but he was never the same, from what I understand. It took him over a year to recover and move on with his life, and not long after that his Tua lover dropped my infant mother on their doorstep before walking away once again."

"Wait a minute." I held up a hand as I tried to digest this. "A year? I thought babies had to be in the womb for nine months?"

Iannis shrugged. "Time moves differently in the Tua realm. In any case, my grandfather's wife was gracious enough to take my mother in as her own, and they raised her as best they could, considering she had powers they didn't know what to do with. Eventually she became too much for them to control, and they handed her over to the Dromach, a sect of mages in Manuc who are specially trained to deal with the Tua and charged with maintaining the walls that separate Recca from their realm. It was amongst them that she met and married my father, nearly a thousand years ago."

"A thousand?" I echoed faintly. "Just how old does that make you?"

Iannis smiled slightly. "I believe it's not polite to ask one's age."

I snorted. "That only applies to women, and you know it."

My eyes narrowed as I considered him. "So what exactly did you inherit from your half-Tua mother, then?"

"For one, a longer lifespan than the average mage," Iannis admitted. "Barring accidents such as tumbling from an airship, I might live to three thousand years of age, if not longer. My lifespan is one of the reasons why my heritage is little known – most mages of my age are nearing the end of their life and show signs of it, when they aren't using illusion to disguise their wrinkles. It is easy enough to fabricate a history for myself."

"By Magorah." I shook my head. "So when I'm old and grey and lying on my deathbed, you'll still be baby-faced?"

"I don't know that baby-faced is the right term, but yes." A troubled expression briefly crossed Iannis's face. "But as a half-mage, your lifespan should be longer than the average shifter's."

"Well that's good to know," I said lightly even as my heart sank. For some reason, even though it didn't matter, I didn't like the idea that Iannis would look exactly the same as he did now when I was old and grey. I wondered if he would become more aloof with age, or if he would soften up and show more emotion as the years went by. And what about me? Would I become more stern and emotionless like the mages, the more I spent time among them? Or would I retain the wildness of my shifter heritage?

"Okay, so being a quarter Tua means you live super long and you get to run fast, amongst other things?"

"I have a few other tricks up my sleeve, like my healing talent, but yes." Iannis inclined his head, his lips curling up at the corners. "I can actually run much faster than what you've seen, but there was little point in leaving you and Fenris in the dust. Besides, I'm accustomed to hiding my speed, since if my peers noticed they could easily deduce that I'm not a full-mage."

"Lord Iannis, are you in there?" the Finance Secretary called, interrupting our conversation as he rapped on the door. "I have urgent news."

Iannis was instantly behind my shoulder as I undid the locks and opened the door. The Finance Secretary was dressed in blue-black robes, the Canalo Mages Guild emblem sewn onto his breast. There was a tightness around his eyes as he inclined his head briefly at me, then swept into the room with a large leather notebook tucked underneath his arm.

"You look agitated, Cirin," Iannis remarked as I shut the door behind him. "What is this urgent news?"

"I just got word that Zavian Graning is resigning his post as Federation Minister. We're expected to cast votes for his successor on the last day of the Convention, so I suggest you start thinking about your choice now."

"Resigning?" Iannis asked, sounding highly alarmed. "Why?"

"For health reasons, apparently." Cirin perched on the edge of one of the white sofas, his dark eyebrows drawn together in a frown. "I've no idea as to the nature of his malady, but it must be very serious to prompt such a sudden resignation. When I arrived at the Convention the Minister did seem a little lackluster, but I didn't think he was that ill."

"This doesn't make any sense," Iannis argued. "The Minister is a mere four-hundred years old – he should still be in excellent health."

"Umm, I hate to interrupt," I said, "but are we talking about the same Minister who's presiding the Convention?"

"Yes," Iannis said tightly. "Along with his staff, he organizes the Convention every two years. When it is not in session he ensures Federation law is executed in the various states, and maintains the Federation's foreign relations."

"His office is also tasked with bringing any Chief Mage or

other high-ranking official who violates the Great Accord in any way to justice," Cirin added.

Such as Fenris, I wanted to say, but I kept that bit to myself – I doubted the Finance Secretary was privy to Fenris's true identity. Part of me wanted to say that the Minister could fuck off, but the more rational part of me recognized that if Iannis thought his sudden deterioration was suspicious, there was likely a larger game afoot. It sounded like this Minister was even more important than Iannis. "Do you think the Resistance is involved with this in some way?"

The Finance Secretary's black brows rose. "How so?"

"Well I mean, they were responsible for the attack on Iannis's ship," I pointed out. "They didn't want him to arrive at the Convention, and I'm wondering if this is why. Maybe they planned to get rid of the Minister for some reason, and took you out because they feared you might be voted in to take his place?"

"Me?" Iannis scoffed. "I doubt that would happen. I've not been a Chief Mage long enough. Traditionally, such votes are a mere formality, as the retiring Minister has always suggested his successor. If Graning has not nominated anyone, that would indeed be unusual."

"I'm not so sure you aren't a contender," the Finance Secretary said, tapping his square chin thoughtfully. "From what I've been hearing, the Minister's Office has been very impressed with the way you've been cleaning up the Mages Guild and ferreting out key players of the Resistance in Canalo. Add to that the fact that you've just come back from the dead, and you may be more popular than you realize."

"Hmph." Iannis folded his arms across his chest. "I've no plans to become the next Minister, and I would like to know what exactly this malady is that's befallen our current one. The logical step is to make an appointment to see him."

The Finance Secretary shook his head. "As far as I under-stand it, no one knows where he's being kept."

"Now that *is* suspicious," I said just as the grandfather clock in the living room let out a low *gong*. We all looked up to see that it was eight o'clock now – where had the time gone?

"We'd better get going," the Finance Secretary said as he briskly got to his feet. "The session starts in less than half an hour."

"Very well." Iannis set down his coffee cup. "After you finish your shopping, head back to the Capitol Building, Miss Baine. You may not be able to attend the Convention itself, but you can still hang about and make good use of your hearing. See if you can find out anything about the Minister's illness or location, the Resistance, or anything else that might be of use."

"Does that mean you're giving me permission to wander around the Capitol Building?" I asked hopefully. The building was three stories, after all, and I was sure there were all kinds of secrets I could ferret out.

"If it gets us the information we need, I don't care what you do," Iannis said. "If we don't find out what is going on with the Minister, especially now that the Resistance is becoming so bold, the Northia Federation may soon turn down a path of destruction the likes of which it has never seen."

And with those ominous words, he swept out the door.

23

"Oh, oh oh! We should totally get him these."

Annia arched an eyebrow as I pulled a set of daffodil-yellow robes from the rack. "Do you *want* the Chief Mage to cut off your head and put it on a pike outside the Capitol Building?" she asked with a smirk.

"I don't believe that particular color would go very well with Lord Iannis's complexion," the clerk sniffed from behind his counter a few feet away. I glanced over my shoulder to see him push his small, round spectacles up his nose and give us a superior glance. "Perhaps try the maroon robes on the other end."

"Excellent idea," I told him, then turned away so I could roll my eyes. "It was just a joke," I muttered as I reached for the maroon robes the clerk had indicated.

"I figured after all the time you'd spent at Solantha Palace, you'd have realized mages don't have a sense of humor."

"Well yeah, but that guy's *human*," I complained.

Annia laughed. "Yeah, but he spends all his time catering to mages. Clearly their attitude has rubbed off on him."

"I guess so," I said as I continued to look through the rack. My fingers stopped at a set of dark violet robes with lace edging the collar and cuffs, and I grinned as I pulled it out. "Surely I can get away with this though, right?"

Annia snorted as she gave the robes a once-over. They had silver buttons that traveled from just above the navel to the high collar that would brush the underside of Iannis's chin. A ridiculous amount of lace frothed from the collar, covering the topmost buttons, and although there was less of the stuff at the cuffs, I knew it would look similarly ridiculous. The paisley pattern that was subtly woven into the fabric was a nice touch too.

"If the Chief Mage looked about a thousand years older, these would be perfect for him," Annia said.

"I'm not so sure about that," I muttered. Based on what Iannis had told me this morning, he would look exactly the same a thousand years from now. Shaking my head, I put the garment back. We'd already spent half the morning shopping for ourselves – it was time to wrap this up and get back to the Capitol Building so I could start gathering information.

"Why so serious?" Annia asked twenty minutes later as we walked out of the tailor's shop. Aside from the new red and silver robes I was wearing, I left empty-handed – the tailor promised to have the robes and my new ball gown delivered to the hotel room by mid-afternoon. "You looked pretty sour-faced when I met up with you at the café this morning, too."

"It's just that there's a lot going on." We stopped at the curb so we could hail a cab. I lowered my voice so that passersby wouldn't hear, and explained to Annia about the bad news the Finance Secretary had delivered this morning.

"Well shit," Annia said as a hansom cab pulled up. The driver, who sat behind the cab rather than in front of it, waved us forward, and we climbed into the cab and settled in for the ride. "Do you think the Resistance has actually managed to brainwash one or more of the delegates onto their side?"

"The Federation Capitol Building," I called to the driver, then turned my attention back to Annia as he cracked his whip, urging the horses forward. "They converted Argon Chartis, didn't they?"

"Well, yeah, but he'd already fallen from grace, so to speak, and was hungry for revenge. These guys are all either Chief Mages or have powerful positions in the Mages Guild. What could the Resistance offer them that they'd be willing to trade their cushy positions for?"

"More power?" I shrugged. "Perhaps they've managed to convince some disgruntled mage that the Resistance has the upper hand and is going to win. Otherwise, I don't see why any mage would throw in their lot with them."

"Yeah, well with the way things have been going lately, that might not be far off from the truth," Annia said darkly as we rolled up the hill toward the Capitol Building. "I mean, you've already uncovered two separate conspiracies, Naya, and that's in Canalo alone. How many other dangerous pots are the Resistance stirring across the rest of the Federation?"

"It all seems to come back to the Benefactor," I mused, drumming my fingers against my thigh. "He's the one stirring all these pots, and if we can catch him and take his spoons away, we might be able to stop this."

"Yeah, well good luck with that," Annia said as the cab rolled to a stop in front of the Capitol Building. "I have a feeling that with this bunch, finding the Benefactor is going to be like digging for a piece of dirt in a mound of soil."

"You're probably right." I shook my head, then leaned in and hugged her. "Say hi to Fenris for me, will you?"

"Will do. Try to make it back home in one piece." Annia winked at me, and I winked back before I turned around and let the driver hand me down from the cab.

I trotted up the steps of the Capitol Building in my new

robes, and though the guards studied me with a critical eye as I passed, they made no move to stop me from entering. Unlike yesterday evening, the entrance hall was swarming with activity, both humans and mages alike bustling to and from the building and looking very official. In the center of the entrance hall was a large, mounted map of the building, and I stopped to study it, trying to figure out where I wanted to go. It looked like the main assembly room was located in the Great Rotunda on the first floor, surrounded by smaller meeting rooms. There were a few clerical offices down here, but most of the offices were on the upper floor, on the opposite side of the building from the banquet hall. I wondered if there was anyone up there right now worth eavesdropping on, or if everyone of importance was in the Convention.

Knowing the only way to find out was to go up there, I walked through the entrance hall. I passed a coffee shop on the corner as I turned right, heading for the stairs at the other end of a secondary hall that would take me to the stairs. Unfortunately, there were two guards guarding the steps, and as soon as they saw me they both stepped in front of the staircase, blocking my path.

"I'm sorry, miss, but these stairs are for authorized personnel only," the guard to my right said. There was a hint of apology in his tone, but he spoke firmly. "Is there someone in particular you're looking for?"

"No," I admitted, giving the guards a sheepish smile. I really wanted to vault over their heads and dash up the stairs, but the female mage I was pretending to be wouldn't be able to do that, so I had to behave. "It's just that I'm not allowed into the Convention, so I was hoping to find a place to sit and work." I lifted the leather portfolio that I carried in one hand, which had papers and a notepad in it so I could pretend to be doing something useful if need be.

"If you need a place to wait, I'd suggest the coffee shop." The second guard pointed back down the hallway. "There is lots of comfortable seating, and the beverages are very good. But you can't go up these stairs."

"Thank you." I briefly inclined my head to the guards, then turned around and walked back to the coffee shop I'd passed earlier. My stomach growled at the scent of fresh pastries, and though I was disappointed at this setback, there were actually quite a few mages sitting at the glossy wooden tables and chairs that I could listen in on. Approaching the dark granite countertop and the glass case of pastries next to it, I ordered a plate of muffins and a large cup of coffee, then brought my fare to the rear of the store, where the walls were lined with cushioned booth backings. I rested my back against the dark green velvet as I settled in at one of the little tables and prepared for a long afternoon.

As I chewed on a blueberry muffin and studied the mages chatting away at the tables, I noticed that a number of them were also surreptitiously studying me. It occurred to me that these mages probably saw each other at the Convention every other year, but I was a new face, and they weren't sure what to make of me.

"Have you noticed that Lord Iannis seems a little...different, from the last time we saw him?" a redheaded mage asked her dark-haired companion.

"How so?" the other mage, also a female, asked. She picked up her white china espresso cup between dainty, painted fingernails and sipped at it like she was having coffee with the queen of Sandia instead of sitting around in a coffee shop with a fellow underling.

"He seems distracted, as if his mind isn't entirely on the Convention." The redhead traced the rim of her coffee cup with her forefinger. Her expression gave little away, as was the case with most mages, but it almost seemed like she was pouting. "I was in the Great Rotunda this morning before the session started, and watched him talking with the Chief Mage of Nayra. It just seemed like his mind was elsewhere."

"Well I can't say I'm that surprised, considering he arrived so late, and that he brought his mistress along."

"Mistress?" The redhead's pale blue eyes widened.

"Yes. You know, *her*." The brunette looked over her shoulder and met my eyes. I smiled politely and shifted my gaze back down to my papers, pretending that I hadn't heard what she'd just said – as far as they knew, I was too far away to hear their conversation.

"Really?" I looked back to see that the redhead's brows had shot up. "Well she's got a pretty face, but someone like Lord Iannis could do a great deal better."

"Oh I'm sure it's just a fling," the brunette said airily. "I suppose even the most distinguished Chief Mage is bound to let their hair down occasionally like lesser mortals, but she doesn't look like she's doing much more than shuffling papers back there. I can't see that she'll serve as more than a passing interest for someone like him."

My jaw clenched at that, and I had to force myself to relax. Yeah, so maybe I *was* doing little more than shuffling papers over here, but I was definitely more than a piece of ass to Iannis.

"More than" would imply that the two of you are sleeping together, a voice in my head reminded me.

I sighed. I needed to get off this train of thought before I drove myself crazy with it. Ever since we'd kissed back in the mountains I kept expecting something more to happen between Iannis and I. Each time we were alone together we seemed to be teetering on the edge of something, yet it never went anywhere. What was he thinking? Was he regretting the kiss? Had he brushed it off as something that had happened while he was under the influence of magic? Did he want more? I couldn't figure it out, and worse, I still couldn't figure out exactly what *I* wanted. Yes, I was attracted to him, and yes, my body wanted him, but my *mind* kept telling me it was a bad idea.

"Did you hear about the Minister's decision to resign?" a mage two tables to my left asked. "I couldn't believe my ears when I got the news this morning."

"Quite shocking," the mage sitting across from him agreed with a solemn nod. "Perhaps he's older than we realized. Who do you think is going to replace him?"

"I've heard that Lord Cedris ar'Tarea is being considered."

"The Chief Mage of Rhodea?" The other mage sounded incredulous. "That's one of the smallest states in the Federation! Surely you're joking."

"Not at all," the first mage said. "He seems to have very strong connections with the Minister's office, and his record, from what I've been told, is impeccable. I hear he has a very strong chance."

"That's ridiculous. If his record is impeccable, it's only because he doesn't have enough things to do to get him into any kind of trouble."

The conversation quickly devolved into an argument, and I tuned them out, seeking out other bits of conversation. To my surprise, Lord Cedris came up quite a few times in conversation as a popular candidate. I wondered if he really *was* as well connected to the Minister's office as some seemed to think, or if perhaps the Benefactor had a hand in increasing his popularity. I would have to ask Iannis about it when I saw him next.

"Excuse me," a man said, drawing my attention away from the buzz of conversation. "Are you Miss Sernan?"

I looked up from my cup of tea – I'd switched from coffee after cup number three – to see a tall mage standing just in front of my table, dressed in dark, silver-embroidered robes that were a cut above what the other mages in the coffee shop were wearing. He had jaw-length, curly black hair, a square jaw, and a complexion like coffee-tinted cream. I went still as I noticed that his bottle-green eyes were the exact same shade as mine, and a chill went through me – I'd never met someone with my exact eye-coloring before.

Come on, Sunaya. It could just be a coincidence.

Maybe, but I didn't like coincidences. I couldn't quite reconcile his youthful face with the fuzzy image of my father that I'd conjured in my head, but this guy had the same curly black hair that I did, too. I tensed as I searched his green eyes for any sign of recognition, but there was none.

"Yes, I am Narina Sernan," I finally said. "Who are you?"

"Oh, forgive me. My name is Coman ar'Daghir." Without asking, he pulled out the chair opposite me and sat his bony ass down in it. "I've been curious to meet you ever since I heard that you were part of Lord Iannis's entourage. I've accompanied my own Chief Mage to the Convention for at least a decade now, and I don't believe I've ever met you."

"This is my first Convention," I told him, picking up my cup and taking a sip of my tea. "I'm one of several assistants who work in Lord Iannis's office, and the one he usually takes along with him was unable to make it this year."

"Is it true that your airship crash-landed in aboriginal territory?" Coman asked curiously. "And that you were taken prisoner by the Resistance?"

"It is." I narrowed my eyes, trying to guess at what he wanted. He was the first to come out and directly ask about that, even though I knew the others had to be thinking about it.

"That must have been terrifying. Were you tortured for information?'

"I would rather not speak of it, if it's all the same to you," I said, thinning my lips. I set down my teacup, and I didn't have to pretend to feel as if he'd rubbed my fur the wrong way. If this guy really was my father, he sure didn't seem to know it. Shouldn't he be having some inkling that I was his daughter? I mean, supposedly he'd put a spell on me so my illegal magic would remain hidden. Surely that meant he cared *somewhat*.

Or maybe he's just not your father and you're reading too much into this.

"Oh forgive me, I didn't mean any offense," Coman tried to assure me. "It's just that so many people are avoiding the obvious question. And by that I mean, why was Lord Iannis's ship attacked in the first place?"

"I imagine it was to stop him from reaching the Convention," I allowed cautiously, curious to see where he was taking this. "But as to why exactly, I'm afraid I don't know."

"I see." Coman looked momentarily disappointed, but he rallied quickly. "I don't suppose you have any idea who Lord Iannis is planning to vote for to replace the Minister?"

"I haven't seen him since we heard the news this morning," I admitted. "He was troubled to hear about the Minister's rapidly declining health, and I imagine he'll think deeply on this matter before he makes any kind of decision. Last I knew, he was planning to secure an appointment to see the sick Minister for himself."

"Well if he does I would love to hear about it, as none of us have any idea where the Minister is." Coman shrugged, then checked the timepiece on his wrist. "In any case, I must be going now. Pleasure meeting you, Miss Sernan."

I watched Coman go, trying to discern if there was anything else about him that would prove he was related to me. But he was a man, of course, so any genetic similarities beyond our facial features would be hard to determine. I certainly didn't have his broad shoulders or the extra six inches of height. He turned the corner and disappeared from my sight, and I committed his name to memory. I would do some digging into this guy and see if I could unearth anything that would give me answers.

The afternoon wore on, and I sat there for several more hours pretending to do administrative work while I listened to the conversations around me. Interestingly, Iannis's name also popped up a number of times, confirming the Finance Secretary's theory that Iannis was a possible contender for the position. Following Coman's lead, several more mages came by and struck up conversations with me, slyly trying to discern which way Iannis was planning to vote. I evaded, playing the vapid bimbo secretary as best I could while also pretending to be a mage. The mages weren't fooled, though – from the snippets of conversation I caught when they thought I couldn't hear, they figured I must know *something* as Iannis's mistress.

To be fair, there was a kind of logic to that – I knew from my work as an enforcer that men tended to tell all kinds of things to the courtesans they spent time with, and those women could be a wealth of information if given the right incentive. But then again, Iannis was notoriously tight-lipped when he didn't want to talk about something – I doubted I would get anything out of him even if I *was* sleeping with him.

Checking my watch, I noticed that it was getting close to five o'clock, and with nothing interesting to overhear for the last half hour, I packed up and headed out. I had a ball to get ready for, and the dress I'd bought for it was calling my name back at the hotel.

24

I was sitting in front of the vanity mirror in my room, doing my makeup, when I heard the front door open. My heart sped up a little as I caught a whiff of Iannis's scent, and I had to force myself to sit in the chair and finish what I was doing so I didn't rush out there with only half of my lips painted red.

"Sunaya?" Iannis rapped on my door. "Are you decent?"

"As decent as I'm ever going to be," I called back as I finished putting on my lipstick. I put the small tube down on the vanity counter, then pursed my lips as I considered the various clips and pins scattered across the countertop. I wanted to fix my hair in some kind of fancy up-do, but hairstyling wasn't my strong suit. Made me wish I was the kind of person who had a maid, or someone who specialized in this kind of stuff.

The door swung open, and I turned in my chair to face Iannis as he entered. He opened his mouth as if he were about to say something, but stopped short when he saw me sitting at the vanity in my finery.

"Well, this is new," he murmured appreciatively. "Stand up and let me see you properly."

The husky note in his voice sent a thrill through me, and I

rose to my feet without even thinking about it. A faint blush rose to my cheeks as Iannis studied me from head to toe, his violet eyes drinking in my form with a kind of intensity I'd only experienced from him a handful of times. I'd chosen a red satin dress for the occasion, with a corset-style off-the-shoulder bodice and a tulle skirt that flared out from my waist. Tiny crystals were scattered throughout the fabric of the skirt, and also in the tulle that overlaid my breasts and sleeves.

"I see that you've done a decent job of spending my money today," Iannis said softly as he crossed the room to me. His lifted a hand, and a shiver of longing passed through me as his fingers traced my bare collarbone. "Although perhaps you could use a bit more practice, since I don't see any jewelry on you."

"I haven't had a chance to put it on yet," I responded, my voice slightly strained. The *serapha* charm was tucked into my bra since I couldn't openly display it, so I'd bought a crystal necklace and matching earrings that were still sitting in their boxes on my vanity. "Or do my hair yet, as you can see."

"Leave your hair." His fingers moved to my curly locks, which were still slightly damp from the shower. "I like it the way it is." He wrapped a curl around his finger and rubbed the pad of his thumb against it, instantly reminding me of the time he'd cornered me in the living area of his suite. That had been the same day he'd announced to the Mages Guild that he was making me his apprentice, and I'd been pissed as hell that not only had he not bothered to consult with me beforehand, but he was still refusing to give any serious attention to the silver murders. In response to my insults, he'd backed me up against the bookshelf and half-threatened, half-teased me, and just like then, a spark of heat lit in my lower belly as he toyed with my hair, the heat of his hand brushing against the curve of my cheek.

"I don't understand." I stepped back, the spark of heat quickly turning to anger. "Why do you keep doing this?"

Iannis's hand abruptly dropped back down to his side. "Doing what?"

"Leading me on," I snapped. "You get this look in your eyes like you want to fuck me, and it scares the shit out of me. And then after you get close, you change your mind and we act like nothing happened." Closing the distance, I fisted my hand in the front of Iannis's robe and dragged him forward, feeling a perverse amount of satisfaction as his eyes widened. I bet the bastard had never been manhandled in his life. "I fucking *kissed* you, Iannis. I pressed my naked body up against your chest and you *liked* it. Are we going to keep pretending that didn't happen?"

Iannis's eyes sparked dangerously, and the air between us thickened with power as he leaned in close. "Do you really want to go down this route?" he asked softly, and the hairs on the back of my neck rose in response to the menace in his tone.

"We're already on the path, so I don't see why not," I snarled, fed up. "I think it's about time you put up, or shut up."

"And just what do you expect me to do, Sunaya?" Iannis's hand clamped around my wrist, fingers tightening painfully, but he didn't remove my grip from his clothing. "Shall I sweep you up into my arms and carry you up the hill and into my palace, in full view of the other mages? Just how do you think it will look if the Chief Mage of Canalo breaks the rules and starts sleeping with his apprentice?"

"I know the rules as well as you do," I growled. "Which is why I don't understand why you're leading me on like this when you know better."

Iannis's jaw clenched. "I'm a man, and I have needs just like anyone else. Despite whatever differences we may have, and all the reasons why I should pretend you are no more attractive than a plucked chicken, you are a beautiful woman, and when you look like this..." His other hand curled around my waist, fingers sinking into the satiny fabric. "How can you expect me not to want you?"

"What, so you're telling me you're just a man who can't control his desires?" I snapped, not sure if I should be pleased or offended.

"I *am* controlling my desires," Iannis growled. "That's why I haven't stripped this dress off you and tossed you onto the bed yet. Or any of the other times I've wanted to."

"Yet?" My breath quickened at the idea, and my eyes involuntarily flickered to the bed behind him.

Iannis's eyes darkened. "This discussion is over," he said tightly, stepping back.

"No, it isn't!" I tightened my grip on his robe and dragged him back. "You don't get to say things like that and just walk away!"

"I can do whatever I want." Iannis's voice simmered with barely suppressed fury. "I'm your Master, and the Chief Mage of your state of residency, Miss Baine. I believe that makes you my subject, not the other way around."

He grabbed my wrist again, and I yelped as a shock of energy bit into my skin, forcing me to let go. Iannis whirled around, his robes swirling around his ankles, and I shook with rage, my claws biting into my palms and dripping blood onto the carpet.

"So I guess you won't care, then, when I go into heat next week and find someone else to warm my bed?" I spat, unable to resist one last parting shot.

To my surprise, Iannis froze in the doorway. "What?"

"You heard me," I bit out. "Next week."

Iannis turned slowly, his eyes hard, but I noticed his face had paled a little. "Explain."

I arched a brow, keeping my expression flat, but inside I was pleased I'd actually snagged his attention. "I would have thought you mages knew everything about us shifters, seeing as how you created us."

"I'm afraid that particular event happened before my time," Iannis said tightly, folding his arms across his chest. "So you'll have to enlighten me as to why you absolutely must have a male in your bed next week."

I sighed, sitting down on my vanity chair again as some of the fight abruptly went out of me. "Twice a year, shifter females go into heat in a fashion vaguely similar to what animals do, although thankfully not the same because otherwise we'd be forced to birth cubs constantly. You'll forgive me if I don't understand the exact science behind it, but we have a fertility cycle that culminates into ovulation every six months, and during that one week we're completely consumed by the need to have sex. We become off-the-charts horny, and if we don't have a male to help us release the tension we go bat-shit crazy and we can't focus on anything else. Think of it as a drug addict suffering without his fix, except that it only happens twice a year. And we have really nasty tempers and lethal claws and fangs."

"That last part is certainly true." Iannis sighed heavily as he sat down on the edge of the bed. "I had heard of this phenomenon in shifters, but I hadn't realized it was quite so... intense. It must be terrible having to deal with this." He actually sounded a little appalled.

"Well, in a way it is, but the sex is pretty damn good." He scowled at that, and I couldn't help but smirking a little. "But since you're not available, I guess you'll never find out."

Iannis clenched his jaw as he surged to his feet, and I watched in fascination as he began pacing back and forth in front of the bed. Part of me couldn't believe I was actually saying these things. But as I'd told Iannis, we were already going down this route, so I figured I might as well go all the way. Was talking about this really going to make the situation any worse at this point?

"This wasn't supposed to happen this way," he muttered.

My brows shot up. "Which way was this supposed to happen?" I asked, intrigued at the idea that there was actually a plan in his mind.

"I thought..." Iannis hesitated. "I thought that when your apprenticeship was over and the mage community had no choice but to recognize you as mage, that I could approach you as something more than a mentee. I thought that I would have *time*." His eyes lifted to mine, and there was such distress shimmering in their iridescent depths that for a moment I actually felt bad for him. "I failed to consider your own constraints and limitations."

"Wait a minute." I couldn't believe what I was hearing. "You've been planning to pursue me this entire time?"

"I wouldn't say the entire time," Iannis said dryly. "But as we've spent more time together...I couldn't help but ponder it. You're quite unlike anyone I've met, and your...outlook on life has pushed me to see things in ways that I might not have otherwise. I am intrigued by what we might accomplish together."

I grinned a little at that. "You know, if I didn't know any better, I might think the great Lord Iannis is admitting that I've helped him become a better Chief Mage."

Iannis smiled a little. "Let's not get ahead of ourselves."

I laughed at the absurdity of the statement. "We've gone a couple years ahead of ourselves with this conversation," I said, shaking my head. "I mean seriously, just how long is it going to be before my apprenticeship with you is done, anyway?'

"Around ten years."

"Ten YEARS?" I grabbed the edge of my vanity table to keep myself from falling out of my chair, and gaped at him. "You're joking, right?"

"Not in the least." Iannis's lips thinned. "Which is why the news that you have to have sex twice a year is very unsettling."

"Are you fucking serious?" I shook my head, unable to wrap my head around the audacity of his statement. "Let's sweep that aside for a moment and focus on the fact that you expected me to be celibate for *ten years.* Just because I only go into heat twice a year doesn't mean I haven't had sex more often than that in my lifetime. What do you think, I'm some kind of monk?"

"I wasn't expecting you to be celibate the entire ten years." An uncomfortable expression crossed his face. "I was just hoping that perhaps, if you did take lovers between now and then, that you wouldn't be parading them past me and that they would be flings. I was also prepared for the possibility that you might find someone else to strike up a relationship with, which in a way would have been a relief."

"By Magorah." I shook my head, not at all knowing what to make of this. "Do you think this is just some kind of game of chess, Iannis? That you can move the pieces around, and if things fall into place properly I'll swoon into your arms at the right moment when you're ready for it? You've lived longer than I can even fathom. Haven't you figured out by now that life doesn't work like that?"

"It is precisely because I am so long-lived that I think in such terms," Iannis pointed out. "Ten years isn't so long to wait. I often think in terms of decades, if not centuries."

"This is just too much." Agitated, I pushed to my feet and began pacing. "I don't know how this could ever work. You and I are so ridiculously different."

"You are half-mage yourself," Iannis pointed out softly. Somehow he was in front of me, and he took my hands as I stopped short in front of him. "And though the world considers me a full-blooded mage, I am not."

"Yeah, but the part of you that isn't mage is even more

ancient and alien." I bit my lip as I looked into his face. The feel of his hands wrapped around mine sent a current of warmth through me, and I wanted so badly to soften. "Honestly, I don't know why we're having this conversation, Iannis. Unless you're willing to break your rule about waiting ten years before you can touch me, this is never going to work."

Iannis frowned. "We could get married," he suggested. "The Mages Guild wouldn't like it, but there wouldn't be anything they could do about it."

"*Marriage?*" I gasped, wondering just how much crazier this conversation was going to get. "You and I haven't known each other that long, and marriage is an eternal commitment. Are you going to tell me that you love me and want to be with me forever and ever?"

"I believe I've proven on more than one occasion that I care for you," Iannis said tightly, hurt flickering in the depths of his violet eyes.

I sighed, then reached up and touched his face. "I believe that, but caring for me isn't the same as love." I searched his gaze, wondering if I might see something in them that would convince me that emotion actually did exist in Iannis, but his eyes were shuttered now and I couldn't read him. "Who's to say that you and I won't get sick of each other in a hundred years, and then what? We're stuck together for life. I'm not going to give up my independence just so you won't have to suffer embarrassment if someone catches us together." I dropped my hand and turned away.

"I am not thinking merely of my embarrassment, Sunaya," Iannis pointed out quietly. "Your safety would also be at stake if we became lovers and were found out."

"I get that, but..." I raked a hand through my hair, trying to figure out how to explain my feelings. "This might seem strange to you, but shifter relationships are very physical. I can't marry someone that I've never made love to. I just can't."

"Are you saying that if I took you to bed that you'd marry me?" Interest lit Iannis's eyes.

Another thrill rippled through me, and I ignored the little voice that shouted *"Yes!"* in my head. "Can't make any promises, but we'd be moving in the right direction." My body simmered with need just thinking about it, and I fought the urge to wet my freshly-painted lips with my tongue. I remembered all too well how his body looked and felt beneath those robes, and with all those years of experience behind him, I couldn't help but think he would be a fantastic lover.

Iannis was silent for a long moment. "I will have to consider it," he said finally.

"Alright." I shrugged and turned back to the mirror, as if the decision he was pondering was no big deal. "But just remember, you've only got a week."

"Perhaps." He was suddenly behind me, and a thrill zipped through my nerves as his fingers slid beneath my chin and tilted my face upward. "But there are some things I can do in the meantime."

He lowered his face to mine, and my breath hitched. "You're going to get lipstick all over your face," I warned breathlessly.

"I don't care," he murmured, and I closed my eyes as his warm breath fanned across my face. I tilted my head back, and our lips met, a whisper of skin on skin that electrified me. Heat exploded in my belly, and I longed to press my body against his, but I was sitting in the chair and facing the wrong way. Annoyed, I nipped at his lower lip, and he growled, then gripped my lower jaw and pushed his tongue past my lips. The dark, exotic taste of him filled my senses, and I moaned, gripping his forearm hard as I fought to bring him closer.

The next thing I knew, he'd scooped me up into his arms and

was kissing me so hard that I could barely breathe from the intensity of it. My body was burning up as he pressed me down onto the mattress, my heart jackhammering so wildly against my chest I was sure he had to feel it. And through my lust-drenched brain, I wondered if we were actually going to do this now. Were we finally going to give in to the desire that had been pulling us together almost from day one?

Eventually Iannis lifted his head from mine, his violet eyes smoldering as he looked down at me. I reached up to trace the flush that had spread across his alabaster cheeks, and he pressed his hand against mine, holding it to his cheek. It was an incredibly tender moment, one that was completely at odds with the savage way he'd kissed me, and for a heart-stopping second I wondered if maybe he really *could* love me.

"You must understand," he said quietly, his thumb stroking the back of my hand, "that after living as long as I have, it's difficult for me to make hasty decisions. But," he added, his voice growing husky again, "I'm beginning to think you'll be more than worth it if we do decide to do this."

And with that, he rolled off the bed and left me lying there, staring at the ceiling and wondering just what the hell had hit me.

25

An hour later, Iannis and I climbed into the carriage I'd had the concierge call for us, and we were off to the ball. The Finance Secretary and the other delegates had come to collect us, but because Iannis and I had spent so much time arguing, we hadn't been ready to leave. Iannis had ordered them to go on ahead without us while we'd finished getting ready, which meant that we would be arriving fashionably late. The fact that we'd also be arriving separately from the other Canalo delegates would raise eyebrows, and only further the rumors that I was Iannis's mistress.

Then again, after the way Iannis had kissed the breath out of me earlier, was I really so far away from becoming exactly that? My lips tingled in remembrance even as I pressed them together in distaste. I didn't like the term "mistress" – it implied that I was a kept woman, which was far from the truth. But since we weren't married, I guessed that was the only other title they could fall back on for me.

I looked away from the window at Iannis to find that he was watching me, and the air thickened between us instantly. Not wanting to deal with the tension, I decided to give him a debrief, which was something I needed to do anyway.

"You might want to know that I learned a couple of things when I was hanging out at the coffee shop this afternoon."

"Oh?" Iannis asked, relaxing back against the velvet upholstery. "I'm surprised you didn't mention that back at the hotel room."

"I was going to, but we were sidetracked," I said dryly. "From what I've been overhearing, a Lord Cedris ar'Tarea is apparently the frontrunner as the next Minister."

"The Chief Mage of Rhodea." Iannis nodded. "I've heard rumors to that effect too, though I can't quite fathom why he is such a popular choice. He governs a small state and has little experience with international affairs."

"That's what one of the mages in the coffee shop was saying. I also heard several people mention that you were a prime contender as well."

"Hmm." Iannis's lips thinned. "Between the two of us, I certainly believe I would be the better choice as the next Minister. But I would rather not leave Canalo so soon in my political career."

"Yeah, no kidding." If Iannis became the next Minister, there was no way he'd have any time to train me. "A bunch of people came up to me and asked how you were going to vote. I guess maybe I should tell them you're voting for yourself," I joked.

"Very funny." He did not look amused.

"That reminds me," I said, my eyes narrowed. "One of the mages who tried to chat me up was a Coman ar'Daghir, and he kind of looks like me. A *lot* like me."

Iannis went still for a moment. "Eye and hair color do not necessarily equate blood relation."

"But you're not denying that he *is* a blood relation," I accused, folding my arms across my chest. Iannis said nothing, simply staring blankly, and I ground my teeth in frustration. "Oh come on! You *have* to tell me who my father is. You can't keep me in the dark about this."

"You're not ready to know yet."

"What the fuck does that mean?" I fisted my hands in my skirts, just itching to slap some sense into him. "How the hell do you expect us to work together if you insist on treating me like a child that needs to be kept in the dark?"

"It's not a matter of age, but experience." Iannis's eyes hardened. "Acknowledging your parentage publicly is going to open up a world of problems that you won't be well-equipped enough to deal with until you understand the magical world and its rules far better. Once you are finished with your apprenticeship, I will happily divulge your father's identity."

"Once I'm finished with my apprenticeship?" I echoed in disbelief. "But that's not for another ten years!"

Iannis sighed. "Answer me honestly. Is there really any burning reason for you to know his identity right now?"

"Other than the fact that he's my father and I want to?" I answered sarcastically.

"Yes, and just what would you do with that information?" Iannis challenged. "Are you going to run off to reconnect with the father who abandoned you, while the Northia Federation is on the verge of calamity? Is it truly so important that you discover the identity of a mage who clearly does not want to have anything to do with you, right this very second?"

"No," I admitted tightly around the lump swelling in my throat. I glanced away, blinking back tears of anger and grief. Apparently the wound of my father's abandonment was more tender than I'd realized.

"I haven't told you who he is precisely because I do not wish to cause you unnecessary distress," Iannis said gently. "Believe me, if circumstances change and this knowledge becomes necessary, I will tell you."

I let out a deep breath, then turned to face Iannis again. "You know, I could just ask Coman myself," I pointed out.

"Let me save you the trouble," he said dryly. "Coman is not your father, and if you ask him about it he will likely be rather confused. Your inquiry will merely raise suspicion and questions that we would rather not deal with, since you are here as Narina Sernan, *not* Sunaya Baine."

"I guess you have a point." My lips twisted as I acknowledged that logic. If I was going to ferret out more information about the identity of my father, I couldn't very well do it as myself.

"I do find it very interesting that Coman approached you, however."

"And why is that?"

"Because he is Lord Cedris's Legal Secretary."

"What?" My eyes widened. "What was he doing out in the coffee shop then, instead of the rotunda?"

"He may have come there during an intermission for refreshments," Iannis speculated. "More likely, though, Lord Cedris sent him out specifically to question you and try to find out more information about me, since he believes I am his direct competition."

"Huh." I pressed my lips together as I considered that. "He was asking questions about our time at the Resistance camp," I recalled. "I don't know why that information would be of relevance to Lord Cedris, though."

"The fact that he is asking might suggest that he has an interest in the Resistance somehow," Iannis said, frowning. "Although he could have just been digging for dirt."

"Well maybe we can find out more at the ball tonight," I suggested hopefully.

"Indeed. Our main objectives tonight are to discover exactly where the Minister is sequestered, and to determine if Lord Cedris's sudden popularity is legitimate. It defies belief, but after all that has happened we cannot exclude the possibility that he is somehow allied to the Benefactor or the Resistance."

"I'm guessing that means you're going to rub a lot of elbows and I'm going to listen in on as many conversations as possible?"

"Yes. And since you are not a delegate, you'll attract less notice if you sneak off somewhere that guests are generally not supposed to be."

The carriage rolled to a stop, and I peered out the window to see that we were in a long, long line of carriages dropping ball guests off at the Grandham Hotel, which was where the ball was being held. Guess we weren't the only fashionably late ones. It took us a good ten minutes before our carriage pulled up in front of the entrance, and I tried to act aloof rather than self-conscious as Iannis helped me down from the carriage. Reporters and photographers crowded near the entrance, and I had to force myself not to flinch as camera bulbs flashed and reporters shouted questions at us about the upcoming vote and who we thought the next Minister was going to be. Blinded by the flashes, I clutched Iannis's arm and allowed him to guide me up the stairs and through the doors.

Oh well, at least we'll look good for the photographs, I thought as we passed through the elegant lobby. Uniformed staff greeted us respectfully and directed us toward the ballroom, which was several hallways away. I'd picked out a set of royal blue robes for Iannis, with winged shoulders and golden vines that shimmered as he walked. A gold satin sash belted around his waist, and the ensemble enhanced the contrast of his broad shoulders to his tapered hips. Only the tips of the dark blue leather boots with gold buckles I'd bought for him could be seen, but they were my favorite part of the outfit. I would have bought a pair for myself if they had come in my size. I'd commission a similar pair for myself once we got back to Solantha, if I ever had any money of my own again.

One problem at a time, Sunaya.

"Welcome to the Convention Ball," another hotel staff member greeted us at the entrance to the ballroom. Like the other staff, he was dressed very smartly in a suit and tails, and he held a clipboard and pen in his hands. "May I have your names, please?"

"Iannis ar'Sannin, Chief Mage of Canalo, and Miss Narina Sernan."

"Yes, of course, my lord." The man bowed deeply, then extended a hand toward the entrance. "Please enjoy your evening."

We stepped into the ballroom, and I tried not to crane my neck as my eyes took in the enormous space, which was packed to the gills with delegates and invited guests. The walls were painted a pale, creamy gold, and soared past the mezzanine balconies to meet the ornate crown molding that bordered the ceiling. The ceiling itself was fairly plain, the only adornment a large, stylized flower painted in the center, and hanging from the middle of the flower was a single chandelier that cast the huge room in a muted yellow glow. Wall sconces set in the pillars that lined the walls and supported the arches of the mezzanine provided additional light, but the overall effect was subtle, creating plenty of shadowed corners for attendees to lurk in and whisper to each other when they weren't socializing with the main crowd.

I remained on Iannis's arm for the first half hour as introductions were made, but as time went on more and more female mages began to flock to him, slyly flirting, and he took to the sport like a duck to water, coaxing information out of them the same way they were trying to do to him. I knew there was a purpose to it all, but I hated the way these women dismissed me or gave me thinly disguised looks of derision. So I was more than happy to let a handsome young mage sweep me off to the dance floor before the jealousy monster trying to rear its ugly head made me do something stupid.

I danced and socialized for a good hour with the delegates and their guests, making small talk while surreptitiously testing the waters to see if anyone knew anything about the Minister's whereabouts or Lord Cedris's campaign. A good number of the guests were humans, wealthy socialites who had enough pull in their own circles that they merited an invitation and flew in across the country to mingle with these high-ranking mages. None seemed to have any more information about the Minister than I did, however, and there was also frustratingly little to be learned about Lord Cedris. I gleaned some speculation that he'd made agreements with key mages to push for certain types of legislation, but nothing concrete.

Of course this would all be much easier if I could actually ask questions, but nobody wanted to divulge any information to me since I was an outsider, and I didn't want to draw suspicion my way. The mages who did talk directly to me mostly just wanted to pump me for info about Iannis anyway. Hopefully he was having better luck than I was.

Lord Cedris himself was present, of course, and he diligently circled the crowds, talking and laughing and rubbing elbows. He was tall and lean, dressed in a set of red and white robes that did nothing for his long, pale blond hair and haughty, aristocratic features. I saw Iannis speak with him for a few moments, but Cedris seemed much more interested in talking up the other delegates, presumably to persuade them to vote for him.

"Good evening, Miss Baine. It's a pleasure to see you again," a low, throaty voice came from my right.

I jumped at the sound of my real name, nearly spilling the glass of champagne I was nursing, and turned to see Thorgana

Mills standing next to me, a smile on her glossy lips. The owner of Mills Media & Entertainment was resplendent in a white mermaid-style gown that clung to her willowy figure, and her ice-blonde hair was swept into a classy up-do and secured with a diamond-encrusted hair-clip.

"Good evening, Mrs. Mills," I said in a low voice. "How are you this evening?" It figured someone of her great wealth and status would be invited here, and I cursed myself for not donning a better disguise. I had worked for her as a bodyguard on occasion, and she had seen me in Iannis's palace not that long ago.

Thorgana laughed lightly. "You have gumption, I'll give you that," she said, "daring to show up at such a public event so thinly disguised and expecting no one to recognize you. You seem to be moving up in the world. You could not have afforded that dress on an enforcer's income."

"Indeed." I smiled apologetically, though what I really wanted to do was smash her in the back of the head with my champagne glass and lock her up somewhere before she blew my cover. "I hope you won't rat me out, Mrs. Mills."

"Not at all," she said, still smiling. "I admire your audacity. I'm sure Lord Iannis is making good use of your valuable talents to gather information and support so he can secure his title as the new Minister."

"Oh I don't know about that," I demurred, lifting my glass of champagne to my lips. I took another sip as I studied her over the rim of my glass, trying to figure out what her angle was. Was she just toying with me for the hell of it? "Lord Cedris is a very strong contender."

"It certainly seems so, though I can't understand why exactly," Thorgana mused. Her perfectly plucked brows drew together in a faint frown. "There are dozens of Chief Mages who are more qualified, Lord Iannis included. I would think that

Lord Iannis would be confident enough in his abilities to not be intimidated by Lord Cedris?" she prodded.

"Perhaps," I allowed. It seemed like she was trying to get me to confirm that Iannis was running for Minister, and just because he wasn't didn't mean I was about to let anyone know that. "I suppose you'll have to ask him yourself."

"Oh I have, and he's just as tight-lipped as you." Thorgana laughed again. "It seems that you are learning well from him. He wouldn't give me any details about what happened after his airship crash-landed in the middle of nowhere, either."

"Well you *do* own several newspaper companies," I pointed out with a teasing smile. "I think you can understand his reluctance to share information he doesn't want distributed by the media."

"Oh how silly." Thorgana waved a hand as if the notion was ridiculous, but even though she appeared to be little more than diamonds and silk on the outside, I wasn't so sure that Iannis's caution was misplaced. After all, she *was* the owner of the company, wasn't she? "I have little to do with the business I inherited from my father. It pays for my jewels and parties, but I leave the muck-raking to my managers."

"Of course." I smiled indulgently. My nose told me she wasn't lying, but there was something about the way she said it that made me unsure whether to believe her protestations.

"Well, I suppose I ought to get back to my husband," Thorgana said with a little sigh. "I'm done here, but my husband isn't, so I must be the dutiful wife and finish making the rounds with him. Don't worry, though," she added with a wink. "Your secret is safe with me."

"Enjoy the party," I murmured as she walked gracefully back to her husband, who was schmoozing with a couple of delegates in Cedris's camp. I toyed with one of the jewels in my skirt, still trying to discern exactly what it was about my conversation with Mrs. Mills that made me uneasy.

I didn't have long to dwell on it, though, because Coman passed in front of my line of sight, and something about his purposeful gait gave me pause. He wore a pair of dark maroon robes shot through with silver threading, and the embroidery sparkled in the light as his robes rippled about his tall form. I thought perhaps he was going to join the group of mages clustered near the hors d'oeuvres-laden tables to talk to his boss, but Lord Cedris was no longer amongst them. Instead, Coman headed for the ballroom exit. Senses tingling, I handed off my half-empty champagne glass to a waiter, then made my way across the room as quickly as I could without drawing attention. Coman could just be looking for the restroom, but my intuition told me that he was up to something.

I stepped out into the hallway and looked to my left just in time to see Coman's robes follow him into a room about thirty feet down. The door clicked shut, and I frowned as I heard him slide a bolt into place. The sign on the door proclaimed it to be a smoking room, as did the noxious odor of tobacco and cigarette ash that lingered on the air outside. It didn't make sense that Coman would lock it unless he was meeting someone in private.

Knowing it would look odd if I stood outside in the hall to listen in, I tried the door to the right of the smoking room and found that it was a broom closet. Sandwiching myself between a large mop bucket and the wall, I closed my eyes, put my ear to the thin wall, and focused in on the conversation occurring in the other room.

"You have an excellent chance at securing the vote tomorrow," Coman was saying, sounding quite pleased with himself. "If only half of those still undecided throw their support behind you, the odds are better than even."

"You say that, but quite a few of the delegates I talked to

tonight seemed to be favoring Lord Iannis," Lord Cedris remarked. The dark undertone to his smooth, cultured voice suggested he was not happy about this.

"Yes, but you have the upper hand," Coman insisted. "I've spoken to the mages we discussed, and all but one promised their support in exchange for raising the gold production cap of their respective states. Some actually sounded offended that Lord Iannis had not approached them with similar promises. You have many key players on your side."

"Just as well." There was a pause. "How is the Minister faring? All of this will come to nothing if he recovers or if someone discovers the truth about his illness. Has anyone tried to visit him?"

"Not since we moved him to that house on Blixton Road," Coman reassured him. "The number of guards we had outside the last location were drawing too much attention, so I've lightened the detail. Nobody is likely to go looking there since it's on the south side of town, and besides, it may not matter soon. From what the guards tell me, he is not improving."

"So much the better." Lord Cedris sounded satisfied. "We ought to get back to the ballroom before we are missed."

I held my breath as I listened to them exit the smoking room, and waited until their footfalls had long faded before I cautiously let myself out of the closet and went to report what I'd learned to Iannis.

26

Excitement thrummed through my nerves as I re-entered the ballroom – I was sure we could manage to locate the Minister with the information I'd overheard in the broom closet! Plus, it sounded like Lord Cedris *was* trying to rig the vote, and it was definitely suspicious that he seemed to be the only delegate who knew where the Minister was. If we got our hand on the Minister and brought him back to health, we could bring Lord Cedris's campaign crashing down.

I navigated the sea of colorful and bejeweled guests, searching for Iannis, but between the crush of bodies, the loud chatter, and the amalgamation of scents, it was like searching for a single flower in a sea of blossoms. Not seeing him amongst the groups of gossiping mages, I made my way to the dance floor to check if he was out there twirling some female on his arm.

Long fingers curled around my upper arm, and a familiar, lightly-accented voice murmured in my ear, "Would you care to dance?"

"Iannis." The name escaped me like a sigh, and I turned to face him. A slight smile played on his lips, and his iridescent eyes shimmered in the muted yellow light from the chandelier.

He offered me his hand, and as I placed my palm in his, an electric current ran between us, sending heat rippling through me like a gust from a sirocco. I allowed him to lead me out onto the ballroom floor, and though I felt the stares from the other dancing couples as their swirling robes and skirts brushed up against us, my eyes were locked on his.

Gently, Iannis took my right hand in his, then slid his other hand behind my left shoulder blade. I wrapped my fingers around his upper arm, mimicking the other couples, and just like that we were waltzing with the rest of the dancers.

"The rumor that we are lovers has spread through the delegation like wildfire, and is being used to discredit my so-called campaign," Iannis murmured, amusement dancing in his eyes. "We might as well give them something to gossip about."

"If I didn't know better, I'd say some of my rebellious streak is beginning to rub off on you." I grinned, enjoying this side of Iannis that few people ever saw.

"Perhaps." The tips of his fingers caressed my exposed upper back, sending a lick of heat through my spine. "I do wonder if perhaps I should consider the role of Minister. If we are left with Lord Cedris as our next leader, the Federation will not be in safe hands."

"Maybe." I leaned in a little closer so that my words wouldn't be overheard. My breasts brushed against his chest, and the words momentarily caught in my throat. "But before you start worrying about that, we should visit the current Minister ourselves and see if you can't do something about his illness."

Iannis's dark brows shot up. "Have you discovered his location?" he asked, his lips hovering a few inches from mine.

"I have," I confirmed, my voice a little breathless. "I snuck into a broom closet and overheard Lord Cedris and Coman talking about it." I recounted to him exactly what I'd overheard.

Iannis's expression never changed while I spoke, but by the

time I was done his eyes were sparkling dangerously. "It sounds like Lord Cedris knows exactly why the Minister has fallen ill, and is keeping him sequestered to prevent anyone from helping him. He should be surrounded by physicians and healers, not just guards."

"That's kind of what I'm thinking too." I hesitated for just a moment. "Should we go and get him tonight?"

"We'll get him now." Iannis's mouth tightened. "The vote is tomorrow, and if the Minister is as gravely ill as Coman indicated, we cannot afford to delay."

"Do you think it'll be suspicious if we leave early?" I turned my gaze toward the dancers around us, who were still casting surreptitious glances at us.

"You could feign an illness of some kind," Iannis suggested. "If you swoon in my arms, I'm sure no one would think it suspicious."

"I'm not swooning," I started to snap, then caught the glint of amusement in his eye. "You're teasing me."

"It is remarkably easy to do."

I caught myself just as I was about to roll my eyes, then instead hunched forward a little and pressed a hand against my abdomen. "Oooh," I groaned, just loud enough that the dancers near us would be able to hear.

Iannis placed steadying hands on my shoulders. "Are you alright?" he asked, playing along.

"I think those salmon canapés didn't agree with me." I braced a hand on his forearm, as if for support. "Perhaps it's best that I turn in for the night."

"I'll make sure you're seen back to the hotel, then." He tucked my arm in his and guided me carefully off the dance floor, as if not wanting to move too fast lest he upset my stomach. I kept my hand placed over my abdomen, allowing lines of strain to tighten my face, and the dancers who saw us hastily cleared a path. Guess they weren't really into the idea of getting projectile vomit on their finery.

I stiffened momentarily as I caught an excited whisper. "Can she be expecting his child?"

"Why else would he be so solicitous of a mere assistant?"

I bit back a snarl at that. I wanted to give those two gossips a piece of my mind, but I had bigger things to worry about, so I bit my tongue and kept moving.

"Leaving so soon?" The Finance Secretary approached us as we headed for the exit.

"Ah, Cirin." A faint smile curled Iannis's lips. "I'm taking Miss Sernan back to the hotel as she isn't feeling well, but I'd like a word with you. Would you mind following us outside?"

"Certainly." The Finance Secretary's expression never changed, but curiosity flickered in his dark blue eyes as he fell into step with us. We made quick goodbyes to the variety of mages who came up to us, then boarded the elevator and asked the operator to take us down to the second floor.

"What is it that you wanted to speak to me about, Lord Iannis?" the Finance Secretary asked once we were out on the front steps awaiting our carriage.

Iannis glanced around to make sure no one was within earshot, then leaned in. "Miss Baine has discovered the Minister's whereabouts."

"Is that so?" Cirin's eyebrows winged up as he turned his gaze toward me. "How did you manage that? I've made discreet inquiries of my own, but I've yet to turn anything up."

"Yeah, well, you don't have my super-hearing skills." I tapped my left ear, then grinned as Iannis and Cirin both gave me vaguely annoyed looks.

"The how is not important at this moment," Iannis said impatiently. "Miss Baine and I will go see the Minister now. It is likely we will be bringing him back with us. Apparently Coman ar'Daghir, Rhodea's Legal Secretary, is hiding him somewhere on Blixton Road, on the south side of town."

Cirin frowned. "I'm gathering it's no coincidence that the Chief Mage of Rhodea is the frontrunner as the Minister's replacement?"

"You can put money on that," I assured him.

"Alright. I'll prepare a room for the Minister, and discreetly tell the rest of our delegation." Cirin hesitated. "Are you sure you will be alright on your own? I could always put one of the other delegates on this and come with you."

"No, Miss Baine and I will be fine."

"Very well." The Finance Secretary bowed deeply. "Good luck, to the both of you." His eyes met mine for a heartbeat longer than necessary, assessing me, and then he was gone, headed back up the stairs and to the light and laughter of the ballroom.

I let out a breath I didn't realize I'd been holding. "Are you sure he can be trusted?"

"Cirin is ambitious, but loyal," Iannis said. "He's gotten to where he is because of me, and he won't damage that alliance."

The carriage the concierge had called for us pulled up, and a footman jumped down from the rear to open the door and help us climb in. Iannis gave the driver directions in a low voice, and the vehicle bumped and jostled along the streets as it headed over to the South Side neighborhood.

"So what's the plan?" I asked, reclining against the plushy upholstery. "Are you expecting me to fight the guards in this dress?" I could do it, of course, but I was growing fond of the garment and I didn't want to ruin it.

"Of course not," Iannis said "We'll use magic to distract the guards and then sneak in."

Iannis used illusion magic to disguise us, swapping out our finery for dark, unassuming clothing and hooded cloaks that would hide our faces. The carriage came to a stop, and I stepped onto the cracked sidewalk and looked around while Iannis paid the driver and gave him instructions to wait until we returned. Sewage and brine laced the air, and many of the houses here sported peeling paint, rickety fencing, and dingy windows. Every third streetlamp or so was cracked, casting the neighborhood in more darkness than it perhaps deserved, and I couldn't help but think that Lord Cedris had chosen a good location to hide the Minister. No one would think to look for him in a rundown neighborhood like this.

It took a bit of searching, but we found the house several blocks up, sitting in the middle of a wide, unkempt yard that prevented the other houses from cozying up to it. I picked out three guards total, two by the front porch and one by the rear, a dead giveaway in this poor area.

"They set wards set around the perimeter," Iannis murmured as we studied the rear of the property from across the street. "Likely to prevent the Minister from leaving. I will need to disable them in order to get him out safely."

I sighed. "Are you *sure* we can't just knock the guards out?"

"Doing so will only alert Lord Cedris," Iannis reminded me. "I'd like to keep him in the dark about this until after the vote."

"Oh alright." I huffed out a breath, crossing my arms over my chest. "We'll do this your way."

Iannis muttered a Word, and the streetlamp posted on the sidewalk outside the rear of the house flickered twice before plunging the street into darkness. The guard, who had been lounging against the two-story house's faded siding, straightened up with a curse and fumbled for his flashlight. In the time it took for him to find it, Iannis and I darted across the street and up the back steps, our feet making no sound as we alighted on the porch.

The guard's eyes widened, and he opened his mouth to say

something, but Iannis held up a hand and the man stopped. His lips moved, but no sound came out, and I gathered that Iannis had frozen his vocal chords just like Fenris had done to me back when I'd been mouthing off to the Council.

"*Vyagari,*" Iannis whispered, and the guard's eyes glazed over. "You will open the door and let us through, and you will not tell the other guards about this." Power resonated in his voice, sending chills down my spine. "When we come out again, you will lock the door behind us and forget that we were here."

The guard did as he was commanded without hesitation, stepping aside and holding the back door open for us. We stepped into the kitchen, and I grabbed hold of the knob and closed the door myself, making sure that it made no sound so that the guards out front wouldn't hear anything.

"You have to teach me how to do that sometime," I said under my breath.

"It's not as easy as simply speaking a Word," Iannis said dryly. "Suggestion magic requires many hours of practice to become even passably good."

"Well I guess that's why I keep you around," I muttered as I passed him. There was little point in searching the entire house when I could follow my nose, which had quickly caught the stench of sickness and the underlying scent of a male. I traced the scent upstairs, and Iannis followed close behind me as I led him to a bedroom at the end of the second-story landing.

"By Magorah," I muttered, clapping a hand over my mouth as the stench grew stronger. "Maybe you should wear a mask or something, Iannis." I couldn't catch human illnesses, but the sheer intensity of the smell made me wish I had something to cover my nose and mouth.

"I'm afraid these handkerchiefs will have to do," Iannis said, producing two large ones from his sleeve. I took one from him and pressed the piece of silk to my nose, then sighed in relief.

My sense of smell was too keen for it to block the stench, but it made the smell slightly more bearable.

With our handkerchiefs over our noses, Iannis pushed open the door, and we entered the sickroom quietly. The air was stuffy and hot, which wasn't surprising because the two windows were tightly shut, the drapes closed so securely that not even a sliver of moonlight filtered into the space. My eyes could barely pick out the shapes of the furniture, so I focused on the large bed that dominated the rear half of the room and the occupant within it.

Raising my hand, I conjured a ball of flame to provide some illumination. The blue-green flames flickered in my hand, just bright enough to permeate the darkness, and I could clearly see the man who was bundled up in the bed. His long, yellow hair was plastered to his head with sweat, and angry red scabs marred his already sallow complexion. Dark circles rimmed his closed eyes, and he let out a reedy moan as we moved closer.

"Damnu air," Iannis swore as he gently pulled back the blanket. The Minister's pajama pants and shirt shielded me from the worst of it, but the open collar and exposed hands and feet showed that scabs had spread all over his body. "He has chicken pox."

"Chicken pox?" I scowled, searching my memory for what little I knew about human disease. "Isn't that something only children get?"

"Generally, yes. But if one hasn't had it as a child, they can be infected later on in life, and the disease is often fatal to adults." Iannis pressed his left hand against the Minister's forehead, and the man groaned again. "It is also highly contagious in the early stages, and extremely resistant to magic healing."

Iannis spoke several Words aloud, and I pressed my lips together in thought. "If it's so contagious, I suppose it makes sense that he was placed under quarantine. Shouldn't the Minister's office have demanded the other mages be tested for the disease, since they were all likely to have been in close proximity with the Minister for at least a week?"

"Yes." The hand Iannis placed on the Minister's forehead began to glow. "The fact that they didn't do so is highly suspect."

I pressed my lips together, but said nothing more, only fetching a chair for Iannis so that he could sit and focus on healing the Minister. I opened the door to the corridor wide to let in some cleaner air before we all choked, then stood by and watched as Iannis worked his magic. A good hour passed as Iannis fought to drive the infection out, sweat beading on his brow as his jaw clenched with the strain. Watching Iannis heal the Minister gave me a new appreciation for him – he'd done this for me several times now, but because I'd been unconscious I had no idea it was such a strain on him. Or perhaps this disease was especially tough to beat, as he'd said.

Finally, Iannis removed his palm from the Minister's forehead and sat back in his chair. "It's done," he exhaled, sounding both pleased and tired. There was an undercurrent of relief in his tone that suggested this healing had not been a sure thing at all. I wondered if other mages without his Tua heritage could have managed.

The Minister blinked open chocolate-brown eyes, and in the light of my flame I could see his complexion was much healthier. All the scabs had fallen off or disappeared, and there was no trace of pockmarks on his now-smooth skin. Confusion filled his expression as he pushed himself to an upright position.

"W-where am I?" he asked a little more loudly than I would have liked. His eyes fixed on me. "And who are you?"

"Shhhh." Iannis's voice was hushed, but soothing, as he drew the Minister's attention to him. "It's Iannis, the Chief Mage of Solantha. This is my apprentice, Sunaya Baine. You've been very ill, sir, and we came here to heal you."

"Ill. Yes." The Minister pushed a hank of sweat-laden hair

from his handsome face. "I do recall not feeling very well and taking to my bed, but I don't remember how I ended up *here*." He cast a dubious look at the humble room and wrinkled his nose.

"The story that was given out to the Convention was that you were too sick to receive visitors, in quarantine for your own good," Iannis said tightly. "But after some discreet questioning, we have determined there is a more sinister plot behind your quarantine."

"What do you mean?" the Minister demanded in a querulous voice. "Who would dare?"

"I think we should table this discussion until after we've gotten out of here," I interrupted, casting a nervous glance toward the window. The Minister had lowered his voice a bit, but he was still too loud, and I *really* didn't want to tip the guards off to our presence after we'd worked so hard to go unnoticed.

"Yes, I agree." Iannis stood up, then helped the Minister to his feet. "Miss Baine, help me escort the Minister downstairs. Once we have him safely back in the hotel suite, we can go over everything and decide what to do from there."

27

I *can't believe I'm letting Iannis disguise me as Secretary Asward,* I grumbled to myself, arms folded across my chest as Iannis worked. We were standing in the living room area, and the delegate I was impersonating was sitting on one of the couches next to Bosal, drinking coffee and looking down his ugly nose at me. Said ugly nose now disfigured my own face too, and I could not wait for the time when I would be rid of it. But for now, there wasn't anything I could do about it.

"I don't understand why you're taking Miss Baine along instead of me," Asward complained yet again, and I rolled my eyes. Iannis had already explained to them what had happened with the Minister and why they were staying here so that the Minister and I could go to the Convention without being seen. "I understand why the Minister has to attend, of course –" here Asward stopped to incline his head respectfully at the Minister, who was standing next to me, "but Miss Baine has no legitimate reason to attend the Convention. It sets a terrible precedent."

Iannis turned slowly to face Asward. "Are you questioning my authority, Secretary?"

Asward's round face blanched. "Of course not, my lord. It's just that –"

"Then the matter is settled. You and Secretary Bosal will stay here until I call for you. It will not do to have either of you anywhere near the Capitol Building while the Minister and Miss Baine are in disguise. Have I made myself clear?"

"Yes." Asward lowered his gaze, but the way he pressed his lips together told me that he wasn't at all pleased with the decision.

As Iannis turned to apply the Minister's illusion, I retreated to the island counter where the Finance Secretary was sipping his coffee so I could pour myself another cup. Iannis and I had stayed up late into the night briefing the Minister and discussing strategy. After the two of them had gone to bed to recover from their mutual ordeal, I'd catnapped on the couch, keeping my senses trained on the door in case any guards or Resistance soldiers came barging through the door looking for the Minister.

"This is going to be an interesting day," Cirin murmured over his cup of coffee.

"No kidding." I took a long sip, savoring the rich aroma and flavor. "The delegates are going to be in an uproar."

"I believe we're ready now," the Minister said in Secretary Bosal's voice. Aside from the more formal robes he wore, he looked exactly like the delegate. I touched my own head of hair, which was distressingly short and mousy and completely unlike the mane of curly black locks I was used to. But I was just going to have to get used to that – I only had to wear this disguise for a few hours, and honestly I was lucky Iannis had convinced the Minister to let me attend in the first place.

The traffic-heavy carriage ride to the Capitol Building was long and filled with tension. I looked out the window and tried to focus on the passing scenery and ignore the fact that my elbow and thigh were literally rubbing up against the most powerful man in the nation. Iannis had disclosed my true identity to the Minister, and though the man was courteous enough not to say it in front of me under the circumstances, he was not pleased that Iannis had chosen a hybrid apprentice. But the Minister had thanked me, albeit reluctantly, for rescuing Iannis from "those dangerous savages" and ensuring he made it to Dara for the Convention. I guessed that his ingrained disapproval of shifters warred against the fact that without my reconnaissance skills, he might well have been dead by now.

Despite my nerves, I couldn't help my fascination as I entered the Great Rotunda for the first time. It was a huge, round room with a domed ceiling that soared impossibly high, pushing through the second story to crown the top of the building. A golden fresco made up entirely of runes swirled out from the center, and rimming the dome were small, arched windows that allowed sunbeams to filter in and bathe the room in light.

The seats were organized theater-style, with four rows that spanned the length of the room, except that in front of the red-covered chairs there were gleaming wooden tables where the delegates could set pen and paper and glasses of water. Each seat was designated by a golden place card on the table, announcing which delegate was to park his behind there, and small sheets of paper and pens had been set out at each station. Iannis led us to a group of seats in the top row, closest to the end. To my dismay, I was seated between the Minister and the Finance Secretary rather than next to Iannis, but there was little I could do about it. I cast my gaze to the center of the room, where a long desk had been set up, flanked by two smaller ones. Four mages sat at the largest desk, members of the Minister's office who were running the Convention in his stead. Typewriters were set up at the smaller desks, and I assumed the mages clacking away at them were assistants or secretaries of some kind.

"Delegates," a silver-haired mage called, and the way his voice reverberated throughout the room told me his voice was magically magnified. "The Convention is now in session. Please take your seats."

There was a loud, collective rustle of clothing as the mages who were still standing obeyed, and then silence fell across the room. The silver-haired mage tapped his throat, then leaned in and conferred with the other mages at his table in hushed tones.

"That is Federation Secretary Yaris Brung," Iannis told me. *"He mostly deals with foreign affairs, but he is also known to be the current Minister's right-hand man."*

"Gotcha," I replied, keeping my eyes trained on the conferring mages.

"There is other business to attend, but we will start with the vote for the next Federation Minister," Secretary Brung announced. He picked up a black, rectangular box with a small slit in the top and spoke a Word, and the box began to levitate. "Before you, you will find pen and paper. Please write down your candidate of choice, and place your vote in the box when it comes your way."

Before the procedure could start, a tall, elderly mage I had not noticed before asked for the floor.

"You may speak, Lord Ortho."

"The Chief Mage of Suluris," Cirin whispered for my benefit.

"Secretary Brung, has the ailing Minister not made some recommendation about his successor, as is the custom?"

Brung looked uncomfortable for a moment, but replied quickly enough, "No, Lord Ortho, most regrettably. Perhaps Lord Zavian felt too weak to do so. In any case, he deemed it best to leave the decision up to the Convention itself."

Iannis and the disguised Minister exchanged a quick glance.

I could sense the Minister's shock at what had to be a brazen lie from a trusted subordinate, and imagined that he would be planning swift retribution against the traitor very shortly.

The box floated toward the delegate sitting at the end of the first row, and I watched as it hovered there, waiting while she carefully wrote out her choice on the piece of paper, then folded it neatly before placing it in the box. Out of the corner of my eye, I saw the Minister sit up straight, and I could only imagine how he must feel at having to sit here and watch the other delegates vote on his replacement as though he were already dead. His eyes narrowed as he watched the progress of the box across the room, and I half-wondered if he was somehow using magic to see how the delegates were voting. But there was no trace of the strong, burnt-sugar scent of a recently cast spell, so I figured he was just speculating.

I waited with bated breath as the box circulated around the room, going up row by row to allow each delegate to cast their vote. When it arrived at Lord Cedris's section, he took his time slipping the piece of paper into the box, and there was a distinct smirk on his handsome face. Pompous ass. He was probably voting for himself anyway.

Eventually the box sailed up from the fourth row and straight to Iannis, hovering in front of him while it awaited his vote. I glanced over just as Iannis was folding his piece of paper in half, and nearly laughed out loud when I saw what he'd written on it.

"*Do you really think I'd be a good choice as the next Federation Minister?*" I asked, allowing laughter to creep into my mental voice.

"*Considering that this vote hardly matters, I thought I'd have a little fun.*" The humor in Iannis's words made my lips twitch. "*I'm sure you would revolutionize the Northia Federation if you were in office.*"

"Oh, you have no idea."

The box went to the Finance Secretary next, and then to me. I poised my pen over my piece of paper, and I could feel the Minister's eyes on me, practically burning a hole through my cheek. With a straight face, I quickly wrote *Minister Zavian Graning* on the slip of paper, then tucked it into the box.

The Minister smiled faintly, and I'll be damned if he didn't incline his head ever so slightly at me in approval.

When the box came to the Minister next, he picked up his folded piece of paper, then held it over the box for a moment as if he were about to drop it in. But after a few seconds, he put the piece of paper back down, then plucked the box out of thin air.

"Secretary Bosal, what is the meaning of this?" Secretary Brung demanded as the Minister stood up.

"I'm sorry, but I cannot vote for a new Federation Minister," he said in Secretary Bosal's voice, and just like that the illusion dropped away, revealing his true form. "Because you see, Secretary Brung, I *am* the Minister."

There was a beat of silence as everyone stared slack-jawed at the Minister, and then the entire room erupted. As the delegates shouted and argued amongst themselves, I watched the blood drain from Lord Cedris's face. His dark eyes glittered with rage, and I could practically taste his bloodlust from across the room.

"Minister!" I warned as I noticed Coman discreetly coax Lord Cedris from his seat and lead him through the sea of delegates. "Lord Cedris is getting away!"

The Minister's eyes flashed as he followed my gaze, and I pressed my hands against my ears as I watched him tap his fingers against his throat in preparation. "SILENCE!" he roared, his voice reverberating through the walls and floor, and all chatter ceased. "In light of recent events, I am ordering the arrest of Lord Cedris ar'Tarea, Chief Mage of Rhodea, as well as the other members of his delegation."

"On what charges!" Lord Cedris demanded, his face turning beet-red as all eyes swiveled in his direction.

"Attempted murder, conspiring against the Federation, and aiding the Resistance, which is an act of treason," the Minister snapped, and a collective gasp rose from the rest of the delegates.

"This is preposterous!" Lord Cedris shouted, sounding on the edge of hysteria now. He tried to make a break for it, but several other mages hit him with spells, and he froze into place. I sat back in my chair and watched with supreme satisfaction as the Minister had Cedris and his delegates clapped in rune-covered irons. But as they were dragged out of the room, I knew in my heart that this was only the beginning, and our work was far from done.

28

Outrageously enough, the Minister and his Secretaries refused to allow me to attend the interrogation. I wasn't even allowed to listen outside. Iannis attempted to argue on my behalf, but the Minister was adamant – I wasn't supposed to be here anyway, and he'd already extended enough "liberties" by allowing me into the Convention to attend the vote. Now that he had his position back, Lord Zavian was rapidly reverting to type – the very kind of self-satis-fied, rigid high mage that the Resistance wanted to overthrow.

Liberties, my ass, I seethed as the carriage took me back to the hotel. I wanted to take the liberty to punch the Minister right in his supercilious face. But that would probably get Iannis in trouble, so I'd tamped down on my rage and left the building as instructed.

When I got back to the hotel room, there was nobody there – the other delegates must have gone back to their own suite. Tears sprang to my eyes now that nobody was around to see them, and I blinked rapidly before they started trickling down my cheeks. It wasn't fair. I'd rescued Iannis, we'd saved the Minister, and we'd captured Lord Cedris. I should have been on top of the world, dancing and celebrating and feeling triumphant. How was I supposed to exist in a world like this? A world where all sides consistently shunned and belittled me? How could I stand up for my ideals and fight for what was right, if the powers that be continued to stomp me into the ground every chance they got?

Fuck this, I thought angrily, shoving one of the couches against the wall. I wasn't going to languish in this stupid hotel suite feeling sorry for myself. If I had to stay here and wait for Iannis, the least I could do was make good use of the space. So I pushed all the living room furniture up against the walls, changed into a tank top and pants, and I did something I hadn't had a chance to do in a long time.

I trained.

Training wasn't so much about keeping in shape – my job as an enforcer, not to mention the grueling trip over the past week, did a good enough job at that – but about honing my skills and sharpening my focus. Nevertheless, I worked through the usual strength and flexibility exercises before moving on to basic punches, kicks, rolls, and stances.

By the time I started on my first form, my bare arms were covered with a light sheen of sweat and most of the stress had drained from my body. As I glided through the motions, striving for grace rather than power, my troubled thoughts drifted away, and Roanas filled my mind instead. I could almost picture his tawny lion's gaze watching me, and the sensation made me ache with sadness and happiness all at once. I missed him more than words could convey, and there were many times I wished I could hop on my bike and ride over to his house so I could talk my cases over with him.

But even though I couldn't visit Roanas at his home anymore, I could still draw comfort from my memories of him, and wrap them around myself in times of trouble. Training was the perfect way to do that – with every kick and punch, every pivot and crouch, I could feel my mentor's presence and encouragement almost as if he really were here with me.

By the time the door swung open, I was in the middle of my fourth form, so deeply focused that I didn't even stop. I ducked an imaginary opponent from one end, then spun out of my crouch to crescent kick the one behind me, my foot whipping through the air at inhuman speed.

The sound of my flesh slapping against Iannis's palm as he caught my foot jarred me from my trance-like state, and I jumped, then lost my balance. Thankfully Iannis let go of my leg and caught me around the waist before I toppled to the floor.

"I see you've done some redecorating," he murmured, his violet eyes sparkling with amusement as he drew me closer.

"Yeah," I said, my voice a little breathless – and not from the exertion. His chest was nearly touching mine, and the heat from his body felt good against my sweat-slicked skin. "I thought you'd appreciate it if I refrained from adding smashed furniture to your hotel bill."

"Indeed," Iannis agreed. He reached up and brushed a damp curl from my forehead. "I apologize for sending you back to the hotel, but I am glad you found an outlet for your frustration."

"It's alright." I licked my lips as his fingers trailed fire across my skin. "I know that despite your 'I'm all-powerful' attitude, you can't control everything."

Iannis scoffed lightly. "I never said that I was all-powerful."

"No, but you sure act like it most of the time." Grinning, I danced out of his reach, not because I didn't like him touching me but because I liked it a little *too* much. Despite the fact that I'd thoroughly enjoyed the kiss he'd given me, I didn't think it was a good idea to let him do it again after I'd given him an ultimatum. If he wanted me, he was going to have to make a decision before I'd let him take any more liberties.

I just hoped he decided before I ran out of time.

"So, are you going to tell me about this interrogation?" I asked as I plopped down on one of the couches that I'd shoved against the wall. "I hope it's not all bad news."

"As a matter of fact, it's not." Iannis sat down on the opposite end of the couch, twisting his body sideways to face me and leaning an arm on top of the white upholstery. "Lord Cedris doesn't know who the Benefactor is."

I turned my head to scowl at him. "I thought you had *good* news."

"He doesn't know who the Benefactor is, but he admitted that someone *did* contact him about a month before the Convention with blackmail photographs of a rather sordid nature," Iannis continued blithely. "Professionally taken, too. This person would only communicate to him via post and parcel, but they basically promised him the position of Minister if he followed their instructions, and threatened to expose his indiscretions if he balked. If those photos had been published, Cedris would have had to resign from office and face trial by the Convention."

"Huh." I pressed my lips together as I absorbed that information. "Does that mean we're supposed to forgive him or something?"

"Certainly not. He should have come to the Minister immediately with a full confession, and would have gotten off with a much lighter penalty. Instead he's guilty of treason for his dealings with the Benefactor, since it's clear his actions were benefitting the Resistance. He knew about the planned attack on my dirigible, which is why he was so displeased when I arrived at the Convention after all. The Benefactor must have reckoned that my presence would make it harder for Cedris to swing the vote, so they tried to eliminate me to ensure he would get the position. Secretary Brung was being blackmailed for different reasons, and was told that the Minister would fall ill several days before any symptoms appeared. It was between the two of them that they were able to isolate the Minister so effectively."

"By Magorah." I shook my head at that. "If one of the Secretaries is capable of being blackmailed, then the Benefactor probably blackmailed or bribed additional delegates to help swing the vote."

"I agree." Iannis nodded. "Those who strongly campaigned on Cedris's behalf are being rounded up and interrogated as well, since unsurprisingly none of them are coming forward. The Minister is putting together a special task force to track down the Benefactor and eradicate the Resistance, and he's asked me to be part of it."

I jerked. "And are you?"

"Of course." Iannis frowned at my reaction. "How could I not? The Federation will never be safe until this madness is stopped."

"I know, I know, it's just that..." I scraped my hands through my hair and tried to figure out how to say this.

"What is it?" Iannis's tone softened.

I lifted my gaze to his again. "It's just that I know the Minister isn't going to want me anywhere near this task force, and you're going to be so busy there's no way you're going to have time to train me." A lump formed in my throat.

"Ah, but that's where you are wrong." Iannis smiled. "I told the Minister in no uncertain terms that you've been invaluable in uncovering all these conspiracies, and that if he wanted me on the task force you would be working with me." The smile turned into a smirk. "He said that since you're my apprentice I can do whatever I want, but of course that was just his way of saving face while agreeing."

I laughed a little at the twinkle in his eye. "How clever of you."

"Indeed." His face grew serious again. "But whether or not

he agreed, I already made a promise to you that I wouldn't neglect your training again, Sunaya. I will reduce your apprenticeship duties at the Mages Guild so that you have more time to focus on spellcasting and other lessons. I suspect we will need the extra time as members of this new task force in any case."

"No kidding." I bit my lip as another thought occurred to me. "Did Cedris or Brung say how the Minister caught the disease in the first place?"

"The Benefactor was in charge of the arrangements, so I assume he somehow made it happen. I just don't understand how such a thing is possible without magic." Iannis frowned.

"Perhaps that is why nobody else caught it from the Minister, if it's supposed to be so contagious." My mind was spinning with the implications. If the Benefactor could target specific enemies with common ailments, what prevented him from spreading some plague that killed only mages, or worse, only shifters?

"If I asked Noria or Elnos, I'm pretty sure they'd say it's the power of human science and give me some fancy term or something that I can't pronounce." I smiled a little, but my heart sank as I remembered the turmoil I'd left behind in Solantha. Would Noria still be there, or had she run off to join the fight by now? I hated the thought of us becoming enemies. Was there any way I could warn her about the task force, without at the same time being disloyal to Iannis or helping the Resistance? I needed to convince Rylan to get out as well, although I doubted he'd want to talk to me after learning I'd used his name to infiltrate a Resistance camp.

"You should pack your things," Iannis said as he rose. "We'll be leaving for Solantha in the evening."

"Alright," I said dully. I hopped off the couch and headed back to my own room, my heart heavy. Even though I'd accomplished what I'd set out to do here in Dara, I was dreading the idea of going home.

29

Considering what had happened the last time Iannis had travelled on a dirigible, plus the fact that the Resistance was probably even more focused on eliminating us, I should have been a bundle of nerves during the flight home. But I was so tired from this long-ass ordeal that not long after we left Dara I conked out, sleeping like the dead for most of the flight.

"Miss Baine." Iannis gently shook me awake. "We're here."

I cracked open my eyelids and looked out the window just as we passed over Solantha Bay. Despite the fact that I was dreading what I'd find on the ground, I couldn't help but grin as I watched the morning sun crest over the horizon, pink and gold flames rippling across the water and making the Firegate Bridge glow. I couldn't even explain how relieved I was to see the bridge still standing there in all its fiery glory – the Resistance had already tried to destroy it once, and I'd half expected to find it blown to smithereens. If it was standing strong, I hoped that meant Solantha was too.

But as we drew closer to the Palace, I saw groups of humans crowded outside the property just beyond the protective wards, and my sharp eyes picked out picket signs that many of them waved. I couldn't make out what they said, but I imagined the words were angry, if the number of guards trying to corral the protesters were any indication.

"By Magorah," I whispered as horror creeped up my chest. "Just what is going on down there?"

Rather than landing at the airport, which would force us to brave the angry mob to gain entrance to the Palace, Iannis ordered the pilot to land us in the middle of the palace gardens, well within the protective wards and away from the angry protesters. A light breeze tugged at my hair as I disembarked from the dirigible, bringing the kiss of the ocean with it, and for a moment I forgot about the protestors on the ground. But then I caught sight of Director Chen and Fenris waiting for us, and their grim faces reminded me all over again.

"Welcome back, everyone," Director Chen said, her voice solemn. "I am glad to see you have all arrived safely."

"You sure don't look glad," I pointed out. "Is there something going on we should know about? Such as why there's an angry mob trying to storm the Palace downstairs?"

"Many things, and none of them good," Fenris confirmed. He forced a smile, no doubt noticing the worried look on my face. "But we're hoping that now that you are back, Iannis, things can be settled."

"What things?" Iannis demanded, looking between Chen and Fenris. "What more has happened in my absence?"

Director Chen sucked in a deep breath before she spoke. "Because my appointment was never formally ratified, the Council decided to rule in your stead and completely shut me out while I was leading the search. They called for the arrest of anyone who has known or suspected ties to the Resistance, which in their very broad definition is half the city."

"*What?*" Iannis's voice sizzled with fury.

"It's true, Iannis." Fenris's voice was heavy with sorrow. "Not only that, but they've arrested the families of all these 'suspects' as well. Prominent business owners, enforcers, media employees, and many, many others have been taken, including Inspector Lakin and most of the Baine Clan. If not for the fact that I returned aboard Director Chen's dirigible with Resistance prisoners in tow, I suspect I would be sharing their fate."

"Are you fucking kidding me?" I shouted, furious at the idea that Lakin, who when last I'd talked to him had been working hard to protect shifters from the fallout, had been swept up by the Mages Guild's misguided attempts at seeking justice. "Iannis, we have to fix this." I nearly grabbed his sleeve before I caught myself.

"Set up a meeting with the Council in thirty minutes," Iannis said between gritted teeth. "I want to get to the bottom of this, and I mean to do it *now*."

THE MEETING WAS A BLOODY AFFAIR, and I got to watch from the sidelines as Iannis ripped each and every one of the Council members a new hole. Omonas tried to fight back, pointing out that it was Iannis's fault that he hadn't made sure to ratify Chen's appointment, and in response Iannis set his robes aflame. It would have been gratifying to watch the fat bastard shriek and scream if he hadn't also decided to rip off his robes, but apparently the fire Iannis had used couldn't be put out by normal means, and it consumed the robe to ashes before winking itself out.

After that, none of the other councilmen dared to raise a voice against Iannis, and he told them in no uncertain terms that they were never to pull a stunt like that again, and that as of today he would be ratifying Chen's appointment. He also told them that they needed to immediately release any citizens they'd imprisoned that they didn't have *hard* evidence against, and that if it wasn't done by the end of today he would see them all removed from their positions and new Council members appointed.

Seeing that he had matters well in hand, I slipped out of the Palace in disguise, briefly integrating myself into the mob outside as a human so I could get into the city itself. Now that I was on the ground, I could read the picket fences clearly, and they said things like "FREE MY FAMILY" and "DEATH TO ALL MAGES" and "GIVE THE POWER TO THE PEOPLE." A huge part of me wanted to tell these people to stand down, that it was okay now, that Iannis was back and their loved ones would be returned to them, but there was no reason they would believe me, and in any case I needed to check on my friends.

Wishing for my steambike, I considered changing into beast form and running down to the Port. But running around as a jaguar after my entire clan had been arrested was probably a bad idea, so I decided against it and hoofed it down to Witches' End instead. The five-mile walk was even more depressing than the mob outside the Palace – the once-clean streets were now strewn with refuse from the piles of uncollected garbage bags rotting on the sidewalks, storefronts were smashed in or boarded up, and the few people out on the streets walked quickly, eyes darting around nervously as though expecting someone to jump at them from the shadows or through a broken window. The streets stank of garbage, grief, and fear, and it made my heart hurt.

Worse, though, was the fact that Comenius's glass storefront was now covered in plywood, battened down and closed to the public. For a heart-stopping moment I feared that he'd skipped town, but when I ran up the side entrance and pounded on the second level door, he answered.

"Oh, Naya." He threw his arms around me, and we both squeezed each other so tightly I wondered which of us would bust a rib first. "I am so glad to see you've come back safely."

"I thought you'd left," I told him as he let me into the apartment, my legs shaky with relief. Elania was just inside, and I embraced her too, soaking in her exotic scent. "So many shops are closed, and when I saw yours was boarded up, I feared the worst."

"We're still here, and we're alive and well," Comenius said gently. "Elania and I decided it would be best to close up our shops until this disaster blows over."

The sound of a toilet flushing caught my attention, and I turned to see Annia walk out of the bathroom. Her eyes were unusually dull, her shoulders slumped, and she barely managed a smile when she saw me.

"Hey." I rushed over to her, my heart sinking faster than a downed ship as I embraced her. "What's going on?"

"Noria's gone," Annia muttered as she hugged me back. "When I came home, Mom was crying in the living room and clutching an old photograph of her. She told me that Noria had left the day before to join the Resistance."

"No." I felt the bottom drop out of my stomach, and I pulled back to stare at Annia. She only gazed back at me woodenly, no sign in her face that this was a joke or prank. "Fuck," I exhaled.

"Yeah, fuck." Annia let out a bitter laugh as she threw herself onto Comenius's sofa. "Here I was, rushing off with you to save the Chief Mage so I could cash in on that huge bounty, when what I really should have been doing was sticking to my sister's ass like glue and making sure she didn't do anything stupid."

I let out a sigh as I sat down next to Annia on the couch. "It's not your fault," I told her. "She was going to do it anyway –"

"*No.*" Annia sat up straight, tears thickening her voice as she glared at me. "Don't you fucking dare say that. That's like saying it was inevitable, that there was no fucking choice, no fucking *chance* for me to change her mind." Her voice shook as she balled her hand into a fist. "That's like saying it's *fate*, and I don't believe in that shit." Her dark eyes burned, as if daring me to challenge her so she could plow her fist into my face.

"You're right." I dropped my gaze, partly because I didn't want to fight one of my best friends, and partly because she *was* right. "I'm sorry. I shouldn't have said that."

"Here," Comenius said gently, placing two cups of tea down on the coffee table in front of us. "Drink this."

"I need whiskey, not tea," Annia muttered, glaring at the cup as though it were personally responsible for all her woes.

"It'll help soothe your nerves." Comenius lifted the teacup and offered it to her. "Come on, Annia. You can't keep going on like this."

Annia didn't say anything to that, but she did take the teacup. I took a sip from mine, and sighed as the hot, soothing blend slid down my throat and warmed my stomach. Comenius's tea wouldn't solve my problems, but it would make me feel better, and right now I needed all the pick-me-ups I could get. "Thanks, Com."

"You're quite welcome." Comenius sat down heavily in the wicker chair and regarded me with a troubled look. "I hope your return means that the Chief Mage is going to do something about this catastrophe. The humans and shifters who haven't run off are targeting anything connected with magic, which is why I've had to close down my shop. With the constant riots and lack of authority to get the population under control, the streets aren't safe. Just the other day, the fortuneteller who works next door was beaten and raped in the street on her way home. Elania and I spent all night healing her, and now she won't leave her apartment."

"By Magorah." I dug the heels of my hands into my eyes,

unable to cope. "That's fucking awful. Iannis has yanked the Council back into line, and he's working on getting all the wrongfully imprisoned citizens freed, but I don't know how long it'll take to bring the city back under control."

"I'm afraid it will take much more than that to get Solantha back to normal," Elania said sadly. "The Mages Guild has broken the trust of the people, what little there was of it, and they will not easily be reined in again."

"Which I'm sure is exactly what the Resistance wanted," I said bitterly.

"That wouldn't surprise me at all," Comenius commented. "Many of the humans and shifters who've fled the city have run right into the arms of the Resistance. Including Noria," he added softly with a glance at Annia.

I visited with Comenius for a little longer, but there wasn't much more to say, so in the end I decided to head back to Rowanville and see how my apartment had fared. As I'd expected, my section of town had not been spared by the vitriol rolling through Solantha. Anti-mage graffiti covered once-pris-tine boutiques and storefronts, windows were either boarded up or shuttered, and the only signs of life were the occasional set of eyes that peeked through window curtains as I passed.

But the worst thing by far was the envelope stuck to my front door with a knife, both blade and paper crusted with dried blood. There was no name on it, but since it was stuck to my door I had to assume it was for me. I carefully removed the knife and envelope, then eased into my apartment.

I'd half expected the place to be trashed and graffitied, so I was relieved to see that it was exactly the way I'd left it, dirty dishes on the counter included. I tossed the knife and letter onto the coffee table, then went through the coming-home ritual of hanging up my coat and shoes, washing the dishes on the counter, and cleaning any blood or grime off my weapons. It might sound silly, but after all I'd been through, I craved a slice of normality before I tackled the bloody letter.

Eventually I ran out of things to do, and with my kitchen cleaned, my couch cushions plumped, and my surfaces dusted, I sank down onto the couch with the letter in my hand. I used the bloody knife to slit the envelope open – because hey, I might as well – and with a shaking hand unfolded the single page inside.

Sunaya Baine,

Despite multiple attempts to plant your feet onto the correct path, you have chosen the wrong side. Your efforts to thwart our plans have been noted, and retribution will be swift.

The note was typed and unsigned, but it didn't take a genius to figure out who'd sent it. With a sigh, I ripped it up, then tossed the pieces into the air. The Resistance might think they were my biggest problem, but they were just one more big bad bully trying to stomp me into the ground because I didn't fit their mold. But if they thought they were going to get away with this, they were just as wrong as everyone else who'd tried to break me.

"Get in line," I whispered as I watched the paper fragments flutter to the floor like confetti. "Get in fucking line."

To be continued...

Sunaya Baine's adventure continues in **Marked by Magic**, Book 4 of the Baine Chronicles. Make sure to join her mailing list so you can be notified of future release dates, and to receive special updates, freebies and giveaways!

Join at www.jasminewalt.com/newsletter-signup

If you want to keep up with Jasmine Walt in the meantime, you can like her Facebook page, and follow her on Twitter, Goodreads, and Amazon.

DID YOU ENJOY THIS BOOK? Please consider leaving a review. Reviews help us authors sell books so we can afford to write more of them. Writing a review is the best way to ensure that the author writes the next one as it lets them know readers are enjoying their work and want more. Thank you very much for taking the time to read, and we hope you enjoyed the book!

GLOSSARY

Aryn: employee at the Sandin Federal Bank.

Baine, Sunaya: a half-panther shifter, half-mage who hates mages and has a passion for justice. Because magic is forbidden to all but the mage families, Sunaya was forced to keep her abilities a secret until she accidentally used them to defend herself in front of witnesses. Rather than condemn her to death, the Chief Mage, Iannis ar'Sannin, chose to take her on as his apprentice, and now she struggles to balance her shifter and mage heritage.

Baine, Melantha: Sunaya's cousin, and daughter to the Jaguar Clan's Chieftain.

Baine, Mafiela: Chieftain of the Jaguar Clan and Sunaya's aunt.

Baine, Mika: a young jaguar shifter, daughter of Melantha Baine.

Baine, Rylan: one of Chieftain Baine's least favored children, and Sunaya's cousin. He is an active member of the Resistance, with the rank of captain.

Benefactor: the name the Resistance call their anonymous, principal source of financial support. According to Sunaya's investigations, this mysterious criminal has many different irons in the fire.

Canalo: one of the fifty states making up the Northia Federation, located on the West Coast of the Northia Continent.

Canalo Council, usually just the **Council:** a governmental body composed of eight senior mages, supposed to advise the Chief Mage and substitute for him in case of sudden death.

Capitol: building in the capital Dara, where the Convention of Chief Mages meets every other year to conduct governmental business.

Chen, Lalia: the current Director of the Canalo Mages Guild in Solantha. She serves as deputy to Iannis ar'Sannin, the Chief Mage.

Chartis, Argon: former Director of the Canalo Mages Guild, dismissed by the Chief Mage for insubordination and attempts to undermine the Chief Mage's authority.

Chieftain: a title used to distinguish the head of a shifter clan.

Comenius Genhard: a hedgewitch from Pernia, owner of the shop Over the Hedge at Witches' End. Close friend of Sunaya Baine, employer of Noria Melcott, and lover of the witch Elania.

Creator: the ultimate deity, worshipped by all three races under different names.

Dira: mage, one of the secretaries at the Mages Guild.

Danrian, Warin: regional manager of the Sandin Federal Bank for Canalo, who turned out to be one of the Benefactor's henchmen there. He was behind the illegal Shifter Royale, as well as coordinating the bank's dodgy credit scheme for shifters.

Dara: capital of the Northia Federation, located on the east coast of the Northia Continent.

Dromach, the: a sect of powerful mages in Manuc who are specially trained to deal with the Tua, and charged with maintaining the walls that separate Recca from their realm.

Elania: girlfriend of Comenius; a witch specializing in potions, with a shop in Witches' End

Enforcer: a bounty hunter employed by the government to seek out and capture wanted criminals. They operate under strict rules and are paid bounties for each head. While the majority of them are human, there is a strong minority of shifters, and even the occasional mage.

Enforcer's Guild: the administrative organization in charge of the Enforcers. Also, the building from which the various Enforcer crews work under their respective foremen.

Fenris: a clanless wolf shifter as well as good friend and confidant of Chief Mage Iannis ar'Sannin. No known last name.

Firegate Bridge: Solantha's best-known structure, a large red bridge spanning the length of Solantha Bay. It is accessible via Firegate Road.

Captain Galling: the human captain of the Enforcers Guild in Solantha City, appointed by the former Chief Mage and Council.

Garai: the largest and most populated country on the Eastern Continent. Garaians are known for slanted eyes and ivory skin as well as their complicated rune-like alphabet.

Garidano, Cirin: Finance Secretary of the State of Canalo.

Gor, Faron: shifter, Chief Editor of the Shifter Courier, the Solantha newspaper for the shifter population. He provided important information to Sunaya during the investigation into the Shifter Royale.

Great Accord: a treaty struck by the ruling mages centuries ago which brought an end to a devastating war known as the Conflict. It is still the basis upon which mages rule their countries and territories. All new laws passed must be in accordance with the provisions of the Great Accord.

Halyma: shamaness of the hills Coazi and chief shamaness of the entire Coazi tribe, due to her outstanding magic talent.

Hennis: a jaguar shifter, butler in the home of Mafiela Baine, the Chieftain of the Jaguar Clan.

The Herald: the main newspaper in Solantha City, geared towards the human majority population.

Iannis ar'Sannin: Chief Mage of Canalo. He resides in the capital city of Solantha, from which he runs Canalo as well as the Mages Guild with the help of his deputy. Originally a native of Manuc, a country located across the Eastern Sea.

Incidium: a powerful illegal drug that produces euphoria.

Kalois: a rare foreign plant which masks the smell of silver so well that shifters can be drugged or poisoned despite their sensitive noses.

Kan Zao: a mental and physical martial art tradition from Garai.

Lakin, Boon: a jaguar shifter from Parabas, recently appointed as Solantha's new Shiftertown Inspector following Roanas's death. Sunaya and he are friends and occasional allies. It was a case he investigated and discussed with Sunaya, that led to the eventual exposure of the Shifter Royale.

Laniren; Tyron, Myrna, and **Tylin:** a wolf shifter family residing in Shiftertown in Solantha. The teenage son, Tylin, had been kidnapped to fight in the Shifter Royale.

Loranian: the difficult, secret language of magic that all mages are required to master.

Mages Guild: the governmental organization that rules the mages in Canalo, and supervises the other races. The headquarters are in Solantha Palace. They are subordinate to the Chief Mage.

Magi-tech: devices that are powered by both magic and technology.

Main Crew: the largest group of Enforcers in the Guild. They are generally favored over the other crews and get the most lucrative dockets.

Manuc: an island country off the west coast of the Central Continent.

Magorah: the god of the shifters, associated with the moon.

Maxon, Brin: former Enforcer on the Main Crew, partnered with Nila Romana.

Melcott, Annia: a human Enforcer. She is a close friend of Sunaya's, and Noria's older sister.

Melcott, Noria: Annia Melcott's younger sister. A gifted inventor, she regularly tinkers with mechanical devices in between her college classes and her part-time job at Comenius's shop.

Mills, Thorgana: human socialite, who inherited ownership of The Herald in Solantha and several other newspapers, as well as other companies across the Federation. She only resides in Solantha part-time. Sunaya used to do occasional bodyguard gigs for her in the past.

Nevin Rindar: lion shifter and reporter for the Shifter Courier, who disappeared some weeks before Sunaya began investigating the Shifter Royale kidnappings.

Northia Federation: a federation consisting of fifty states that cover the entire northern half and middle of the Western Continent. Canalo is part of this federation.

Over the Hedge: a shop at Witches' End selling magical charms and herbal remedies, belonging to Comenius Genhard.

Pandanum: a base metal used, amongst other things, for less valuable coins.

Parabas: a city north of Solantha, outside the state of Canalo.

Pernia: a country on the Central Continent, from which Sunaya's friend Comenius Genhard hails.

Prison Isle: an island in the middle of Solantha Bay that serves as a prison for Canalo's criminals.

Privacy Guard: a company leasing uniformed guards to governments and other institutions all over the Federation.

Ragga, Elnos: Noria Melcott's boyfriend. He is a student at Solantha academy and one of the few mages who believes in equality amongst the races. He and Noria can often be found working together, developing new magi-tech devices.

Randor, Wilam: executive at The Butcher's Block, a meat-packing company that advertises in the Shifter Courier.

Recca: the world of humans, mages, and shifters.

Residah: the mages' book of scripture that holds Resinah's teachings.

Resinah: the first mage, whose teachings are of paramount spiritual importance for the mages. Her statue can be found in the mage temples, which are off-limits to non-mages and magically hidden from outsiders.

Resistance: a movement of revolutionaries and malcontents planning to overthrow the mages and take control of the Northia Federation. Over the past months they have become bolder and more aggressive, using terrorist attacks with civilian casualties. They are financially backed by the still-to-be identified Benefactor.

Romana, Nila: a human Enforcer on the Main Crew and Brin Maxon's partner, known for relying on her looks first, her fighting skills second.

Rowanville: the only neighborhood of Solantha where all three races mix.

Sandin Federal Bank: a bank with branches in all fifty states of the Federation; its Canalo manager was Danrian Warin. It was shut down after Sunaya brought a scheme of "interest-free loans," financed with illegally mined gold, to the Chief Mage's notice.

Serapha charms: paired amulets that allow two people, usually a couple, to find each other via twinned stones imbued with a small part of their essence. Normally, only the wearer can take a serapha charm off.

Shifter: a human who can change into animal form and back by magic; they originally resulted from illegal experiments by mages on ordinary humans.

Shifter Courier: Solantha newspaper specifically geared towards the shifter population.

Shifter Royale: an illegal underground betting concourse where kidnapped and drugged shifters were forced to fight against each other, sometimes to the death. Discovered and exposed by Sunaya, with help from Boon Lakin and Annia Melcott, after her cousin Mika had been kidnapped by the organizers.

Shiftertown: the part of Solantha where the official shifter clans live.

Shiftertown Inspector: a shifter appointed by the Shiftertown Council to police shifter-related crime. He has deputies who assist him. The position is currently held by Boon Lakin, a jaguar shifter, appointed after the murder of his predecessor Roanas Tillmore.

Sillara Tarenan: a shifter Enforcer and early victim of the silver murders.

Solantha: the capital of Canalo State, a port city on the West Coast, home of Sunaya Baine.

Solantha Palace: The seat of power in Canalo, where both the Chief Mage and the Mages Guild reside. It is located near the coast of Solantha Bay.

Solin Endeman: a human, employed by Warin Danrian to sell tickets to the Shifter Royale.

Taili the Wolf: in shifter legend, the very first shifter (a female).

Tanzarite: a rare semi-precious stone.

Talcon, Garius: the former Deputy Captain of the Enforcers

Guild. Sunaya discovered he was in league with Petros Yantz, the man behind the silver murders, and killed him in self-defense.

The Twilight: a bar in Rowanville where Sunaya used to bartend.

Tillmore, Roanas: The former Shiftertown Inspector and father figure/mentor to Sunaya. He was poisoned while digging into the silver murders, prompting Sunaya to take over the investigation.

Traxtoline: an explosive material, expensive and unstable.

Tsu-Wakan: a Coazi warrior whose tribe lives on the Mexia plains

Tua: a legendary and highly dangerous race of very long-lived beings with powerful magic, who sometimes cross from their own world into Recca, most frequently in Manuc.

Turain: a small town north of Solantha, where the Shifter Royale took place.

Ur-God: the name the humans call the Creator by.

Vanit, Laro: foreman of the Enforcer Crew to which the late Sillara Tarenan belonged.

Witches' End: a pier in Solantha City, part of the Port, where immigrant magic users sell their wares and services.

Yantz, Petros: the former Chief Editor of the Herald. He fled the city after Sunaya discovered he was behind the silver murders, and is still at large.

ACKNOWLEDGMENTS

As usual, thank you very much to all of my beta readers and ARC readers who've contributed to making this book better. I'd like to give a special shout-out to Victoria Newman in particular. Of all my beta readers, you've been one of the most thorough, and I greatly appreciate the time you spent helping me take this book to the next level. I'd also like to thank Carmen Lund, one of my biggest and earliest fans. You always make me feel like a rockstar. <3

I'd also like to thank Mary Burnett, my writing partner and editor. We've had a pretty wild ride with this series so far, and I can only hope things will get even better and brighter.

I'd also like to thank my fellow indie authors, particularly Rebecca Hamilton, Pippa DaCosta, J.A. Cipriano, Chris Fox, and Domino Finn. The indie community is so helpful and support- ive, and I've learned a lot from you all. Thank you for continuing to be awesome. :)

Finally, thank you to Judah Dobin, my super-talented illustrator, and my biggest fan. I know without a doubt that I wouldn't be doing any of this without your encouragement and support. Love you lots. <3

ABOUT THE AUTHOR

New York Times and USA Today Bestselling Author Jasmine Walt is a devourer of books, chocolate, and all things martial arts. Somehow, those three things melded together in her head and transformed into a desire to write, usually fantastical stuff with a healthy dose of action and romance. Her characters are a little (okay, a lot) on the snarky side, and they swear, but they mean well. Even the villains sometimes.

When Jasmine isn't chained to her keyboard, you can find her working on her dao sword form, spending time with her family, or binge-watching superhero shows on Netflix.

Want to connect with Jasmine? You can find her on Twitter at @jasmine_writes, on Facebook, or at www.jasminewalt.com.

ALSO BY JASMINE WALT

The Baine Chronicles Series:

Burned by Magic

Bound by Magic

Hunted by Magic

Marked by Magic

Betrayed by Magic

Deceived by Magic

Scorched by Magic

Tested by Magic (Novella)

Forsaken by Magic (Novella)

The Nia Rivers Adventures

Dragon Bones

Demeter's Tablet

Templar Scrolls

Serpent Mound

Eden's Garden

The Gatekeeper Chronicles

Marked by Sin

Hunted by Sin

Claimed by Sin

The Dragon's Gift Trilogy